SUFFRAGETTE
to Death

A White House Dollhouse Mystery

Barbara Schlichting

SUFFRAGETTE
to Death

Barbara Schlichting

Copyright © 2018

Dedicated to all the First Ladies, former and present.
Bless them for all they've done for our country.

Books by Barbara

Single Titles

THE BROKEN CIRCLE

White House Dollhouse Mystery Series

SPANGLED to DEATH
WORD to DEATH
CLUED to DEATH
SUFFRAGETTE to DEATH

HISTORICAL FICTION

BODY ON THE TRACKS

POETRY

WHISPERS FROM THE WIND
Blood Red
Bike With Me

PICTURE BOOKS

Red Shoes by Barbie Marie
Martha Washington: HER FIRST FEW DAYS AS FIRST LADY

NON-FICTION

Immigrant Snap Chat

You can write to Barbara Schlichting at

schlichtingbarb@gmail.com.

You may also contact her through her website.
www.barbaraschlichting.com.

If you so choose, you may sign up for the newsletter
on the website.

Chapter One

I woke early to a beautiful summer day.

Before leaving home, I kissed my handsome husband, Aaron, and walked out the door. The walk to my White House store near downtown Minneapolis, brought me past several ground-out cigarette butts near the bar appropriately named Pracna on Main. The rest of the way wound near the Mississippi River and a small park where children played, plus the old Grain Belt Brewery, now a library. There's also a bike trail. In a few short minutes, I was unlocking the store's back door.

I wanted to spend a few minutes with my assistant, Nancy. Nancy bears an uncanny resemblance to First Lady Edith Wilson. I'm not the only one who's noticed; when Russ Lippmann, a Woodrow Wilson biographer, director and owner of the neighborhood theater met Nancy, he immediately sought her for a role. His Rose Garden Theater featured historical plays about First Ladies and he thought Nancy would be perfect for their new play about Edith Wilson.

I promised to help Nancy learn her lines, as it would give me a chance to find out more about Edith Wilson. I knew only a bit about her, and wanted to learn more.

The back door was still locked, so I knew that Max, my upstairs renter, wasn't up, and that Nancy hadn't arrived. The security code was Dolley Madison's birthdate. After punching it into the pad, I opened the door and stepped inside.

In the workroom, I found a doll's head carved, which meant that Max (who was also my employee), had spent the previous evening carving it. It's my job to paint the doll's head. Today I would paint Edith Wilson's face. My clients liked the natural look of my dolls. I sew the inaugural gowns, but not the Presidents' outfits. Those are easily purchased from a store in New Jersey. When the dolls are ready, then they're sold with the appropriate White House dollhouse. With my cell phone, I took a moment to send Max a message to tell him the head was beautiful. As I hit send, a new message popped on the screen from Nancy. She wanted to know if a blueberry muffin and coffee were on the agenda? Of course I said, yes!

I walked into the showroom, and took a minute to glance around. I made sure that the autographed pictures of First Ladies balanced evenly and that my framed doctoral diploma hung behind the computer where the checkout counter and cash register stood. Another wall featured my collection of miniature dollhouses and beside them my Penny dolls. I gave them a once-over with a duster, pinching my nose to avoid the particles.

Two days ago, I'd purchased Wilson memorabilia from a First Ladies descendant only online site. I'd purchased Edith Wilson's dollhouse and number of her papers plus a diary. I'm distantly related to Dolley Madison, and the site is privately owned by an Adams descendant. I wanted to show the dollhouse to Inga who owns the antique store on the opposite end of the block from the theater. I displayed it near the storefront window to draw in customers. My shop is just a short hop, skip, and a jump from the Mississippi River, which flows over St. Anthony Falls. The falls once harnessed energy to mill Gold Medal and Pillsbury flour. The other side of the river is downtown Minneapolis. This neighborhood is home to some of the oldest buildings in the city. Not far down Main Street is the historic Stone Arch Bridge, built by James J. Hill, the railroad magnate. I was pleased that our location fit right in with all the nearby historic sites.

I gazed out the front window. The cobblestone street slowed a few motorists, but not all. Russ Lippmann walked past, heading toward the theater. He glanced in my direction, changed his course, and entered my store.

"Russ, how nice of you to come in."

"I'm sorry I haven't taken the time to look around." Russ smiled as he gazed around the room. "My mother would love one of these houses."

"Who was her favorite First Lady?"

"Oh, probably Abigail Adams. She loved how Abigail told John not to forget the ladies."

"Our first champion for equal rights," I said. "It's too bad that Abigail had such trouble with arthritis and couldn't travel much. She wasn't in the best of health once John became president."

"The historical White House is so plain compared to the one we have nowadays, isn't it?"

"Yes, and more gracious looking, I think."

"More welcoming—like come in and have a look around," Russ said. "I love it. Once the production run is finished, I'll bring Mother down here to take a look."

"Thank you. I'm looking forward to it."

Russ walked out the door. I watched him as he headed toward the theater and thought how his silhouette reminded me of the former president, Woodrow Wilson. I turned toward the sound of the back door opening.

"Hey, Nancy." I waved her over. "How much do I owe you for the muffins?"

"Forget it, Liv. I'm just happy that you're here. It's hard learning all these lines, and then Russ gave me a different script last night," Nancy said. She set the bag of muffins down and handed me my coffee cup.

"What? Tonight's your opening. Besides, he can't do that, can he? He's not the playwright," I said. I noticed that Nancy's brown eyes were bloodshot, and her usual neatly combed, long brown hair was unstyled. Her outfit was a wrinkled summer dress. "What'd you do? Sleep in your clothes?"

"No. I grabbed them from the clothes basket." She gulped down the muffin. "Didn't eat much except a bag of popcorn last night. I'm starved."

"Let's see that script." I took it from her offered hand. "I've read through it once because I had wanted to audition for the first lady role. Neither the president nor the first lady were depicted very well. What pages did he change?"

"Pages twelve through fourteen and further into Act Two as well," Nancy said.

"Russ is not the playwright, is he?"

"No. Ann Michel is," Nancy said. She flipped through the pages to the cover, and handed it to me for a look.

"This doesn't make any sense. The script is rewritten so that it depicts more about Edith Wilson's role in the White House as First Lady especially when her husband was seriously ill. The new title explains her role to a tee, *Meet Presidentress Edith Wilson*. How she handled the Suffragettes and how she supported him during the war," I said. "The script must be unlicensed, for the rewrite to legally happen." I flipped through it and read the marked changes in the first few pages. "What's he talking about here, anyway?"

"Unbelievable. -You'd think Russ would know better." Nancy's eyes opened wide.

"He's the Wilson biographer and probably doesn't want a dim light shown on the president." I frowned. "Still, I think you'd better speak to the director or producer."

"I'll talk to the stage manager, Linda." She sat down and stared up at me. "Now what do we do?"

"We rehearse the lines just as they were written." I opened to page one. "Where are you having trouble?"

"Right..." she got up and touched the spot on the page, "There."

"Okay. Why don't you go from, 'You can call me Mrs. President.'"

Nancy began to speak her lines: "You can call me Mrs. President, but truly, I relay to the President what's important, and he dictates what's needed, and then signs it. And I hand it over to the proper cabinet member."

I read the other parts and corrected Nancy as needed. At the end of Act I, I said, "That was good. Only four places where you were a bit off."

"Yes, but what's going to happen when Russ hears me recite these lines and not his rewrites?"

"Did he redo the script which refers to the Suffragists and the Night of Terror? The lines had surprised me because President Wilson's Fourteen Points happened in 1919 and the Suffragist movement in 1917. The women protested outside of the White House for six days." I read further. "He's deleted all of this! I can't believe it! Women almost died for the right to vote." Fuming, I stared at her. "He can't remove this. Those women fought hard. They lost their homes and families to march for equality."

"I know. That's what makes me so angry," Nancy said.

"I agree. When do you rehearse next?" I asked, scanning the script.

"Ten." She glanced at the clock. "Fifteen minutes."

"Talk to the stage manager." I handed back the script.

"You're right, I will," Nancy said. She finished her drink and threw all the paper scraps into the garbage. "As a matter of fact, I think that I'll do it right now."

"Walk softly and carry a big stick, as Teddy Roosevelt once said." I nodded my approval. "By the way, will you be able to work in the store today?"

"We're supposed to rehearse this morning and our call is five-thirty for this evening's production. Act I begins at 7:00 sharp." She brushed herself off. "I was hoping to go home and take a nap after rehearsal. I'm beat."

"If you need to, you can get some shut-eye here. Maybe Max will let you use his couch."

"I'll text him."

"No matter what, Aaron and I will be in the audience tonight. Break a leg!"

"Thanks! But, I hope not!"

Nancy left, and I strolled to the front door and unlocked it. After turning the Closed sign to Open, I went over to the computer and decided to do a search on the origin of the expression "break a leg." The source said that actors considered it bad luck to wish each other "good luck," so they said "break a leg" instead. It fit under the guise of superstition.

I clicked from the site and opened a file about Edith Wilson and another on Woodrow. I wondered why Russ would want to change history? It was wrong. Everyone knew that Wilson had been near death after a stroke and the First Lady took over the office, dictating and running the nation as if she was president.

My cell phone rang just as a customer entered. The call was from Aaron, so I let it go to message. Glancing at the customer, I said, "Good morning. How may I help you?" She looked vaguely familiar, but I was unable to place her.

"Just here to look around." She stopped right beside Edith Wilson's antique dollhouse. "This isn't for sale, is it?"

"No." I shook my head. "I just purchased it and believe it had belonged to Edith Wilson." I walked over toward her. "You're awfully familiar. If you don't mind my asking, who are you?"

"Linda — I'm the stage manager at the Rose Garden Theater. You've probably seen me walk past your window, that's all." Her tall, thin frame towered over me by a few inches. Her short blonde hair sparkled in the sunlight streaming through the window. She said: "Nancy just showed me what Russ did to the script."

"And?" I held my breath.

"I told her to say the original lines. You can't change them now, especially since she's not a professional actor. It's nerve-wracking enough for actors onstage without worrying about brand-new lines. The audience watching you, synchronizing your movements with your lines, stage light and sound changes, listening to the other actors recite, is really hard for a non-professional. I plan to speak to Russ in private when I get a chance," Linda said.

"I'm glad." I took a deep breath, and said, "It's not right to trim history. The stories of the Suffragists and the struggle for equal rights need telling."

"I agree. We still don't have the ERA, but at least we have voting rights, thanks to those women."

"Good! We're on the same side." I smiled and turned my attention back to the dollhouse. "I haven't had a chance to look closely at this."

"Well, I need to get back. I wanted to let you know not to worry about Nancy. She's doing a great job."

"Thank you," I said. Linda's smile lit up her face as we shook hands.

"See you later," she said.

Back by the computer, I withdrew my phone and listened to my voice mail. "Honey, can't make it to the opening tonight. I've been assigned another shift. Done at eleven. We'll have all day tomorrow. Kisses." I clicked from the message, and said, "Shoot!" aloud. I didn't want to have to go alone to the theater, but this type of situation happens when you're a policeman's wife. I took a deep breath to try and shrug off the disappointment before redialing.

"Liv? Sorry," Aaron immediately responded. "It can't be helped."

"Where will you be on patrol?"

"Right nearby. I'm going to try and sleep a little bit longer," Aaron said.

"Good, you need your sleep," I said. "I'm picking up some flowers for Nancy on her opening night, or do you think I should wait until after the show and give her a long stem rose?"

"Whatever you think is the thing to do."

We disconnected and I called my grandma for her opinion about flowers. Her suggestion was a single long stem rose at the end of the performance. I made a quick phone call and ordered one from the nearby florist, Yellow Daisy Floral. After, I logged into my store's website and noticed that there'd been a number of views over the previous few days, and I hoped the picture of the antique Edith Wilson dollhouse would draw them into the store. I answered a few questions concerning First Ladies before logging off the site.

The morning fled by with a couple customers coming inside for a "look and see" stroll between the aisles. I was all caught up for the moment on sewing the inaugural ball gowns so I removed my quilt pieces from the bag I stored nearby. During the down time, I worked on quilt squares. This particular quilt was called the Texas Star which once was known as the Dolley Madison Star. I'd finished piecing a block together in the workroom when Max entered, carrying an Edith Wilson dollhead. He also had to tell me that tonight he planned to carve another Barbara Bush doll since a customer inquired about her yesterday. He made sure that we always had one doll to spare of each First Lady.

"Have you heard from Nancy?" I asked before he walked out.

"She's upstairs on the couch." Max removed a cigarette from his pocket.

"Catch you later." I knew he wouldn't return anymore today. Carving dolls and looking after the store was his main job, but for extra cash, he picked up odd jobs. I never really knew what or where he worked besides his store hours. Basically, I trusted him to take over when I had to be gone and Nancy wasn't here. I respected his privacy.

I glanced at the clock and realized that it was time for lunch. Down the block was a hamburger joint, and I purchased one to go plus a glass of iced tea. The rest of the afternoon was spent sewing Edith Wilson's inaugural gown. The black charmeuse satin trim on black velvet gave me a headache. I set the tiny gown aside to finish on another day. I picked up Barbara Bush's royal-blue gown and stitched the velvet bodice and skirt. I finished the gown and readied it for the doll, which I still needed to paint.

It was time for me to lock up and head home. After placing all the fabric scraps inside a container and cleaning the work area, I went to the front and locked the door, switching the sign from Open to Closed. I grabbed my bag, and locked the back door behind me as I walked out.

Once home, I ate a quick dinner and got myself ready for the theater. I checked to make sure the tickets were where they should be in my bag, that I had my phone and keys before leaving the house. I started the car, backed from the garage, and pressed the remote control to shut the door. It didn't take long before I was purchasing the rose, and driving the car toward the theater. I parked in my usual parking spot behind the store, and walked around toward the front of the building.

I pulled out my phone and sent a message to Nancy, saying, "*Good luck.*" It didn't take long before I receive a response, which said, "*Thanx!*"

Once inside the main lobby, I took a few minutes to read the wall-hung playbills and peruse pictures and short bios about each of the actors. I grinned while reading Nancy's because there was a mention of the store.

When the auditorium opened, I showed my ticket, grabbed a playbill and went to sit. The soft music conjured up the Wilson era. Sitting right up front, I watched as the properties manager gave a final peek at the stage. The stage manager, Linda, walked out the side entrance speaking into her headphone. I placed the long stem rose across my lap. I missed Aaron beside me. Suddenly my phone chirruped and I glanced at it. Aaron had sent a message saying that he was entering the theater and not to leave my seat, no matter what.

His message didn't make much sense. My first thought was that he had changed shifts with someone. A moment later, the music suddenly stopped, and a hush fell across the audience as we waited for the actors to take their places. I watched as the spotlight hit center stage, illuminating Linda.

"Ladies and gentlemen, please remain seated. Something has happened. The performance is delayed. We will keep you posted." She walked off the stage.

Removing my phone, I texted Aaron. *"What is it?"* When he didn't respond within thirty seconds, my natural curiosity took over and I became restless. Finally, a response. It read, "keep cool." *What the heck did that mean?*

Within a few minutes, people began walking toward the exit doors. Suddenly, Aaron walked on stage, wearing Linda's headset.

"May I have your attention, please?" He waited a moment, then repeated himself. After another few moments, the crowd quieted. "I have some bad news. The doors are locked, and we'll have to take everyone's name and phone number before you'll be allowed to leave. There's been an accident and tonight's performance is cancelled." Aaron glanced down at me, and quickly looked away.

Linda took back the headgear, and said, "The theater will offer a full refund, or you can use your tickets next week when we'll reopen this production."

I looked up at Aaron, who shook his head.

The person behind me shouted, "What happened?"

"No one is to leave without giving their full name to a police officer. There are several officers stationed by the main lobby doors. The back doors are off-limits."

I got up, and briskly walked toward the dressing rooms to check on Nancy.

Chapter Two

I accidentally stepped on someone's toe.

He said, "Watch it, lady!"

"Sorry!" I kept going until at last coming to the backstage curtain. I knew my way around since I'd walked through the building many times during the renovation. Once backstage, I bumped into the stage manager.

"Linda, where's Nancy?" I put my hand on Linda's shoulder to get her to look me in the eye. When I saw the look in her eyes, I shivered. "What happened?"

"I went to call 'places,' for starting," Linda said. She covered her face, and then blinked at me. "I can't begin the performance unless everyone is in their designated place. Nancy never showed." Linda looked away and then back again. "I went to the dressing room and found her slumped over the makeup table. I called her name."

"Did she answer?"

"Yep. I thought her eyes looked hazy." Linda thought a minute, and continued, "She held up two fingers—you know—like this, but said 'five'." Linda held up her fingers like a 'v'. "It seemed odd. I called for the medics because she just plain didn't seem right and her speech was slurred."

"I'd like to know why the police are involved," I said, furrowing my brows. "Can I see her?"

"The medics are with her. I doubt you can get into the room."

"I'd like to try."

I followed close behind as we walked through a wall of uniformed police officers and EMTs, presumably from the outside ambulance. Suddenly I came to a halt when Aaron stepped out from beside another officer.

"Oh no, you don't, Liv. You go home."

"What?" I crossed my arms and stared at him. "Nancy's my friend and employee. I have a right to know what's going on. Besides, maybe I can help." I shrugged. "I'll keep out of the way."

"Take her into the office," Aaron told a younger officer.

"Can't I at least see her?" My face flushed as the beginning of a horrible thought began to creep into my consciousness. I peeked around him and saw Nancy. The medics were carefully lowering her onto the gurney. I realized that I may not ever be able to speak to Nancy again.

"The body is still warm, she hasn't been dead for too long. Odd skin tone," a medic stated. The medics began preparing her for the ambulance.

"Interesting," Detective Mergens said, jotting it down in his notebook.

"How can she be dead? She was healthy when I texted her before the performance," I said, puzzled.

"Let her in," Detective Mergens said, stepping from the room. He looked at me and said, "I figured since it had to do with a First Lady and it happened right beside your store, my partner and I better come right away. I sent a couple of uniform officers, just to be safe." He nodded to Aaron. "Officer Reynolds, let her take a look."

"Follow me," Aaron said.

I did as told, and stayed right behind my husband. Nancy looked peacefully asleep and her upswept long hair still in the Edith Wilson hairstyle. A rather large hat lay on the dressing table.

"She can't be dead," I said. A nearby chair was brought over and I sank into it. "When I saw the police, I wondered if something awful had happened. I feel miserable. Nancy was a good person and a friend."

"Do you know her next of kin?" Detective Mergens asked.

"She wasn't married. I'm sure I have her parents' number on file, but I don't recall offhand."

"Don't worry, we'll locate them. It would be helpful if you could look around and see if anything appears different, or out of place," Detective Mergens said gently.

Tears flooded my eyes as the medics covered Nancy with a sheet and wheeled her from the room.

"Give me a minute to pull myself together," I said. I wiped my eyes dry and took in a few deep breaths. I glanced around the room. "A pot of Irish shamrocks? That's odd for opening night. Her parents weren't able to make the opening because they're on vacation. Nancy's between boyfriends," I said.

"Interesting. I knew you'd be able to help us out," Detective Mergens said. To a nearby officer, he said, "Let's bag the plant if for not no other reason than it's odd for an opening night performance." He continued, "Can you tell us anything else?"

"Not really." I looked over to Aaron. "I feel just sick for her and her poor family."

"Linda, right?" Mergens said, shifting his gaze to the stage manager. "Is this how she was when you saw her?"

"Yes. Nothing looks disturbed," Linda said.

"What is that smell?" I asked.

"Funny, I hadn't noticed any smell," a voice said from where the costumes hung. Detective Erlandsen came around the corner holding up a long, velvet dress and said, "Liv, I thought I heard your voice. Why is Nancy's name on this? And why isn't she in this costume?"

"She wears a different dress in each act," Linda said. She wiped her eyes. "That's for the second act. What she's wearing now is for the first act."

"I believe that she took a nap before the performance up in Max's apartment. Not sure where he is at the moment, though." Now that I'd been able to see Nancy, I wanted to leave. "Was Russ here? He wanted Nancy to completely change her lines last night. Fooling around with the history in the play, changing every line pertaining to the Fourteen Points and the Suffragists. Nancy was very upset about it. I told her to talk to you, Linda."

"She did, and I told her not to worry. It was too late in the game to rewrite lines. She'd never have had time to relearn them," Linda said. "That was crazy on Russ's part."

"Russ, the Wilson biographer?" Aaron asked.

"Yes," Linda and I answered in unison.

"He also owns the theater," I said. "He's a little on the grumpy-grouchy side, too."

"Got it," Mergens stated, holding his pad and pen. "Anything else about anyone that we need to know or you think may be relevant?"

"Not at the moment," I said. "Oh! I dropped my rose someplace out there that I was to give her. I guess it doesn't matter now, does it?" "Can I leave now?"

"You sure can, and you've been most helpful," Erlandsen to me. "If you think of anything weird or different, I want to know."

"I know. First Ladies, and all that." I yanked my bag up higher on my shoulder and let Aaron pull me out of the room and lead me to the outside door. "I'm sick about this, Aaron. What caused her death?" We continued to the car. "She was in good health."

"It's questionable," Aaron said. He opened the car door. "The cause of death won't be known until the autopsy. You know all of that."

"Sure, but then why were the detectives there? They must've had suspicions." I climbed into the car.

"When they heard it had to do with a First Lady, their internal antennas perked up. They worked the last few cases with you or should I say, 'us'? You were always right on target for the how and why of the case."

"Okay. Thanks for the backhanded compliment," I said. "When will you be home? Eleven?"

"My shift ends then, but who knows, now that this has happened," Aaron said. "Straight home now, and text me when you get there."

"I will." I started the engine and slowly drove away. I watched him through the rearview mirror as he hurried back to the theater doors.

Five minutes later I turned into the new subdivision and headed toward my house. As soon as the garage door lowered and I entered the kitchen door. The back of my neck tickled, and I shivered. I set my bag down on the countertop and went to the refrigerator, pulling out a small soda. I popped open the lid and went out to the living room where I turned on the TV. With my feet up on the coffee table, I slipped out my cell phone and sent Aaron a message telling him that I was home. Next, I looked for messages, and found one from Grandma. Grandma and Grandpa were like my parents, having raised me since I was eleven, after my parents were killed in a hit-and-run car accident. We never did find out who was responsible.

Grandma liked to send me messages similar classroom tests, and this one was no different. It read: 1: How was the performance? A) excellent B) good C) otherwise D) icky. 2: Nancy was A) beautiful B) wonderful C) all of the above. 3: Did you remember flowers? T or F.

I answered with a phone call. "Grandma? You'd better sit down."

"Oh dear Lord," she softly said. "Should I get Grandpa?"

"You'd better."

"Be right back." I took a few deep breaths while waiting for her return.

"Let's have it, Olivia," Grandpa said. "Something happen to Aaron?"

"No. Don't even think that," I said. My heart pounded. "It's about Nancy. She's dead. We don't know what happened until the autopsy results are published."

"Tell me about it." Grandpa said. "Where and when did this happen?"

"I suppose those two detectives were johnny-on-the-spot, eh? Eager beavers," Grandpa said. "Quick to jump but not very high."

"Yep. Erlandsen and Mergens. They were right there and they let me look at her. It was awful," I said. I glanced out the window to help refocus. "The stage manager had called for places, but Nancy never made it to her spot."

"Was she feeling okay beforehand?" Grandpa asked.

"I believe so. A little tired and scared to death, but that's understandable."

"Poor choice of words, Livvie," Grandma said.

"I know. Sorry." Tears moistened my eyes. "I did go backstage and saw that the medics were busy looking after her. Aaron was there, and the two detectives. He says they took the case when they heard about the First Lady connection. No one knows if it's foul play or not, or if there's any connection to the store."

"This is awful news," Grandma said. "Anything we can do? Want us to bring you some chicken soup tomorrow?"

"It's too hot outside for that, but thanks for the offer."

"Alrighty. Keep us informed," Grandma said.

"Signing off." Grandpa disconnected.

"Night." I barely got the word out before Grandma had done the same. Suddenly my world was silent. I finished my soda, shut off the TV and hit the sack.

Aaron rolled into bed about one o'clock. I briefly woke to kiss him, then turned over and went back to sleep. My dreams were filled with running lines from the play, and Nancy's voice telling me that nothing was as it seemed.

I woke up sweaty, and went to shower. Afterward, I slipped into my navy blue capris, red top and draped a white scarf around my neck, all in honor of Nancy. She played the role of a patriot, so it seemed fitting to wear the colors of the flag. In the kitchen, I made up a few extra strawberry and blueberry pancakes for Aaron, that he could easily reheat in the microwave. I quickly ate mine. Aaron would later clean up the dishes. I decided to walk to work, so I grabbed my bag before heading out the door.

My thoughts immediately turned to Nancy and the rewritten lines. *Why was it so important? What did I really know about the Wilson's or the Suffragists?* I decided that I needed to read all there was about the Fourteen Points, since they were mentioned in some of the crossed-out lines. Same with the lines about the Suffragists and the "Night of Terror," when Alice Paul and nine other women were jailed and almost died in prison for protesting outside of the White House for the right to vote. *What would Edith Wilson have had to do with these things? Would she have hidden something in a secret First Lady desk drawer in the White House? Or hide something in another location?*

Was Russ trying to change history with his rewrites? Or had he already rewritten history in his biography? The Fourteen Points had to do with peace negotiations and setting up a postwar world. Why would he rewrite the events of the Suffragist movement when it had little to do with the war? Pressing questions that I couldn't answer.

I passed the Lowry Bridge and kept walking down Main Street, below the old Grain Belt Brewery. In the distance, I saw the old Pillsbury Flour tower. Soon the store came into view and I walked around back. While punching in the security code, I noticed a patrol car parked and an officer standing outside the theater's entrance. I entered my store.

"Hey!" Max greeted me from a stool in the workroom. "Here we go again, eh? More questions by the same two detectives. Mergens and Erlandsen and neither know what's what."

"Yep. Unfortunately. I feel sick about Nancy."

"She was a good kid." Max held a cigarette between his fingers. "Phone's been ringing off the hook. That's why I'm here early."

"I was just about to ask. Figures, right?"

"I suppose Ronnie will be wanting a scoop soon, too," I said, frowning. Ronnie Johnson was an old school chum, and he drove me nuts with his photographer's nosiness.

"I thought I'd heard he'd moved to parts unknown." Max stood. "I'm going for a smoke now that you're here. Won't be long. The police will probably want to talk to me."

"I told them that Nancy took a nap in your apartment. She did, didn't she?"

"Yep. She was fit as a fiddle afterwards, too. Didn't look sick at all."

"They'll want to know that," I said. Max passed by me, and I went out into the showroom. As I entered, the phone rang and I hurried over to it. "White House Dollhouse store, how may I help you?"

"I'm from the local Nordeast paper."

"Name?"

"Sam."

"Sam, don't call back because I don't know anything." I slammed down the phone. As I turned on the computer, the phone rang again. I answered with the same line and it turned out to be the same reporter on the other end, and he got the same response. After that, I let all calls go to the answering machine.

I clicked into the Internet and while it warmed up, I went over and opened the front door, turning the sign around. As I did so, I noticed several people lining the sidewalk. Opening the door, I glanced down the block and realized that the line stretched from the theater down to my store.

"Why are you all lined up?" I asked the nearest person.

"To find out if our tickets for tonight are good. Someone was murdered at the show last night."

"Really? That's awful," I said.

"I heard it was the actress." The woman turned back around and I dipped back indoors.

The traffic in my store had grown considerably since it first opened six years ago. In that time, I'd added an extra assistant. Nancy drew in the university crowd, where her girlfriends purchased houses for their moms or vice-versa. I knew I had to place an ad for a new assistant, but hated the thought of replacing Nancy so soon. I decided to wait.

As I began my search for good Wilson biographers, a customer entered.

"Hello!" I said. "How may I help you?"

"Just nosy. Heard about this store and had to stop since I'm in the neighborhood."

"Stroll around. Take all the time you need. Any questions, just ask." I noticed that the middle-age woman walked a little too slowly and stopped a little too long by the antique Edith Wilson dollhouse. "Isn't that a gorgeous house? I just purchased it for fun. It's not for sale." I got up and went over toward her.

"It's very old, isn't it?" She glanced at me sideways then turned away. "I best be gone."

"You from the theater? You look familiar."

"I designed the costumes. Carol." She smiled. "I'm a distant relative of Edith Wilson and wanted to give it a try. They hired me because of my connection."

"Were you there last night when it all happened?"

"No—I made sure the dresses were ready, then left before the show."

"I'm sure we'll meet up again," I said. "Have you taken a look at the gowns for my First Lady dolls? I sew them myself for each First Lady."

"I will."

I took that as my cue to distance myself. Some people just don't like a salesperson hovering near. The ringing phone jolted me, and I went back to my chair. There were four messages to hear plus several hang-up calls. I went ahead and ran a search on Wilson biographers, and ordered one for my Kindle by a well-known biographer. I already had Russ's on my Kindle but hadn't time to read it. The comparison of the two biographers might prove interesting. I picked up my iPhone and downloaded the new purchase. Next, I Googled the Fourteen Points and printed a copy of the document and did the same with the information of the Night of Terror.

I played back the messages and deleted them from the machine after listening. All were reporters wanting information—except one. I kept it for the detectives to hear because it was rather cryptic. A voice said, "They all deserved it."

Deserved what? Who is "they?"

Chapter Three

The evening brought with it much sadness because Nancy's father contacted me, and I didn't know what to say. How can you tell someone that their daughter may have met her death by an act of evil? I listened to the pain in his voice and heard the anguish from her mother in the background. When we disconnected, I hoped the conversation helped ease their pain. My heart went out to them. I wished that I could've helped them in their grief—I couldn't imagine what it'd be like to lose a child.

After we hung up, I was too distraught to read. I pulled out the quilt block directions and measured the fabric for equal lengths to cut. When that was done, I felt ready to tackle more research.

I read through the Fourteen Points, and made a mental note to ask for a copy of the script for comparison purposes. I wanted to know what points Russ zeroed in on. As I pondered the Fourteen Points which the League of Nations (and later led to the United Nations) was based, it brought back memories.

Grandma used to speak of her mother, my great-grandma, and how wonderful it had been for her to vote for the first time. Great-grandma and great-grandpa visited with friends the night before Election Day. My grandma sat in the kitchen with the women, who spoke about how wonderful it would be to cast a vote in the next election. Grandma said that they were giddy with excitement. I gave Grandma a call.

"Grandma."

"It's late, Livvie dear. Past my bedtime. It's nine."

"Sorry." I pushed on. "Grandma, what can you tell me about the night before your mother voted?"

"Not much, dear. I had a glass of milk and cookies. Mother giggled at the thought of voting for the first time. They decided to choose the candidate who seemed the most progressive. They hoped the Equal Rights Amendment would pass."

"We're still waiting for that to happen, aren't we? Today's young women need to fight for their rights," I said. "Good night."

We disconnected, and at the same time Aaron walked in the backdoor.

"I'm in here," I called, and he was soon beside me. "You're home early."

"Rough night. I cut out early since I worked late last night," Aaron said. He placed his arm over my shoulder. "How's your night?"

"Nancy's parents called." I leaned into him. "I feel sorry for them. She was such a polite and conscientious person. She brought in muffins and when I stayed home from the flu virus, she brought me a pot of beef stew to eat. The clients loved her historical knowledge and patience." I glanced at the clock. "This going to be a long day. I look at the houses and think of how Nancy would straighten them. Her grace and charm usually brought in a new sale. I'll really miss her." I dried my eyes. "Tough situation."

"It's a bad deal, but I must ask you to not speak to Nancy's parents anymore until we have the autopsy report and the investigation is complete."

"You sound ominous," I said. I looked up to him. "Like her death is more than suspicious. Max said she looked fine after her nap."

"No comment."

"You don't have to answer." I thought how Grandma used test questions to find out answers, and decided to try it out on him. "True or false."

"Not this," Aaron said. He wagged his finger.

"Poisoned. True or false?"

"I won't answer because you'll trick me," Aaron said.

"Poisoned plant. True or false?"

"I'm zipping my lips."

"Good grief. I'm going to shower and hit the sack," I said. I started to walk toward the bedroom.

"Don't be mad. I just can't compromise the ongoing investigation. You know that." Aaron called out, "Can't help it, honey."

"I know." I'd have to devise another strategy. I snatched my nightie, and went for a shower. By the time I'd finished, Aaron was already in bed.

"Say you're not mad," he pleaded as he opened the covers for me.

"I'm not. Just promise me that you'll find out who would send Nancy a plant for opening night," I said.

"That's up to the detectives to discover."

Crawling in beside him, I decided upon a few unanswered questions. Aaron's "no comment" was satisfaction enough. Nancy had been murdered, I was certain. I hadn't seen any blood. In the morning, I'd do a search on poisons.

I kissed my honey goodnight, and fell fast asleep.

The morning brought sunshine streaming in through the windows and car doors slamming shut. Time for me to get up. I dressed in a vintage dress from the 1950's, which came from Grandma's trunk. When I'd sorted through all of her trunks a few years ago, I found a treasure trove of old dresses, and we were about the same size. I was thrilled. Today, I felt like wearing a dress similar in style to Mamie Eisenhower, in a pink flowered print.

Aaron was already frying bacon and I smelled fresh coffee as I walked into the kitchen.

"You're up early," I said. I crawled in behind my coffee cup, already set on the table. "Court?"

"Yes. Ten," Aaron said.

I glanced at the clock. "You've got two hours to spare."

"I want to read the autopsy report if it's in before I head downtown." Aaron smiled at me. "You look pretty in pink."

"Thank you." I drank my coffee and ate up. Aaron's eggs always tasted better than mine. I do try hard. It's not easy burning so many meals. "Let's put steaks on for supper."

"Okay. I'll pick 'em up on the way home," Aaron said.

We finished our meal and went our separate ways. I drove because the temperatures were supposed to climb and it was already unbearable. It wasn't long before I parked out back and strolled toward my store. Suddenly, I decided to take a side trip down to my friend at Inga's antique shop. I loved Inga. She'd tipped me off about First Lady memorabilia when they'd come on the open market. She also was a good friend of Grandma's through a metro garden club.

She gave me a surprised look when I entered. "Hey. How are you?" I said.

"It's been at least three days since you've been by," Inga said. "What's new?"

"You haven't heard about Nancy?" I said. "I believe she was murdered last night. I'm just sick about it."

"No, I haven't heard a thing. Have a seat, girl, and tell me all about it," Inga said. She brought out an old cane back chair from behind the counter. "Who did it? Any idea? How did it happen?"

I went ahead and relayed the story. "I tried to get Aaron to tell me more last night, but he wouldn't. I may be wrong, but I think she may have been poisoned. I have a hunch it was something applied to a pot of Irish shamrocks someone sent her before the show."

"Shamrocks? Poison? Nancy was such a nice young woman. Where were the shamrocks?" Inga said.

"On her dressing table," I said.

"Hmmmm..." Inga was thinking.

"Could it have been an accident?" I asked, "Like, poison left on a plant from a garden recently tended? Rain usually washes pesticides away flowers."

"See? But why would any poison be on shamrocks?" I said.

"Maybe it wasn't. It could have come from the potting soil too," Inga said.

"It may or not have been deliberate, is what you're saying?"

"Hard for me to say, not knowing all the facts," Inga said.

"True. Until Aaron tells me more, I guess I'm stuck with puzzle pieces," I said.

"Not to change the subject, but that dress looks nice on you. Mamie Eisenhower would be proud. Which reminds me, something came up on Amazon the other day that you might be interested in," Inga said.

"Russ's biography of the President Wilson was trashed by a reviewer," Inga said.

"Send me the link, will you?" I said.

"Will do."

I walked over toward the hat rack because there was a large Victorican style hat displayed. I placed it on my head. "Yikes! Who would want to wear this thing all day? It's like the hat Edith Wilson wore on inauguration day."

"It does, doesn't it?"

I paid for the hat, and walked out the door wearing it on my head. Arriving at my store, I typed in the security code and opened the door. Once inside, I removed the hat, placing it down on the workroom counter where most pieces go when they don't have a home. After turning on the lights, I headed into the showroom, and circled the display tables. All the dollhouses looked in good shape for the day, and not much was out of place from customers rearranging the furniture.

Next I strolled to the First Lady portraits hung above the old President Lincoln desk, and made sure they were even, and rearranged the Penny Dolls. I got the computer started, and began to search for information on pesticides. I found a number of sites to dig into. As I pressed on the first link, the back door opened.

"Liv, what's going on? Any news?" Max said. He strode into the room. "Just got a call from the detectives, and they want to meet me here. They hinted at my apartment, but I said no, here in the store. Why on earth would they want to go to my apartment? It's a dump. Who wants to look at that mess?"

"The big question is who would want to harm Nancy? I liked her, and so did everyone else. What would be the motive? She never spoke badly of anyone. Why not let them look at your apartment?"

"Like I said, it's a mess.

"They just want a quick look-see," I said. I quickly clicked from the site, and got up. A funny feeling came over me as I walked toward him. "Aaron's being pretty tight-lipped at the moment."

"We did figure she was murdered, didn't we?" Max said.

"Indications point in that direction, but until we know for sure…" I said.

"Yeah, right. It's like the other three murders you solved: the missing Star Spangled Banner manuscript, the lost speech from Abraham Lincoln, and Teddy Roosevelt's land deed. We don't really find out much unless we stumble upon it. All clues surround us, but don't indicate any one thing."

"So?"

"I'm tired of snoopy cops, and you finding yourself in the middle of another First Lady murder," Max said. "I'm also scared for your life. You've been injured once before and landed in the hospital and so has Inga."

"Okay," I said. "We don't know if this has anything to do with the President's wife or even if it is a murder." I tapped my chin. "I have some thinking to do. Something's bugging me. I wonder if there's a desk or a personal item that the First Ladies pass down to each other?"

"You should know the answer to that by now, Liv. First Lady and all. You've studied all that long and hard."

"No one knows everything. But thanks for the compliment," I said.

"I'm going for a smoke." He turned, and removed a cigarette from his upper pocket.

I unlocked the front door and turned the sign around. I hoped for a number of customers today since the weather was sunny. I already noticed plenty of walkers or bikers along the Mississippi River trail. The trail circled from the Hennepin Avenue Bridge down to the Stone Arch Bridge, crossing over St. Anthony Falls.

Back at the computer, I was just ready to click onto the link and begin my research on pesticides when the front door opened and detectives Mergens and Erlandsen entered.

"Max's out back having a smoke," I said.

"Okay," Erlandsen said.

The two continued walking. I heard the back door opening and closing, and the voices from the hallway faded. I clicked onto the site when Linda entered.

"Can we talk?" She strode over to me. "It's kinda urgent."

"Go ahead. I'd get you a chair, but the workroom is off limits at the moment."

"I'm between a rock and a hard place," Linda said. She crossed her arms. "I'm at a complete loss. The actors are bugging the life out of me and want the show to go on for Nancy's memory. There's no one to take her place."

"What about the understudy? I thought she had one?" I said.

"She won't do it." Linda shifted from one leg to the next. "What should we do?"

"It's up to the producer and financial backer to decide what happens, not you. Right?"

"That's Russ and he wants to go ahead, but we can't without an actress. I thought of you." She raised her eyebrow and stared at me. "You'd be great."

"No. That's my answer," I said. *Not on your life, missy.*

Just at the nick of time, the workroom door opened, and the men stepped out. I glanced toward the hallway and watched all three enter.

"Linda, we need to talk," Erlandsen said.

"Why? You've already talked to me. I don't know anything else. I promise."

"Just a couple added questions that we just thought of," Erlandsen reassured her. "No need to worry."

"Can we use your workroom again?" Mergens asked.

"You won't be long, will you?" I said.

"No." Mergens shook his head.

"Okay."

"Please," Linda said. "I've got work to do. I don't know anything. Can't you get that through your head?" She turned and rushed out the front door.

Detective Erlandsen dashed after her out the front door and Mergens took the back in case she ran around the block and down the alley. I glanced over to Max, standing there with a cigarette in his mouth. He nodded toward the back door.

"Then come back and talk to me," I said.

"Will do."

My thoughts starting churning. I recalled the number of times Linda was alone with Nancy—and discovered her just before she died. Shivers raced up and down my spine, not an unfamiliar feeling. But I had work to do. I clicked back onto the link and waded through information about effects of too much pesticides on plants. Not what I needed. I needed the effect of pesticides on humans. As I began another search, the front door opened and a customer entered. I closed out of the site, and approached her.

"Hello. I'm Liv, the owner. Can I help you?"

"Love your dress. Where'd you get it?" The woman wore capris, and pushed a baby in small umbrella stroller.

"My grandma's trunk—it was full of these old things. I thought they'd be fun to wear once in awhile."

"Love it!" She smiled, showing a beautiful set of teeth. Her short purple hair and nose ring made me think of my youth.

"Who's your favorite First Lady?"

"Right now, it's Hillary Clinton. She's done so much for our country." She glanced at the White Houses. "Which is hers?"

"That'd be over here," I said. I brought her to the correct White House. "The first White House website was launched during the Clinton Administration." The baby began fretting and wiggling around so I said, "You take your time. Any questions, just ask." I left her and went back to sit by the counter. Within a few minutes, the baby started to wail.

"I'll be back later!" the woman called as she marched out the door pushing the stroller.

"Sure!"

I began to wonder about Linda when the detectives reentered the store, just as Max came in from the back.

"What happened to Linda?" I asked Max.

"I think Nancy's death made a wreck out of her," he said. "She'll be fine."

"We wanted to know a couple things, and she helped us," Erlandsen said. He looked at me square. "I'll tell you this, since you've probably been snooping around and will find out anyway, but the autopsy report isn't available yet. Nancy was a healthy young woman. No allergies on record. No known enemies. No trouble with the law, not even a speeding ticket or driving unbuckled. That's why we have a strong suspicion she was murdered. That brings us to you."

"Me?" I glanced from one detective to the other. "What are you talking about? I didn't murder her. I don't know anyone who would. Nancy was a nice girl. A very good employee. An all-around nice person."

"I realize that. And that's why we wanted to talk to you. You can't deny you have a track record on this sort of case and know about the First Ladies more than most people."

"Here we go again. Max? You were right. First Lady and all." I crossed my arms. "Tell you what. If I come up with any kind of theory, you two will be the first to know."

Chapter Four

After the detectives left, I gave up on my pesticide search and reached for my sewing. I was happy that I'd spent the time last night cutting squares. As I worked on the fabric, piecing the squares together to make the star, my thoughts circled between Nancy, her parents, and the theater. Who would want to kill her? She was so nice. After awhile, I refocused on business and began sorting through receipts and getting a bank deposit ready. So much paperwork, sometimes it gets overwhelming. It seemed like hours, but really only one, when Aaron walked into the store carrying a couple of raspberry iced teas.

"Thanks. It's just what I needed." I took a sip. "What brings you here? How did court go?"

"It was fine. Glad it's done. Caught the guy red-handed. He couldn't get out of it," Aaron said. He sipped his drink. "Hear you had excitement this morning, eh?"

"News travels fast in your world." I leaned back to relax, swishing my straw around. "Why did Linda run?"

"I think," he said, "she thought they were accusing her."

"Nancy had to have been murdered. She was healthy, and never complained of an illness. Everyone liked her. She hadn't an enemy in the world," I said, and studied him. "Admit it."

"The autopsy is being done now. The death was sudden, and unexplained. The detectives are involved because of you and me, and Nancy played the part of a former First Lady," Aaron said. "Tell me about Linda."

"From what I've seen of her, she couldn't kill a fly. She wanted me to step in as Mrs. Wilson. I don't care to do it."

"Stay away from the theater and the entire cast and crew."

"I'd like to compare the original script with what Russ wanted edited out. Nancy showed me her script—I want to go and look for it."

"I don't want you involved in this," Aaron said.

"'I can go right now, if you'd stay here. You can ding me if someone comes in."

"Reluctantly. If you're not back in fifteen minutes, I'm coming over there," Aaron said.

"Thanks." I came around and gave him a kiss before hiking out the back door. The heat of the day took my breath away, and the bright sunshine was blinding. The old brick buildings always thrilled me. To think that our city's founding fathers, the Washburns and Pillsburys may have walked these same streets, along with President McKinley during the 1892 Republican National Convention, and its former mayor, Hubert H. Humphrey, excited me. I smiled as I opened the theater's back door.

Once I stepped inside, the dark backstage hit me like a brick. It took a minute for my eyes to adjust. I stood in the wings on one side of the main stage. Of course, it has to be dark, I thought. The whole backstage area was pitch black except for what belonged to the set.

"Anyone home?" I hollered. "It's Liv." I waited a minute before hearing footsteps approach from behind.

"Linda here. Hold on." She turned on an overhead light, which illuminated a small area. "Don't move. Let me come to you."

"It wasn't like this last night." I stood still. Black sidewalls moved, allowing me to see her. "Why don't you have the lights turned on?"

"There have been a few gawkers coming in to ask questions. I also don't want the police to keep sneaking up on me and asking a million questions. Whenever they're around, the media shows up and gets in the way."

"Why'd you run out of my shop, if you don't mind me asking?"

"All those questions. It's not even declared a murder yet, and they've asked me more than my fair share of questions. I'm starting to feel like a suspect."

"So you got scared and ran?"

"Yes." Linda smiled. "Want to come back with me? I was in the dressing room and trying to figure out what to do with it all. Should I touch anything or not?" She began walking, and I followed. "Be careful of the props."

"I will."

"Don't brush the table, it's loaded with unique items." We stopped beside it. "This is a copy of Edith's diary, the Fourteen Points, Wilson's glasses, and her purse."

"Okay," I said. I noted the items on the prop table. By now, I'd completely adjusted to the light. "Whose hat?"

"Susan B. Anthony. The actress in the play looks a lot like her," Linda said.

"This is all interesting. Are you saying it's really Susan B. Anthony's hat? Not a reproduction?" I said.

"I don't know. It came with all the props. You'll have to ask the property manager, Sylvie."

"How interesting. Show me the dressing room," I said.

We continued our course and at last came to the room. Linda opened the door and let me enter first.

"This is exactly where Nancy was sitting, isn't it?"

"Yes," Linda said. Tears filled both of our eyes. "I can't believe she's gone, Liv. I'm a wreck. I picture her slumped over. I barely remember dialing the emergency number."

"Somehow, we'll manage," I said. "I'm glad that you found her, really and truly. You're a good person, and you looked after her. That's wonderful."

"Thank you." Linda sniffled, and pulled back. After wiping her eyes and blowing her nose, she asked, "Thought anymore about taking her place?"

"What will happen if I don't?"

"The play will fold." She crossed her arms. "We're barely hanging on as it is."

"You're basically volunteers, right?"

"The actors, technical and stage crew are."

"I wondered if you still have Nancy's script."

"It should be lying around here," Linda said. "I'm so glad you'll do it."

"When will the theater reopen?" I asked.

"Next week, if you can learn your part by then."

"We'll see—I'll work on lines over the next few days, but Aaron doesn't want me coming near the theater," I said. We searched through the trash, drawers, and up and down the makeup counter. "I don't see it."

"He'll enjoy seeing you perform."

"I'll tell him that."

"Let me see if I can locate her costumes."

"Sure." I sat in the nearest chair, and scanned the clothing on the floor. I flicked through a stack of scripts from a previous play, Martha Washinington's First Days in Office, and something caught my eye. A doodle. Just like the ones Nancy was always drawing. My eyes opened wide when I realized that it was her's. "Found it!"

Linda re-entered. "I was ready to give up. I searched through all the costume pockets. Even dresses not associated with this play. "Where was it?""

"It was in this pile of old scripts. I recognized Nancy's doodling, and pulled it out." I opened it and out fell a note I quickly slid it into the palm of my hand, and then into my pocket. I didn't want Linda to see it. I held up the script. "It's definitely Nancy's. All those cross-outs."

"Was that a note I saw you put into your pocket?" She placed her hands on her hips.

"Yes, it might be important. I plan to turn it over to my husband, Aaron."

"At least tell me what it says." She tapped her foot.

"Well…" I debated. "All right, why not?" I opened the note and read it out loud: "I'm in danger. If you find this, Liv, you'll know what to do."

"That's horrible." Linda sucked in her breath and sank into a chair. "In danger? From whom?"

"Good question."

"Now what?"

"We must turn this over to the police, right now," I said. I took out my cell phone and dialed Detective Erlandsen's number.

"You have his number?" Linda said. Her eyes flew wide open.

"Aaron's a cop, remember?" I said just as the phone was answered on the other end.

"Liv. What's up?" Erlandsen said.

"I think you'd better come to the theater. I just found something you might be interested in seeing."

"What is it?" Erlandsen said.

"Nancy left a note hidden in her script," I said.

"Don't touch anything else. We're on our way," Erlandsen said.

The phone disconnected, and I gave Aaron a quick call to explain the situation. "I'm going to have to stay a little while," I said.

"I'll get Max to take over, and be right there," Aaron responded before disconnecting.

"The police? Again? I'm never going to get over this. Stay with me, will you?" Linda clutched my shoulder. "Promise?"

"Promise." Something about her unnerved me, but I wasn't sure what it was. What was she so scared about? "Now, can I please have a script to read through?"

"Oh, sure," Linda said. She edged toward the door. "Be right back." Suddenly the lights went out.

"Doggone it!" I said. I stumbled after her. "Linda, stop right now." I flipped on the lights once again.

As I neared the back door, I heard voices. One sounded like Aaron. I ran outside just as he grabbed hold of Linda.

"Gotcha!" Aaron said. He put her wrists in a hold and quickly stood her next to the wall. "Liv, call the precinct and get the detectives."

"Erlandsen's on his way."

At least the reason for Linda running would come to light. If she wasn't guilty, then why run?

"Please. I'm sorry," Linda cried.

"What's the deal here, Linda?" I asked. "Why did you run?"

"The detectives are coming, and they're going to talk to you,"

"Oh—and tell the truth. If you know something that hasn't been told, now would be a good time to tell it."

Aaron held Linda's wrists, but nudged me aside.

At the same time the two detectives, stepped from their car.

"What do you have to tell us?" Mergens said.

"Linda tried to run off again."

"Why?" Erlandsen said. "We'll deal with her right now."

"You should see what I found before speaking to her," I said. "She ran right afterwards." I held the paper out for him.

"Let me slip on gloves and retrieve an evidence bag." Once the bag was opened, he slipped it inside and sealed it. He read the message. "Oh! This is what we need to proceed with the investigation." He handed the bag to Mergens.

"Here's her script," I said, handing it to him.

"Thanks," Mergens said. He bagged it for evidence. "Erlandsen, take her to the theater where she can give you another guided tour and explain why she ran, again." Mergens gave her a hard look. "Anymore running, and we'll book you for obstruction of justice."

"Okay," Linda said.

"I'll be right there after I speak with Liv," Mergens said. "Liv, I want you to tell me exactly what happened."

"Okay." We opened the door and walked inside. "The lights were off when I first entered and I had to call out for Linda," I said. Once we were in the dressing room, we stopped first and looked at where she found Nancy. Linda was pretty emotional."

"Then what?" Mergens said. "Linda went to look for Nancy's script because we couldn't locate it. I flipped through a pile and found it."

"How did you know it was hers?"

"May I?" I picked up the script and pointed to the doodling. "She's done this before, so I recognized it. I opened it, and the note fell out." "I'd asked for an original script and this one to compare and see what Russ had edited out."

"We've already spoken to him. Why do you think he changed the script?"

"No clue. The script doesn't belong to him," I said. I shook my head. "Unless he didn't want the President cast in such a dim light over the Suffragists movement."

"Why do you think Nancy addressed the note to you?" Mergens said. "Do you have any idea why her life was in danger, or from whom?"

"No, I don't." *But I'm going to play her part,* I thought to myself. *It might be the only way to find out the truth.*

"We'll see if there's any prints on them besides yours," Mergens said.

"It's time for me to relieve Max," I said. I knew I must take care of my store. "I'm going to step in and take over Nancy's role. I mean, why not?"

"Not on your life, Liv. I want you safe—not on stage where anything could happen," Aaron said.

"I'm married to a cop, I'll be safe," I said.

"Okay, we'll stay in touch," Mergens said. "We'll keep investigating, and if we have more questions, we know where to find you."

I turned to Aaron, "Are you staying?"

"For a few minutes."

"I need a script. Be right back." I hustled to the theater and found the prop table, took Sylvie's script and returned to the store.

I hustled inside, wondering how hard it could be to learn lines and to act? I recalled Nancy joking about becoming a Broadway star when we rehearsed her lines. As I stepped into the store, I wished that I could hear Nancy's voice once more speaking to a customer. I set the script down on the back corner of the workbench, and dried my moist eyes. I heard Max talking, so I pulled myself together and hustled out to meet the customers.

Max was knee-deep with two snoopy reporters.

"Out! The police aren't here," Max said. He held the door open. "Git!"

"The police are down the block," I said. "Where are you from?"

"I'm from *City Pages*. He's from the *Trib*. Hey, thanks for the tip!" the first reporter replied.

"They just walked in," Max said.

"And now they're gone." I brushed my hands together like getting rid of dirt.

When the reporters were safely out the door, I had an idea. "I'd better give Sylvie, the prop manager a buzz." I ended up leaving her a voice mail about taking her script.

I went ahead and sent a spray of flowers to Nancy's family. Once the funeral was arranged, I'd send one from the store to the funeral home. My phone chirruped, and I realized from the phone number it was Grandma. "Better take this."

At the same time, an older couple entered the store.

"We're here to look at your houses," the woman said.

"My wife wants a house," said the husband "It's our fiftieth anniversary and I told her that she can have anything that her heart desires." I smiled, and thought, how sweet. He continued, "I thought for sure that she'd just want me." He winked at me, and I giggled.

"Sam!" She nudged him.

"Any house in particular?" I strolled closer. "How about Jackie Kennedy?"

"My wife has always liked the Civil War era, after the Lincolns."

"Not really," his wife chimed in. "I liked Eleanor the best. She was a fantastic woman."

"They all were," I conceded. "Did you know that Eliza Johnson, the wife of President Johnson, who was Vice-President and took over after the Lincoln assassination, taught him to read? He wasn't completely illiterate, but she schooled him."

"Oh! I didn't know that. How interesting," the woman responded. "Can you show us the Civil War house and also FDR's?"

"Sure," I said. We strolled to the first. "This is the Lincoln White House." I left them to look and went over to the other one. "And this display is FDR and Eleanor's. Two First Ladies during wartime. I'm sure they'd have a lot to discuss." I smiled. "I'll let you two look around. Take your time."

"What is this lovely miniature dollhouse?" They stood beside the Edith Wilson's house. "It seems quite old."

"Yes, it belonged to First Lady Edith Wilson, and I just purchased it. It's not for sale, only to look at." They continued looking while I checked messages. Sylvie responded saying that she'd make sure that the detectives locked the doors. Grandma wrote: *What do you want for supper?* I'd forgotten that we were supposed to go there. I scrolled further and read: A) Scrambled eggs. B) Unscrambled eggs. C) Grilled salmon and salad. D) Hot dogs on a stick. E) Hot dish on a stick.

I responded C, and sent the message.

Chapter Five

The older couple meandered up to the counter. "We'd like to purchase two houses. One for my lovely bride and the other for our daughter," the man said. When the woman blushed, he said, "Isn't she beautiful?"

"Yes. You two are very lucky." I felt my cheeks warming. "Which houses are you talking about?"

"The Civil War and Eleanor's."

"All right. I can get it all packaged up within the half hour, if you want to have a seat or keep looking around?" I quickly texted Max, *Sale. Come.*

"I'll look around. These houses are beautiful. What a marvelous store." The woman smiled.

As she strolled away, the man removed his credit card, and handed it over. "Bet you need this."

I started tallying when Max entered. At the doorway, he asked, "Which one?"

"Two." I turned toward him. "Lincoln and FDR."

"Got it." To me, he said, "Aaron's back to help carry them." To the man, he asked, "Where's your car?"

"Out front."

"Thank you." I handed him back his card, and he shoved it into his wallet. "I hope that you'll enjoy them."

"We will," the woman said, coming up beside him. "The dolls look so natural."

"Max carves the heads, I paint them. I also sew the inaugural gowns, but not the men's wardrobe. They're too tedious."

"They're gorgeous," the woman said.

"Thank you."

'When I finished up the paperwork, Max and Aaron carried the boxes to the car, and the customers left.

"Wow! What a day," I said. "Max, Aaron — thanks. You're both wonderful."

"Anytime. Now I'm headed out to my side job. I'll see you in the morning," Max said. With a smoke between his fingers, he headed toward the back door.

"We're going to Grandma's for supper," I said to Aaron. I sneaked a kiss from my husband.

"I work later, you know?" Aaron said. He smiled down at me. "Eat and leave. More or less."

"That's fine. Grandpa falls asleep anyway."

"So does Grandma," Aaron said. He rubbed his chin. "I just found out that Nancy's death has been officially ruled a homicide. Poison. Can't say more than that." He backed away. "The detectives may want me to work a little earlier, but I'll try to wait until after we've eaten."

"Good." I hesitated before continuing, "I have an inkling that this all revolves around the President Wilson and his First Lady. Remember — she all but ran the country when he had that terrible stroke."

"True," Aaron said, pulling me to my feet. "Let's finish up around here and get going."

I followed to the workroom where Aaron carried newly shipped houses from a storage room and set on the countertop, awaiting assembly. I took a few brief minutes to skim through Sylvie's script, and found that it was as I thought. All the lines edited out pertained to the Fourteen Points. Further into the script, I also realized that a great number of pages concerning the suffragists were replaced. Presuming that Russ was the culprit, I wondered why he did it.

"I hope you're not planning to play Nancy's part," Aaron said.

"I'm giving it some thought."

"You'll be in danger the entire time. We have no idea if Nancy's death is related to her work at the theater or something else entirely. Not a good choice, Liv." He shook his head. "No way.'"

"I'm going to take the role. Something tells me that I should do it for Nancy." I also knew that the only way to figure out what really happened was to be part of the cast. "I mean, really? Why not? The motive hasn't been determined."

"I don't like it. By the way, the rose you gave Nancy has been picked up as evidence and brought to the police station. We're assuming it was purchased at the same floral shop as the shamrocks," Aaron said, waggling his finger. "No snooping under any circumstances. Period! You hear me, Miss Nosy?" He gave me a stern look. "I mean it!"

"I'll be extra careful. I'll mind my own business."
"

"I want a text message from you every half hour'. On or off stage. Understand?"

"Yes sir! And thank you."

I needed to gain Linda's trust and find out what lay behind her fear. Something sinister was happening at the Rose Garden Theater. Nancy's murder was the tip of the iceberg, I was convinced.

Aaron stood outside so I wasn't privy to his conversation with the detectives. I picked up the script and began reading them. I knew the Germans viewed the Fourteen Points as imperialistic propaganda since the peace treaty stripped them of an army. As I pondered this, my phone buzzed a message. It was Grandma. When I glanced at it, I rolled my eyes and smiled. A) Salt water B) Wine C) Sour milk D) None of the above.

Chuckling, I chose B. Then I went outside and found Aaron staring off into the wild blue yonder.

"What are you thinking about?"

"Linda and her reasons for running," Aaron said. He glanced at his phone to check the time.

"I want to speak alone with Linda," I said. I crossed my arms. "I don't like how this investigation is going. I don't think Linda could hurt a fly, let alone kill someone. She's too soft-hearted."

"You never can tell." Aaron said. He looked at me. "Don't get involved."

"I'm going to text Linda and ask for her to come here for a minute. I just want to discuss the part. Find out how much Edith Wilson is on stage, that kind of thing." I took a deep breath. "I told Grandma we'd drink wine. The choices were either that or sour milk or salt water."

"All those ABC's, it's like a test in school," Aaron said. "She should've been a teacher."

"I've got things to do at home. Remember what I told you," Aaron said. He wagged his finger at me. "Nothing about the investigation with Linda."

"Right." I watched him leave before heading inside. The backdoor opened as I sat down near the front counter.

"I'm here," Linda called.

"I'm glad you came. We can discuss the script."

"The detectives were so hard on me," Linda sniffled. "Just awful."

"Hold that thought," I said, walking away. "Let me close up."

It took a minute to change the sign and lock the door. Quickly, I pressed the button on the computer to shut it down. "How come you ran again? What on earth is the matter? What's frightening you so much?"

"This play. Nancy's death scared me. There's always something missing. I didn't know about Nancy's lines until now. Hiding her script and then you discovering that cryptic note rattled me," Linda said. She wiped her moist eyes. "I'm starting to think there's more than what meets the eye, but I don't know what."

"What else?" I stared at her. "You have to tell me."

"I don't want anything to happen to you, too," Linda said.

"With Aaron covering my back—it ain't gonna happen. Don't worry so." I waited a beat, then said, "Why would Russ edit those lines?"

"No idea." She shook her head. "I've never liked him."

"Why?" I said. I didn't either.

"There's that pistol on the prop table. Where did that come from?" I said.

"It just appeared. The actress who plays Susan B. Anthony, her diary prop has gone missing," Linda said.

"The copied stage diary? Why?" I said. "We should notify the police about the prop discoveries." Puzzled, I looked aside to give it thought. "What else?"

"The woman who is imprisoned for protesting outside of the White House, Alice Paul. She championed the Equal Rights Amendment. Do you know who that is? I've heard a rumor that a descendant wrote the script," Linda said.

"I wonder who that would be?" I said. I ran my fingers through my hair. *An angle to research?* "Tell me more."

"She and several other women almost died because of wanting the vote." Linda sat straighter, and said, "Another rumor is about Wilson's Fourteen Points."

"The handwritten Fourteen Points given to the President's Cabinet would be worth a fortune, and could change history, if Edith wrote it and not him. You know? Who wrote it out?"

"I never thought of that. Edith as the possible author," Linda said.

"It would prove that she wrote them herself or he dictated them to her. Don't you see? It'd also give credence about who was running the government," I said. I waited for that revelation to take hold before continuing, "That begs the question, why didn't she step in to help the women who were beaten, thrown in jail, and almost starved to death?"

"Now you're back to where we started." Linda stood. "I need to go home."

"And relax. Do you need a ride?" I said.

"Nope, but thanks. I only live a short distance from here. Sylvie said she'll meet me in the morning."

"Okay. I need to know the rehearsal schedule," I said.

"I'll give it to you in the morning," Linda said.

"Good night." I watched her leave, and noticed how slumped shouldered she'd become. I felt sorry for her. I finished locking up, and went out to my car.

It didn't take long for me drive home, where I found Aaron showered and ready to go. My grandparents lived over near Lake-of-the-Isles, in a new senior development. They loved it.

"I hope for another day like today, again tomorrow," I said. "Hopefully, that older couple who purchased the houses will spread the word about my store to all of their friends and family."

"That was great, two houses," Aaron said. He drove from the garage and out to the street. "Mind telling me what Linda had to say? I'm sure that you questioned her. You do anyway, no matter what I say. You're a big snoop."

"Linda is spooked because things come and go and get rearranged on the prop table. I didn't speak to Sylvie, the prop manager, she'll be in the theater tomorrow morning." I said. "She doesn't know origin of the pistol that was on the prop table. Susan B. Anthony's copied prop diary went missing."

"I'll make sure the detectives know," Aaron said.

The greenery refreshed me as we drove and the beautiful colored flowers along the parkway were gorgeous. The lakes sparkled blue against the sunlight. Grandma belonged to the garden club that looked after the Rose Garden across from Lakewood Cemetery. In this cemetery are buried Hubert H. Humphrey, the Pillsbury family, and other notables. After about thirty minutes, we parked out front of the townhome.

We barreled in through the back yard, where we found Grandpa checking out the grill and Grandma sitting and drinking a glass of wine. Two empty glasses and an open bottle of Reisling sat on the patio table.

"I wondered if you got lost. Almost sent you a message," Grandma said. Always on top of it, that's my grandma. "Help yourself."

"I'll take the salt water. Sorry, but I work later," Aaron said.

"Shoot! I wanted to try out some new scotch on you," Grandpa stated, turning around. "Next time."

"Grandma, what do you know about the Right to Vote and the Night of Terror?" Grandma's eyes opened wide, and she took a longer sip. "I'd like to know what you know. Pick your brain."

"Does this have anything to do with Nancy's murder?" Grandma said.

"How did you know that she was murdered?" Aaron said. He'd already fetched himself a glass of ice water, and stood holding it. "You got some kind of radar or did Liv tell you?"

"I never did. I swear." I crossed my heart. "Grandma?"

"I figured she'd been by the sound of it. Nancy was a sweet girl, too," Grandma said. Grandma wiped her eyes dry. "It takes too long for the cops to fess up, that's all. You know, and then get things right. In the meantime, the killer gets away."

"Protocol, Marie. It's not like tv where it's done instantly," Aaron said.

"Grandma? Tell me about the Night of Terror? Why did Wilson let this happen?" I said. I took a sip and waited as she put her thoughts together.

"Want us to barbecue right away?" Grandpa said. He interrupted her thoughts, and I glared at him. "Should I?"

"You two have some kind of code going here?" I said. I glanced from one to the other. "You don't want to talk about it? Fine? I'll dig up stuff myself."

"It's all in the past and not very pretty," Grandma said. "The President's wife never said a word about the women picketing near the White House. Everyone else picketed, why couldn't these women?"

"That's what doesn't make sense. Why not?" I said.

"November 15, 1917, thirty-three women were jailed. The guards were told to beat the women. Well, they did. They chained Lucy Burns' hands above her head and left her like that. Dora Lewis had her head slammed against a cement wall and then beaten up and choked half-to-death. Alice Paul went on a hunger strike and force fed her. Finally, news leaked to the press and they were eventually freed," Grandma said.

"Oh, my God! And neither the President nor First Lady did anything?" I said. When Grandma shook her head, I felt a complete sense of loss for these women and kinship. I had to find out why the line editing had removed those references.

"I wonder if there is a handwritten copy of the Fourteen Points is? I also wonder if there is a letter that excluded the president from acting on behalf of the women, or is this what the Wilson's wanted? Allow the women to be castigated and left for dead?"

Chapter Six

At home, I was left alone with my thoughts after Aaron returned to work. I knew if I started searching about the Night of Terror, I'd be up half of the night, so I chose not to. Instead, I picked up a yellow marker and highlighted my lines. I found an old cassette recorder and recorded the lines before each of mine. While doing so, it made me stop and think. What if all the actor's lines had been edited? But, most of all, who did Nancy fear? Shivers of fear raced up and down my spine. I had trouble shaking them off. I hoped reading the lines, something might click in my memory that would help me in the investigation.

I continued with the recording until finished with the first act. From the beginning, it read like a clip from history until the Fourteen Points, which were altered slightly. I tried memorizing the lines from the first two pages but found it hard to concentrate. I didn't understand all the comings and goings from backstage, and knew I'd have to speak with Sylvie.

I set the following days' needed items in the kitchen near my bag, and went to bed. What Grandma told me about the imprisoned women made me sick, and I couldn't sleep. Next, my thoughts churned about First Lady, Edith Wilson. I poured my heart and soul out in my diary. Did she have a special secret one? If so, where was it? She must've kept many in her day, especially during the White House years. A war president. Of course. There must've been many letters secretly written and passed between her and the president or a close friend. I wondered if they were in the presidential library? I tossed and turned while sleep eluded me.

Aaron quietly folded back the covers about one, and with his comforting presence, I finally fell asleep.

The morning sun streamed through the blinds, waking me. I kissed Aaron before quietly sneaking from the bed. In the kitchen, I started the bacon sizzling and poured myself a cup of hot coffee. I stood near the sink trying to figure out what it was that had kept me up half the night, but decided it was just the remembrance of the jailed women. I shuddered at the thought. Whatever happened to free speech and the right to assemble?

After eating, I went ahead and dressed into my favorite summer dress. It was full of tulips. I donned a sweater to guard against the chilly morning since I planned walking. Taking out a scratch sheet of paper, I wrote: I will see you at 12, 12:30 or 1? Please bring-A) chicken sandwich. B) egg salad C) cooked egg salad sandwich. D) goose burger. PS Please leave a phone message.

With what I needed for the day shoved into my bag, I headed out the door.

The fresh air felt good on my cheeks, and it also cleared my mind. The restless night had left me tired, and I hoped the brisk walk would get my adrenaline flowing. It took about fifteen minutes before stopping at the corner light across from the store. I glanced over to it, and noticed that my neighbor, Mikal, had the light turned on in his small office. Mikal was an elderly gentleman who was a handwriting analyst plus psychic. I loved him. If not for already having a grandpa, he'd be my next choice. I decided to pop in on him.

"Hey you!" I said, opening the door. "Got a minute?"

"For you, Livvie, I've got all the time in the world," Mikal said. His smile covered his face and his blue eyes sparkled. I was sure that the silver moon got its glow from Mikal's hair. "Have a seat."

"Thanks." I sat in the empty chair nearest him. "Have you heard about everything that's been going on?"

"I sure have. Bet you're wondering why I haven't stopped in lately?" The phone rang, and he said, "Don't worry. The answering machine will get it."

"I bet you've been hiding from one of those women again?" I said. I raised a brow. "You're too charming, Mikal."

"How'd you guess?" His laughter filled the room. Mikal attracted women like a flower attracts bees. "She was older than me, I swear. I didn't think anyone could be older than me. I had to change my home phone number. I may have to move."

"Oh Mikal!" I said. I started laughing. When I calmed down, I said, "I'm worried about this play. I'm going to take Nancy's place."

"Write something, and we'll see what happens." Mikal grinned. "For free."

"Okay." I wrote: *Nancy is dead and she was so sweet. I miss her dreadfully because she was a good employee. Then, so many of lines were edited, and that scares me because it may be why she's dead. She'd told me about it and said that she couldn't change the script so close to opening. Once the words are set in your head — that's it.* "Here." I shoved the paper closer to Mikal.

"Hmm, you've got a lot covered here, dear girl," Mikal said. He held up his huge magnifier and brought the sheet to a lamp light. "Hmm."

"Quit saying that. You're scaring me," I said. It felt like needles going up and down my spine. "It's ominous."

"Well…Liv, you'd better be careful," Mikal said. He pinched up his eyebrows. "Don't be in dark places and don't be alone."

"You might as well cancel the acting, then." I sighed. "What else?"

"Beware of trickery. It'll all work out, in the end."

"You mean, I'm not going to be murdered or anything nasty like that?"

"Nope, as long as you keep your wits about you."

"Thanks. I'll dress and stay near the front stage. I'll pretend to be invisible and then nothing will happen. Anything else?"

"I'll buy you coffee opening night."

"It's a deal," I said and stood up. "I'd better get my store opened. Thanks a bunch."

I headed around back to open the door. Once inside, I did my usual circle of the display tables, straightening items while walking by. A couple dolls had toppled over and the dresses needed finger pressing. Afterwards, I stopped at the old Edith Wilson dollhouse and studied it. It seemed slightly askew, as if it'd been turned around, so it was set straight. I wondered if Max had touched it or a customer? By the computer, I got it going.

In the workroom, I grabbed the cassette player from my bag along with the script, and headed out to the showroom once again. I opened the main front door before sitting beside the computer.

No sooner had I logged into the store's website when the phone rang. It turned out to be a customer who needed to know the hours. There were four business related e-mails, so I responded. The fifth caught my attention. It read: Where is it? I forwarded the message to my personal address for later scrutiny. *Where is what?*

With the routine chores completed, I rewound the cassette player, opened the script to the correct page, and began to memorize. I soon learned that my memory, even though I was a mere thirty years old, just wasn't what it used to be. I had a doctorate, no less, and I had trouble memorizing short lines. Good grief!

When a customer entered, I was happy for the reprieve. "I'm here if you need me. Any questions, just holler," I told the young woman. Within a few minutes, her handsome, six-foot tall husband came inside with a toddler straddled across his shoulders. The baby giggled and gurgled as the dad strolled toward her. I presumed they were married.

I held up my script and began reading when I heard, "Miss? What can you tell me about this house?"

"Oh! Coming," I said. I set the script down. In seconds, I was by their sides, and peering down at the historical White House. "This was the first one."

"Really?" The surprised look in the woman's eye was refreshing. "Wow. Where Abigail Adams hung her clothes on the line in the Blue Room?"

"One in the same. The same house that Dolley redecorated and had her parties where she charmed the living daylights out of all the men by serving ice cream."

"And, burned during the war?" She plunked her hands on her hips. "I want this one. Yes, I love Jackie Kennedy. I loved Laura Bush and Michelle Obama but Dolley makes my heart go pitter-patter."

"She does me too. I'm a descendant," I said. I smiled, and tickled the baby's fingers. "I'll make you a deal."

"All right," the handsome hubby responded. "Tell me about it."

"Since your wife's heart goes pitter-patter for Dolley, I'll give you fifteen percent off the regular price."

"You got it." He swung the giggling baby down and handed him to her.

"Let me get my assistant," I said. I reached for my phone and did a rapid message to Max, who suddenly appeared.

"In the workroom," he answered my unasked question. "Which house?"

"Historical." I began ringing up the sale while the man handed over his credit card. While taking care of the transaction, Max went for the house, furnishings, and dolls. "You'll love it."

The woman still strolled around the display tables, and ended up beside her husband. "I'd love one of each."

"I feel like that myself. That's why I opened this place," I said. For some reason, I wondered if she had a job. "Do you live nearby?"

"Within a mile. We just moved to the area," the woman said.

"I could use another assistant if you're interested." I hesitated. "I suppose it's tough with a baby."

"I'll think about it." She held the baby, and started for the door.

Max returned with the larger of the boxes, and said, "Where are you parked?"

"Thanks," I said.

She held the door for Max. "Car's right there." She hustled out with the baby.

"What can I carry?" the man said.

"The furniture, and I'll get the dolls," I said.

Together we carried them out and settled all inside of the car trunk. Max and I headed back inside the store.

"A great day," I said. "Another house. Are you caught up on doll heads?"

"Not anymore," Max said.

"I asked her if she wanted a job. She loves the houses. I think she'd be good. With the baby she'd probably only want part-time."

"We sure could use someone," Max said.

"Do you need me here?" I said. "I want to go to the theater for a few minutes. Mind watching the store?"

"Go ahead."

With the script in hand, I went out the back door, and headed right to the theater's door. I wasn't sure if it'd be open or not. I knew that I wanted to speak to Sylvie about props, but I also figured it was a good time to slide in a few extra questions about Russ and the night of the murder.

The back door was open, so I stepped inside. Fortunately, the light was turned on and I didn't have to squint or call out for assistance. I went straight to the prop manager's office, and peeked inside the open door.

"Sylvie?" I didn't see her at first so I took a couple steps inside the door.

"Right here." She peeked her head out from behind a computer monitor and said, "Over here."

As I walked over toward her, I noticed all the stacks of papers piled high all around her. "Are those scripts or playbills?" My eyes opened wider.

"Oh. It's you. Liv Reynolds." Her eyes shifted to a sheet in front of her, and she slid it underneath another paper. "What can I help you with?"

"I'm taking over Nancy's part," I said. I wondered why she hid the sheet of paper. "I also took your script because I didn't have one."

"Oh, that's right. Linda told me that you might take it," Sylvie said. She shown her bright teeth, and her chubby cheeks. With a stubby finger, she pulled a couple strands of hair behind her ear.

"I'd like to see my props. You know? Figure some stuff out."

"Oh, sure," Sylvie said. Sylvie slid her chair back and stood. "Go ahead."

"Okay." I noticed she moved a book on top of the papers, making me real curious. "To the stage?"

"Right around the corner, backstage," Sylvie said.

"Oh yes. The table with the pistol," I said. I heard her suck in her breath. "Who uses it?" I turned the corner and went back stage.

"Here we are," Sylvie said. She flipped on another switch for more lighting. "The pistol has been removed, as you can see."

"Why was it there?" I said. I studied her. *Was it my imagination that she appeared skittish?* "I'd like to know what props are mine."

"The table is sectioned off by the masking tape." She drew a finger over one strip. "See? A name in right on the tape."

"Oh! I get it. There's Nancy's name. Guess it'll be mine from now on," I said. A lump caught in my throat. "What a sad deal."

"It was. Anyway, she used this pen and here's her glasses. Of course, they're just the frame. Her gloves, purse." She pointed to them. "Whenever someone enters and exits from different places, there's usually time to grab what's needed. If not, like you're entering and exiting from the same place with just a minute between, then we'll move the prop to the needed location."

"We place it all back in this spot."

"Exactly," I said, and smiled. "Is it possible for anyone to sneak in during performance time or before or after without being seen?"

"You mean to steal props?"

"Yes." I was thinking about someone bringing the poisonous plant.

"I see everything. You're thinking about the shamrocks, aren't you?" When I nodded Sylvie continued, "I know your husband's a policeman. Let him do his job." Turning on her heels, she hiked away.

"Thank you!" I called after her.

I marched back to the store, and wondered what on earth made her so mad? Why had she hid the paper? What was on it? I started to wonder if I shouldn't investigate further.

I kept going until entering my store.

"Another customer came and went," Max told me upon entering the showroom.

"What house?" I said.

"It was kind of weird, now that I think about it. She was our first Native American customer. She said a greeting in the Ojibwe language. I once had a girlfriend who was from a Chippewa tribe, and she spoke it," Max said. He massaged his chin. "She stopped by the antique dollhouse."

"Edith's?" I said. He nodded. "Did she ask any questions? Say anything at all?"

"No, that's what was so funny. She stopped, and stared at it," Max said. He slid out a smoke, and held it between his fingers. He reached for his lighter. "She reached down inside of it like she was searching for something. I'm not sure if anything was touched. I should've gone back over and looked inside."

"What did she look like?" I said.

"Tall. Shorts. Brown hair and glasses."

"You just described half the population." I cocked my head. "Remember anything else?"

"Nope. It was weird because no one else has ever done that without asking questions," Max said.

"I'll check it over," I said.

"I'm heading up and working on the heads," Max said.

I watched him leave. My mind raced with ideas. On one hand, I thought about Sylvie. I shoved that dilemma aside and walked over to Edith Wilson's antique dollhouse. I peered down at it and moved the small pieces aside. Nothing was broken. I studied all the furnishings and realized that the bookcase inside of the library was shifted. I removed the small piece and turned it over in my hand. I didn't detect any odd marking on the bookcase. The books were old history books, plus Huckleberry Finn. I set them aright and removed the desk. The tiny sheets were writings from previous presidents.

That discovery brought up another question. Were all the Wilson papers concerning the League of Nations and the Fourteen Points on record? Or had Edith hidden some that she hadn't wanted the public to know about until later since she controlled the president and his staff during his illness?

Chapter Seven

I found it very hard to concentrate for the rest of the day. My thoughts kept going back to Sylvie. I did congratulate myself in learning the lines, albeit not perfectly, for Act I. That made me feel good. I hadn't been told yet about the rehearsal hours. Just as I was ready to close for the day, Linda sent a message. It read: *Rehearsal at seven. See you there.* I responded: *Ok.*

That meant there was little time for me to hurry home, eat, change, and make it back in time. At five-thirty, I hung the closed sign, and locked up. I wondered what to have for supper as I walked home. The walk was nice. The humidity was low, and the temperature tolerable. Noise from cars, busses and voices gave me the energy to walk faster. As I rounded my block corner, I noticed the neighborhood kids playing kick-ball and the little ones riding in plastic bikes. I smelled barbecues grilling from backyards. My stomach grumbled.

Once inside, I yanked out a small frozen pizza and stuck it in the oven while I read Aaron's note. "Sorry, honey. Called into work. Should've let you know but I couldn't help it. Xoxo." I realized that without Aaron's planned sandwich it explained why I was so starved. I sent him a message: Missed you. I have rehearsal tonight at 7.

I went to change into more comfortable clothes. The theater always felt a little damp, so I thought I'd take a sweater. Since Aaron wasn't here to lecture me about case interfering, I figured it as a good time to sneak into the theater before the other actors. I wanted to snoop in Sylvie's office.

After finishing up the pizza and cleaning up, I jumped into the car. It took about five minutes until I parked in the back of the theater. To my surprise, two actors were already entering. As I entered, loud angry voices echoed throughout the area. When I reached the stage area, I realized that it was Russ and Sylvie arguing. I didn't immediately see Linda, who sat in the front row middle, but I sat beside her.

"What's all the fuss about?" I whispered, leaning closer to her.

"Not sure. Something about the Fourteen Points and the Suffragists," Linda said, and gave me a nudge. "How's the lines coming?"

"Almost have the first act down."

"Good." Linda got up as soon as two more actors entered the stage area. I watched her easily climb up onto the stage. "Everyone. Attention."

I glanced around the area and noticed that everyone quit talking simultaneously.

"We have our Edith," Linda said. She lowered her arm, toward me. "Liv Reynolds, please stand." I did as told, and was sure that I had turned three shades of red. "She's the owner of the White House Dollhouse store, right down the block."

"That's me." I sat right back down.

"She's informed me that Act I is coming along. We'll have opening night next Thursday," Linda said. "Between now and then, we'll hold to the already set schedule of evening rehearsals at this time. We'll stay late to go over scenes, if there's any difficulty." She gazed out at us, cupping her eyes against the bright overhead stage light. "Any questions?" When no one answered she said, "Let's get busy. Places!"

I watched as Linda spoke into her headset, and immediately the lights faded. I wasn't sure where my place was supposed to be, but I needn't have worried. Linda jumped down and came right over to me.

"Follow me," Linda said. She led me right to the spot where I was to stand each night for my opening entrance, and Sylvie was right there with the first prop. "When the lights go black, that's everyone's cue to know that the play is about to begin. They'll slowly rise, and you are to enter and walk right over to the desk and sit down."

"How will I be able to see?" I said. I understood why actors get anxious before coming onstage, they're afraid of tripping in the dark.

"Don't worry. There's glow tape and you'll have enough light," Sylvie said.

"Whatever," I said, and thought, sure, and if I fall and break a leg? My nerves were jittery, and I felt like my knees were ready to buckle. I pictured myself standing on stage, falling, with people staring at me. I turned and stared at the back entrance and wondered if I could run out without anyone catching me.

Linda grabbed my arm and said, "I'll walk you through it."

"Thanks." With shaky fingers I opened my script to the correct page. "Is that over there" —I pointed— "my entrance?"

"Yes, and it's on this side, stage right where you'll do your opening lines."

"What should I take out with me?" I said.

"For now, we'll just worry about you knowing where to be and what to do," Linda said.

"Okay." I wasn't sure if I felt better or not, but at least there'd be no prop worries for tonight's rehearsal.

I stood in my assigned place and I noted that the other actors were all in position, but in costume. Tomorrow's another night, I told myself, one rehearsal at a time. Suddenly the background music silenced and at the same time, it became very black. Right after, the lights slowly brightened to a slight glow which gave us enough time to enter and walk to our designated position. The tape really lit up and helped direct me to the correct placement. As soon as everyone was set, then the full lights gradually brightened the stage.

"Edith Wilson!" Linda said, and stared at me. "You're on. As soon as the lights come up—go for it!"

"My cue?" I said. When she nodded, I held up my script and cross read while trying to say the memorized pieces. Every once in a while, Linda directed me to stand in different places or do something physical, such as turning. I stated my final line, "And, the United States will have the final vote."

"Can you repeat that a little louder? Right from the top," Linda asked from the middle of the theater. "Everyone has to hear you."

"Oh." I took a deep breath. "After all the folderol about the Fourteen Points, they just boil down to a recipe for putting everything back the way it was, except for Germany, of course. Everyone gets their land back and the right to sell things to each other." At the end, I realized that this summation must have been written by Mrs. Wilson because the President usually was quite wordy.

"Good! Remember to breathe at the commas. Very good. We'll continue with Act II tomorrow night," Linda said. To me, she continued, "You and I will walk through that earlier. Let's get you here at six."

"Are we done for the night?" Joan Mitchell, the person who played Susan B. Anthony, inquired.

"We're taking a ten-minute break and running through the act once more. It's early yet and Liv has a lot to learn," Linda said.

"Good," Joan said.

My confidence returned and it seemed like a good fit—me and Edith. At the close of the evening, I stood in the dressing room and noticed that the Sylvie had left. While everyone changed or got ready to leave, I sneaked next door and quietly opened the door. Quickly I went to her desk and flicked on the desk lamp. I read a post-it: *Where is it?*

Where is what?

I shut the lamp off and sneaked from the room, and headed straight to my car. During the short drive home, I realized that it was the same question which had been sent to the store's website. *What on* earth *was it that someone wanted?*

I pressed the garage door button, and watched it raise up before driving inside. After lowering it, I went inside the kitchen, closing the door behind me. I went straight to the living room and planned to read through the script once again only to find that I'd left it in the theater. I played through the recorded lines and said what I had memorized then went to bed.

Aaron woke me as he climbed into bed with the news that several people had been questioned about Nancy's death, but no one was charged with the crime. It definitely was cyanide gas that caused the death.

"Who was questioned?"

"I'm not privy to an ongoing investigation's every little bit of it."

"Just say you don't know or won't tell."

"Won't tell."

"Now I won't sleep, but I'm glad that you told me."

My prediction proved accurate. My mind kept circling about the unanswered question: where is it? That had to be the key. I knew Russ was unhappy about the script but would he kill because of it? Did First Lady Edith Wilson try changing the Fourteen Points? I made a mental note to further investigate.

A loud honk from the street below ruined my concentration. I got up and looked out the window, but didn't see anyone and, in turn, climbed back into bed.

The summer sunshine woke me. I kissed Aaron and rolled out of bed. After dressing, I headed to the kitchen and remembered that I'd forgotten my script the night before. "Drats!" I'd have to scoot down and retrieve it. I left Aaron a note telling him my schedule, and that I wouldn't be home until late and we'd have to fend for ourselves for supper. It also occurred to me that he could bring me something at the store to eat for dinner so I added that morsel of information.

Since it'd be a late night, I drove. Backing from the garage, I began to think about the night's rehearsal. I hardly knew any lines for tonight. I waited for the light before I could turn onto Main Street. Three lights later, I turned down the alleyway and parked beside Max's old pickup truck.

I noted that no car was parked in the back of the theater, so my script would have to wait. After opening the back door, I went to the workroom and plunked into a chair. Quickly, I sent a message to Linda, explaining about my leaving it behind.

I got up and walked into the showroom. The hair on the back of my neck tickled as if a blast of cold air had blown. Slowly, I walked up one aisle of display tables and then the next until at last stopping beside the Edith Wilson antique dollhouse. Gasping, I looked at all the tipped over furnishings, broken plates, and book bindings. I slipped my phone from my pocket and took a few pictures, then called Aaron.

"Honey. Answer." I knew he was still sleeping, but didn't ESP work? I left him a voice mail message. Afterwards, I gave Detective Erlandsen a call and he answered on the third ring.

"Liv Reynolds here. Come to the store, right away."

"Now what? I have court within an hour and don't have time."

"Someone's messed with and destroyed a lot of my Edith Wilson dollhouse. You know? The one which had once belonged to her."

"Call it in. Someone will come out and take a statement and pictures. I'll stop by later."

"But…"

"Can't help it." He disconnected.

I stared at the silent phone and growled. "Now what?" I asked myself as I stared at the messed-up house. It took a few minutes to calm down before reporting it. It was ten on the dot, when I opened the front door for business. About ten minutes later, a police officer approached the store.

"Liv Reynolds? Officer Thomas." He entered the store. "I'm here because of a complaint."

"Right here." I showed him the house. I'm sure it wasn't a smirk I noticed, but maybe it was a slight grin, but I couldn't be sure. "See? It's a mess and someone deliberately sabotaged it during the night."

"Wouldn't the alarm have gone off? Have you called your security company?"

"No. I called you guys. My husband is also a policeman."

"Thought the name was familiar." Officer Thomas took a couple shots of the house from different angles. "Anything stolen?"

"Not that I'm aware of."

"I'll write it up and you can sign, or do you want to come to the precinct and fill it out?" Officer Thomas removed a sheet of paper. "What else can you tell me about the dollhouse?"

"It once belonged to First Lady Wilson, obviously an antique, and it's irreplaceable," I replied. Couldn't they see that the house was wrecked and that the person who wrecked it needed to be caught?

"Here," Officer Thomas held out his pen and I signed my name. "Anything else, let us know. My advice is to contact your security and insurance companies."

"I will." I clamped my jaw tight and closed the door behind them. Big help, I thought, as I watched him climb into the squad car.

I went and sat down near the computer and started it. I was furious to think that someone could waltz into my store without an alarm waking up the neighborhood. I was certain that it had been set the night before. I never forget. I found the number in my contact list and gave the Minnesota Nice Security Systems a phone call.

"Liv Reynolds here," I said when someone answered. "Can you tell me why my alarm didn't sound last night when someone broke into my store? Also, how could they break in—period? It's supposed to be burglar proof."

"We'll send someone out to check it over. We've had problems lately with our system."

"You're going to have more problems," I said. "It's awfully coincidental don't you think?" I disconnected in a hurry, still fuming. I wanted to break something. At the same time, Linda entered, bearing the script.

"Thank you."

"You look like you are ready to bite someone," Linda said. She set it down on the counter

"I feel like doing just that," I said. I proceeded to tell her what had happened. "Want to see?" I got up and started walking over to it, and she followed close behind. "Isn't this awful?"

"My gosh!" Linda said. Her eyes opened wide. "I wonder why?" She glanced around the room. "It doesn't look like anything else was wrecked."

"It doesn't make sense, does it?" I picked up one of the books, and the binding bent unnaturally backward. "See? Why do that to a book this small?"

"Are there dolls that go with it?" Linda said.

"No." I shook my head. "Just my White House dollhouses have the presidential dolls. This came with furnishings. Why break the dishes?"

"That was my next question," Linda said. She shook her head, then reached down to touch the bookcase. "Mind?"

"No, go ahead." I watched as she lifted it out, turning it over. "I didn't see any marking at all, do you?"

"I wonder?" Linda said. She brought it over to direct sunlight and studied it. "I might see something, but not sure."

"Where?" I said. She pointed to bottom. "That? I thought it was a minor scratch."

"I don't believe it is," Linda said. She handed it to me. "Look closer."

I held it high. "You may be right."

Just then the back door opened, and I heard, "Liv! You okay?"

"In here, honey!"

"I need to get going. Call me later if you have any questions. I'll see you at rehearsal," Linda said.

"Thanks!" By the time Aaron made it to my side, Linda was out the door.

I softly ran my finger over the mark in question. "I wonder if this isn't the craftsman's mark?"

Chapter Eight

Aaron left after we'd decided that he'd return at five with burgers.

I gave our neighborhood antique dealer, Inga, a buzz. "Haven't heard from you for a while."

"I've been up to my eyeballs with weeding and keeping up with the store," Inga answered. I pictured her dusting the shelves near the check-out counter where she probably sat.

"Have you heard the latest?" I said. I heard a background moan. "How about coming on down when you have a minute?"

"Will do," Inga said.

We disconnected.

The front door opened and a customer entered. "No need getting up. Want to check out the dress on Mrs. Grant." She waltzed right to the house. "Been here before, lookin' around."

"Oh!" I wondered about that. "How nice of you to return." I got up and went over to her. "Mrs. Grant always had her picture done from the side because of an eye problem. I think it was a lazy eye."

"Always wondered about that," the skinny woman said. She smiled, which displayed bad teeth. "Came from money too, and ended up with a poor man."

"Yes, but he rose to power and fame."

"True." She plunked her hands on her hips and stared at the house. "This the Civil War house?"

"First Lady Grant made many changes. She dressed it up. Remember how the White House was called something else many years ago? People's house, which meant everyone could come and take remnants, and they did even though they shouldn't have. She remodeled it, made it elegant once again. Mary Lincoln had also, but by the war's end, and with the assassination, the house had declined in beauty," I said.

"President Grant wrote his biography and then died. At least he had sense to do that."

"Yes, and Mrs. Grant was the first First Lady to publish her memoirs," I said.

"I'll take it."

"Great." I couldn't believe someone would buy a White House dollhouse from such an unknown First Lady. "Let's go to the check-out, and we'll get you taken care of." I texted Max on the way to it. "She also loved living in the White House and loved being First Lady."

"How much?" the woman said.

At the sound of Max's footsteps from the hallway, I turned to face him. "Grant." He glanced at the woman and back, and held up one finger.

"You just want one, right?" I said.

"Yes, ma'am."

"One," I called to him. Turning back to the customer, I asked, "How should we bill this? Cash or credit?"

"Got my cash card." She thrust it out at me. "Best be not more than a thousand."

"Don't worry, it won't be." I started adding it up and showed her the receipt. "Great. Go ahead."

In the meantime, Max carried the box to the counter and set it down. "Got your car out front? There's two more to come, only smaller. They have the furnishings and then the two dolls," Max said.

"My BMW is right out front." She removed her keys from her holey jeans. "Go ahead."

I actually wanted to barf from her bad breath, so I kept my mouth shut and tried to not breathe too deeply. It was a relief to see her go. As soon as she drove from the curb, I opened the front door and hoped for a draught of fresh air.

"BMW?" Max said, cocking his head. "How'd she pay?"

"Cash card." I grinned. "Can you beat it?"

"No!" He reached for a smoke, and gave me his one finger signal before turning and heading out the backdoor.

I went for a dusting cloth before returning to the table. After giving it a good shine, I went to the workroom. As I began assembling the needed items for another identical house, the backdoor opened. I assumed it was Max, then a stranger called out, "Mrs. Reynolds."

"Right here," I said. I stepped out from the room. I noticed the tall, freckled man with the red hair wearing a boyish grin. "Who are you?"

"Minnesota Nice Securities, ma'am. Kenny, here to look at your system." He held a notebook and pen. "Can I get started?"

"I only have the front and back door. The windows, too, I guess." I noticed the Viking ship logo on his blue shirt. "Go ahead."

"You betcha!"

"Any questions, there's me or you can ask Max. I think you met him in the back."

"Yes, yacked a few minutes. We're old buddies. Played football," Kenny said.

"What high school?"

"South."

"I'm a Teddy from Roosevelt," I said.

"It shouldn't take too long," Kenny said.

He started with the front door. I watched from afar as he followed the wires and did certain things to the code box. I turned my attention to the script. I had an awful lot of lines to learn, so I took out the recorder and started with running the lines from the beginning. My lines right after Susan B. Anthony's were especially hard because it showed the hard side of Mrs. Wilson's heart. I couldn't understand why she didn't speak up for women's rights. An hour later, I glanced up to find Kenny standing over me.

"There was a short wire which the alarm was sabotaged. I've rewired it and put in a newer, more efficient box. You'll have to reprogram your code."

"Mighty coincidental since the store was broke into last night. Do you have the old box?" He set it on the counter. "Thanks."

"Don't forget to reprogram it."

"Will do." The door closed and Kenny was gone. I rewound the tape and headed to the back to take care of door.

I was just about ready to open it when Max entered. "It's fixed now."

"Any idea how that happened?"

"No, not for sure, but it appeared as if someone knew what they were doing," Max said.

"As in, not knowing the code but enough about electrical stuff to get themselves inside without being immediately detected," I said. "I'm calling Mergens since Erlandsen couldn't give me the time of day." In the end, I left a phone message.

"Something like that," Max said. He followed me into the workroom. "I'll get a few more houses boxed after I get this one carried out to the table. I was caught up with heads until now. I'll start carving later."

"Thanks, Max. Do you need any extra cash? I'm forgetting to pay you since you're right here all the time."

"I could use a paycheck. I'll go and get your checkbook," Max said.

After the business transaction was completed, I got back to work. While gathering and sorting items for another Grant house, I listened to the recording and repeated the lines. Memorizing the lines for the first and second acts helped the understanding of the movements. I followed Max out to the table, set my goods down and helped him set the table up. After he left, I began with the furniture arrangement. When almost finished, the door opened and Inga entered.

"Over here," I said.

"I didn't see you," Inga said, and walked over to me. "What house are you setting up this time?"

"Someone just purchased the Grant house. It sure feels good to make a sale."

"Yes," Inga said. She stood near the Edith house with her hands on her hips, and gawked. "I can't believe it."

"I was shocked, but the police!" I frowned. "I won't tell you what I think."

"Best not." She held up the book and shook her head. "Why destroy this little thing? It's so tiny, that you can't read it anyway."

"Open the pages," I said. She did. "Do you see anything that piques your curiosity?"

"Are you thinking of a wheel code like what solved the Mary Lincoln impersonator's murder? When we found Abraham Lincoln's lost speech?" When she studied a couple pages, she said, "No."

"I didn't think so, either. I wanted to check what you thought." I held the bookcase, and said, "Linda, the stage manager, thought this was something. Like someone's initials. Aaron thought it was a scratch."

"Do you have a magnifier?"

"I'll get it."

When I returned, I found her sitting by the check-out area. "Be right back," I said. I set the magnifier down and went for another chair, and brought it over. "What do you see?"

"It may be EW, but I'm not sure. It's pretty well scratched. It's like someone put it on so that it wouldn't be mistook for someone else's markings."

"That's goofy," I said. "There's weird things going on around me, and I don't know what it's about."

"Tell me."

"All the script editing from Russ. Then Nancy was murdered. Why would he murder her because of the script?" I wiped my eyes. "Sylvie, the prop person, hid something. Two notes saying the same, 'Where is it? Now the house.' I glanced toward the door. "The electrical wiring had a short in it. The company isn't quite sure how it happened. This all sounds fishy."

"It all adds up to a mystery, but what?" Inga said.

"At least someone agrees with me," I said. I rubbed my chin. "Now, I'm taking over Nancy's part."

"What do the detectives have to say?"

"Not much. I don't think they have any good leads," I said.

"Well, we'll have to keep discussing and maybe something will start to make sense," Inga said. "I've got to get back to the store."

"Sure. Have you been busy?"

"Not bad." She went to the front door. "Really now, keep me posted."

"I will."

I took my duster and began dusting the dollhouses and straightening the furniture other things. As I dusted the historical White House, a customer entered.

"Hi! I'm fascinated by your store. I finally just had to come and see it."

"Good! I'm glad that you came. If you have any questions..." I said.

"Which house is this?" The long blond-haired young woman stood beside me at shoulder level. I figured she was about five years younger. "It's got to be the first, right?"

"Yes! After the War of 1812, President Madison had it restored."

"So this house would be just like it was when Abigail lived in it?" she said.

"Pretty much. They had to furnish the house themselves, and that was an ordeal," I said.

"You're kidding?" She gasped, her eyes wide open. "How on earth did they move everything?"

"Train, coach, buggies. You name it," I said.

"What was Martha Washington known for?"

"She set the precedent for salons and socializing. Getting the parties to come together and talk at informal settings," I said.

"I thought Dolley Madison did that."

"Dolley was the lady who outdid herself with it, getting recipes from all over the country. Championing women, and included recipes from women in newspaper articles. She was a master at diplomacy with southern hospitality and charm."

"Well, I hadn't intended to purchase a house, but I sure feel like one after hearing all of this about the First Ladies," the woman said.

"They are our 'behind the scenes' go to person. Women in need or children, they campaign for that segment of our society," I said.

"I'll take this one."

"Great! Let's go over to the counter and take care of it," I said. Max appeared instantaneously after receiving my message. Within a few short minutes, we had the house loaded and the customer on out the door.

Max strolled through the door after carrying the last box out, and said, "A run on the historicals. Good sign. Americans are interested in history." He grinned. "A few naysayers don't agree, but this proves them wrong."

"I agree. Why wouldn't anyone want to know about the presidents and their families? I realize that not everyone cares to know as much as we do, but knowing how the country started is important and who or what the party in power is all about, is important," I said.

"I'm going to get busy in the workroom," Max said.

"Okay." I stayed seated, and balanced out my daily finances. Next, I checked my e-mails and found there were a number from the website. Most messages asked presidential type questions, which I tried to answer. I was relieved to find that no one sent a cryptic note. I hoped that I'd received the last of them.

I reached for my script and started reading the lines over when the front door opened. It was Russ. Something about his eyes made me think that he was closely related to the president.

"Russ. You look so much like President Wilson. Are you related?"

"As a matter of fact, through my mother we are. I've been told that many times over the years." Russ slightly smiled.

"What can I do for you? Plan to look at the houses?"

"You are not to read the summary about the Fourteen Points. Let me take a look at the script so I can fix it."

"Not on your life," I said. He reached for it, but I was quicker, and snapped back. "It's against all decent protocol to change words before opening night."

"The words are being changed. Period," Russ said. I wondered what his problem was when he shot his arm out and yanked it from my hand.

"Max! Get out here!"

"What?" Max chased out toward me.

"He took my script." I tried unsuccessfully to snatch it away.

Russ started for the front door with it in hand, and Max raced to grab him. I went to stand beside him. Nabbing him by the scruff of the neck, Max easily spun him around.

"Give it!" Max said.

"She's got to stick with what I changed," Russ said. He tucked it behind him, but Max backed him tighter against the wall. "Wilson's legacy must live on."

"Of course it will, you idiot," Max said. He reached for the script and tore it from Russ's grip. "You're not the only biographer in the world."

By now, I was by Max's side, and took the script. "Who do you think you are?" I snarled. "Get out of my store, and don't come back." I opened the door and Max pushed him out. Quickly, I shut it and locked it. "Isn't it closing time?"

"It is now," Max said. He took a deep breath. "What's his problem?"

"It's got to be his ego."

"These theater types have pretty big ones," Max said.

"That's what's so odd. He really didn't write the script. The author based the story on what she knows. I don't see anywhere that it's based on his biography of Wilson."

What was Russ hiding that's so important?

Chapter Nine

Once I'd gathered the inventory for another house, which I planned to assemble in the morning, I worked on the needed memorization. It'd been a hectic day because of customers and Russ leaving me puzzled. Why was he so obstinate about rewriting certain script lines?

I took a moment and printed the Fourteen Points from a website. Not that I understood all of the legal jargon, but most points referred to returning all nations to their original borders from before the war.

Next, I studied the copyrighted script lines, and then the omitted lines. I decided that Russ believed in secrecy. In my opinion, he would've been a conscientious objector to the war. The deeper I investigated, I became more puzzled.

Right after closing, Aaron returned with a burger and soda.

"The detectives never showed. The officers took my statement and left," I told him. I licked ketchup from my finger before wiping my mouth. "They seemed to have pooh-poohed it."

"Don't worry, the detectives have it on their radar." He sipped his soda. "Have you started to straighten it? I want another look."

"Not yet. It's been like Grand Central plus theater people dropping in."

"They know something's up. Nancy's death has them perplexed." He took a hefty bite. "There are no substantial leads, but we don't know about the shamrock."

"They looked fresh. I bet they were delivered earlier in the day from the neighborhood florist where I usually go when flowers are in order."

"I'm sure they've checked them out," Aaron said.

"I doubt it. The detectives don't seem to be on top of anything right now," I said. "Russ, what about him?"

"Russ. What about him? Haven't they questioned him?"

"Don't worry and quit putting down the detectives. They have their hands full with cases and we're short of staff right now due to internal issues."

"Yeah, right." Russ was the likely candidate. But, why kill Nancy? I started getting a sinking feeling someone knew more than what was known, but what? I was going to have to make up a suspect list.

"When will you be home?" Aaron finished his burger, and crunched up his wrapper and threw it away, taking mine with him.

"About ten, or later," I said.

"That late?" Aaron stared at me. "I want you to be careful. As a matter of fact, call me periodically or send me messages."

"Will do, but you needn't worry." I got up and we strolled to the antique dollhouse. "It's one big mess, and was almost ruined." I lifted the tiny book. "Why break the spine? The pages are blank."

"Did you look closer at the bookcase?"

"Yes, and so did Inga. It may be Edith's initials, but we couldn't be sure." I thought a moment. "I'll take care of what I can tomorrow. I'll inspect every piece for odd markings." I glanced up at the clock. "How about walking me to the door?"

"Love to."

Aaron held my hand all the way down to the theater where he entered, following me to the dressing room.

"Remember, honey."

"Yep."

We kissed again, and he left. The actors were just beginning to arrive, and I decided to go in search of Linda or Sylvie. I knocked first on Sylvie's door, and it popped open so I entered.

"Sylvie?" I went to her desk and noticed that she'd filed all papers and what I saw were extra scripts. I left, and set out for the stage area.

"Linda?" I found her with the light crew. "Are we in full costume?"

"Yep. Tonight's the first for you." She studied me a minute before continuing, "You've never put on stage makeup, have you?"

"No." I didn't have a clue what shade because the lights were so bright, and I didn't want to look too sallow. "Bev must soon be here?"

"Any minute."

I left and headed toward the costume room again and grabbed another dress. I'd need several for changes between scenes. Carol, the costume person and makeup artist, Bev, sat in the dressing room and helped dress and undress us as we switched into our costumes. Soon the rest of the cast was doing the same. The woman for Susan B. Anthony sat nearby.

"I'm sorry, but what's your name? It's Joan, isn't it? I'm Liv." I caught her as she finished wrapping her hair up into a tight bun.

"Yep. It's hard coming in like this. Say? Sorry about your friend. Nancy seemed nice," Joan said. She reached down to tie her high-topped shoes. "These things are miserable to wear."

"None of these clothes items are comfortable. How'd they do it?" I couldn't help but to see that her script wasn't marked as mine. "I see that Russ hasn't marked up your script."

"I wouldn't let him near it." Her eyes narrowed. She leaned closer. "He really was angry with Nancy. They fought before she died."

"They did? How do you know?"

"I was right outside the open door." She nodded. "I didn't hear them, but she looked ready to burst. Even slammed her fist on the counter."

"What did Russ do?"

"He made another grab for the script, but she held it firm."

"What did he do?"

"Raised his fist, and walked out," Joan said. "I told the police when I was interviewed."

"That was my next question." I waited a beat before continuing, "One more question, if you don't mind."

"Sure! What is it?" Joan's period dress crinkled from leaning in. "If it's a corset, you're wondering about, I'm not wearing one. Not on your life would I put one of those cages on! I'd faint."

"Me, too, but, that's not what I was wondering." I frowned, not knowing exactly how to proceed so I decided to just spit it out. "Where was everyone when they learned of the show's cancellation?"

"You're wondering if everyone was still in their correct place for the beginning, right?" Joan took a deep breath and said, "I was where I should be. I think everyone else was, too, truly. Um," she tapped her chin, "Linda went from one person to the other before seeking out Nancy." She smiled. "Does that help?"

"Yes," I said. At the same time, Bev entered carrying a box, and set it down near me. "Time for makeup?"

"You betcha!" Bev grinned, and began holding up the compacts.

"Good luck." Joan walked away.

As Bev helped me choose the right shade and showed me how to apply the heavy base, I decided to question her. "Bev?"

"Ah-huh?"

"Do you happen to know who would've been the last person to enter backstage the night of the murder?" I said.

"Why?" Bev's eyes opened wide. "I didn't do it. How could you even think it?"

"No! I'm not asking that." I reached over and gave her a big hug. "I never thought that in a million years. I wondered about the order of the actors entering the backstage area."

"Well..." Bev said, and sniffled. "It's like this...I went to the bathroom so I don't know. The police have already asked a ton of questions."

"Nancy was my employee and a good friend. I'm trying to figure things out for her," I said.

"Well," Bev said. She reached into the makeup box and pulled out mascara. "Wear this shade." She got up. "I'll be helping the Woodrow Wilson guy if you need help with makeup."

"Thanks, Bev." She'd already left and went in search of the Woodrow Wilson actor.

I thought over what had happened, and questioned whether Bev had the heart to murder someone? Using the bathroom for an excuse was pretty lame. I switched gears to Russ. Would Russ kill because of the rewriting? Why would he? He was a well-known and highly respected biographer of many presidents. Why ruin his reputation?

I sent Aaron a message telling him that all was going well.

When finished, I walked out to the theater and listened for instructions. Not too long after, we rehearsed the second act. Fortunately, I'd memorized most of the lines. During the break, I checked for messages but found the inbox empty. Curious, I sent

Aaron another one. It seemed odd to not hear from him.

I took it upon myself to seek out Russ, and discovered him with the sound crew. Two voices rose higher the nearer I came, so I hid in the shadows. Just as I hoped to hear something relevant, their chairs scratched back and Russ stood. I held my breath as he passed before me. I resolved to catch him another time as I wondered if he ever had a moment of never being angry?

Down in the dressing room, Linda began calling, "Places!" I stood to the side and mentally recited my lines. The evening came to close a short time later. Walking to my car and jumping inside felt good. I did a quick check for messages in case Aaron wanted me to stop for something, but there still weren't any. Troubled, I started the car and began driving down the alley.

Two cars followed me out to the main road before I turned toward home. When I neared the first stop light, I looked into my rearview mirror but didn't recognize the driver, which surprised me. I believed that both cars had belonged to theater people. When I slowed down in an effort to force this person to pass, he hugged close to my bumper. At the corner to turn toward my house, the driver sped away, much to my relief.

Once I'd parked in the garage and entered the kitchen, I hollered, "Aaron!" When he didn't answer, I repeated his name as I walked further. In the living room, I found him sound asleep in his recliner and the television set blaring another Twins baseball game. I shut the TV off, kissed my husband's cheek, and said, "Time to go to bed, honey."

After tucking him into bed, I wasn't ready to sleep. I heated a cup of hot chocolate, grabbed my script and sat under a living room lamp to study the lines. I glanced out the front window as a car slowly drove by. I realized that I'd forgotten to draw the drapes. I did so and noticed the passing car was similar to the one which had followed me. I made sure all the doors and windows were locked, including the basement windows. Afterwards, I crawled into bed.

As I lay in bed, my thoughts spun around to Joan and witnessing some sort of angry words between Nancy and Russ, then Max shoving him out the store front door. I was going to have to figure out why he was so angry and adamant to rewrite the lines. I decided to try and track down the author to see if this person could shed light on Russ' reasoning. I also wanted to know more about the technical crew since they had access to the dressing rooms. Eventually I fell asleep, but woke with a miserable headache.

I showered and dressed, joining Aaron in the kitchen. We sat with a cup of coffee and each a toasted blueberry bagel.

"I think someone followed me home." I chewed on my bagel while spreading another dollop of cream cheese. "Fat lot of good you'd have been last night if I needed you. You never responded to my message."

"What message?" He slipped out his phone and read it. "Sorry. I must've had it off." He sipped his coffee. "This is weird, but I feel as if I'd been drugged."

"I have a miserable headache."

"What have we mutually eaten?"

"Nothing except supper, and you purchased it down the street, ham salad sandwiches."

"Right." Aaron frowned. "I'm telling the detectives about being followed."

"You go right ahead." *As if they'll listen!* "I've got to get going." I gave him a kiss, and asked, "Do you work today? This play is putting me off-kilter with your schedule. All this memorizing—it's tough."

"That's okay, honey." Aaron stood. "I work tonight. I'm going to mow the lawn and I'll vacuum. I'll bring you down lunch and supper, so don't worry."

"Thanks, honey." We kissed again and I grabbed my bag before heading out to the car. I wished that I could've walked since it was proving to be another beautiful day and it would help to rid me of my headache.

I realized once turning onto Main Street, that I didn't have any water left in the refrigerator in the workroom. *Did Aaron drink from the water bottle I brought home?* At the next light, I turned onto a side street and parked out front of a neighborhood grocery store, and went inside. After purchasing a small case of six clear water bottles, I finished driving to work.

Max's truck was off to the side and I parked right beside it. The back door was slightly propped open, which didn't sit right. "Max!" I called. Once inside, I shut the back door. "How come the door's open?" I set the water in the refrigerator and continued to the showroom. I still hadn't found Max.

"Max! Where in the world are you?" I stopped in my tracks when I saw Grandma sitting in front of the computer and behind the check-out counter. "What in the world?"

"Caught ya off guard, didn't I?" Grandma cackled, her eyes sparkled. She slapped her palm on the counter. "Grandpa wanted Max to ride and listen to some weird sound the car was making. They left the door open for some reason."

"Good grief! You sure surprised me. Do you know for sure if Grandpa left it open?"

"No."

"I'm giving him a call." When Grandpa answered, I got the answer to my question, that he had. "We've had a break-in Grandpa. Please don't leave the door unlocked." When he agreed, we disconnected. I texted Max. *Was door open?*

"When will they be back?"

"Shortly. Aren't you going to open the store? It is that time, you know?"

"You're right." The woman was johnny-on-the-spot. I got up and unlocked the front door, and also turned the sign around. "The First Lady pictures look crooked." My phone dinged with a return message from Max, which read. *N*

"I wondered if you'd notice that," Grandma said. "Aren't I something ordering you around?"

"I'm going to take care of them," I said. I walked over to the pictures and began to straighten them. Afterwards, I did the same with my other wall hangings. "Have you looked at the mess that someone did to Mrs. Wilson's house?"

"No, I wanted you to show me. Grandpa listens to the police scanner, remember?" Grandma said.

"Follow me," I said. I showed her the broken and destroyed pieces.

"Oh, my! It's terrible," Grandma said.

"I was going to straighten the mess this morning. Why would someone do this?" I said.

"A dollhouse, for pity's sake, too," Grandma said. She shook her head. "There has to be a reason."

"But what?" Just then the front door bell jingled and a customer entered. "Good morning. May I help you?"

"Yes. I'm curious about the John Quincy Adams house?" the older woman said. She wore bright red lipstick and bright blue eyeshadow, which made me think of styles from the sixties and seventies.

"John Quincy and Louisa Adams. It's right over here." I directed the woman to the correct house. "This one."

"How delightful," the woman said. I noticed that Grandma had sat back down and was busy writing. I focused back on the older lady. "The White House was finally starting to become the grand mansion of the country."

"Tell me a little about her. Did she get along with her mother-in-law?" the woman said.

"Abigail certainly was out-spoken and so was Louisa, but I think they came to terms with each other. Life wasn't easy for either of them. Washington D.C. was far away from everything."

"I realize that, but tell me a little bit more about Louisa." The woman's arthritic hand reached out and touched the house. "How had she liked the White House years?"

"She was invaluable with international affairs. Very strong-willed. She loved to dance, wore makeup, which was totally unheard of and made her husband, John Quincy, quite angry many times."

"Now show me Edith Wilson's house," she said.

"The Wilson White House is right over here." I walked her to the house.

"I'll purchase the Wilson house, and pick it up later today," she said. "Mrs. Wilson had an awful lot to hide—suffragists have long memories."

What does that mean? My headache blossomed.

Chapter Ten

My headache seemed to hang around forever, and when I thought it'd never leave, it disappeared. Fortunately, I worked alone and managed to repair the tiny book and upright all the furniture inside of the dollhouse. I stood with arms crossed and stared down at it, and wondered why anyone would try to destroy a dollhouse? While studying the rooms separately, the business phone rang and I went to answer it.

"White House Dollhouse Store, how may I help you?" I sat down and listened as the woman gave a rendition about when she was younger, she'd met Eleanor Roosevelt and how she was so nice. Really, really tall and such a high-pitched voice. She loved listening to her because she was so smart, and that she wanted to hurdle bricks at the President because of his extra-marital affairs. When she'd finished speaking, I said, "You'll have to visit the store and tell me more about the First Ladies."

She replied, "No, thank you. My daughter would want me to buy her one and they're too expensive for my taste." She hung up.

I chuckled for quite a little while and that's when I found Grandma's note. It'd fell to the floor and was tucked partially under the counter. It read: Who did this to the dollhouse? A) A prankster? B) A young snotty nosed kid? (Oops! Might be the same) C) Someone who hates Edith Wilson? D) Someone who hates him. E) None of the above.

Grandma made me crazy sometimes when she left notes like this behind. I printed E and wrote *No clue.*

On the back side of the sheet it read: Who is suspect number 1? A) Stage manager B) Russ the meanie C) Susan B. Anthony D) Audience member.

I wrote: E, *No clue*

Further reading revealed a one liner: Use your knowledge.

That little tidbit set me on edge. It caused a wave of anxiety to rush through me. What knowledge was she speaking about?

I removed a blank sheet from a tablet and started a list. On one side I began writing what I knew.

Linda found Nancy.

Russ badgered Nancy with rewrites.

Russ badgered me for the same reasons.

Russ Badgered Joan, the Susan B. Anthony actress.

Joan warned me about Russ. She didn't know for sure where everyone was standing when Nancy was found.

Sylvie got perturbed when I asked her about props and Nancy.

I overheard a conversation between Russ and techie crew-Tom and Dave.

Cyanide was the poison of choice. Hand delivered shamrocks and in full water vase. I made a mental note to not accept flowers while performing.

On the backside, I wrote: *What don't I know?*

Who killed Nancy and why?

I tucked the paper under a stack of old magazines which sat on a shelf below the register. The computer wasn't running yet, so I turned it on. In a few minutes, I was logged into the store's account and looking at messages. The first six were of interest. One suggestion was that I feature a White House per month and the First Ladies of that era. I responded to each, thanking them for their interest. The final one set my nerves on edge. It was like the last few cryptic messages. "Where is it?"

Once again, I question: Where is what?

The same question went around and around my head. My thoughts went to Grandma's note: use your *knowledge*. Her note was just as cryptic. I shuddered. Just then, I heard the backdoor open and Max's shoes scuff on the floor.

"Max."

"Yep. You came in early. The front door isn't even open yet, I see." He looked over to me. "You look like you've seen a ghost. What's up?"

"Both Aaron and I woke with a miserable headache, which is so unusual. We didn't eat the same thing. Now I feel it coming on again."

"There is a slight, odd odor in here." He sniffed. "You go outside and stand, let me walk around." When I didn't move, he said, "Scoot!"

I did as told, and leaned up against the back wall. What could cause such a headache? I took several deep breaths, then walked to the end of the alley and back. As I approached the door, Max stepped outside, holding a sheet of paper.

"Recognize this?"

"Sure! Grandma's note."

"It smells."

"Oh no." I slipped my phone out of my pocket and speed dialed Grandma. "You okay?" I asked when she answered.

"Yes. A slight headache, but that's vanishing with my second cup of coffee."

"I think we've been drugged as well as Aaron. I'll keep you posted." The next thing I did after disconnecting was to put in a call to Erlandsen. "You'd better get over here. Someone's tried poisoning me, Aaron, and Grandma." I hung up before he responded, and gave Aaron a call. "Get down here right now!" It ended up being a voicemail. "Russ was here after Grandma. It could've been anyone, really. The door's always open. I'm in and out of the back. It could've happened in the restaurant while Aaron waited for the food."

"We don't even know if it's poison, but it sure seems like it." Max's eyes opened wider when he looked at the note still held between his fingers. "I'd better put this down somewhere."

I watched him go back inside, hesitating to follow. How far would someone go to kill me? Why poison me? Lost in thought, I went back inside only to find Max talking to the detectives. Because I'd been outside in the back, I hadn't heard them arrive.

"There she is," Mergens stated, his eyebrow rose. "Max is filling us in."

"Where's Aaron?" Erlandsen asked, glancing around me.

"I left him a message." I took out my phone and looked. "Nope. He should've been here. Oh my God! I'm going home! Maybe I should call for an ambulance right away? He could be unconscious."

"You're not going anywhere, Liv. You look ready to faint. You're white as a ghost," Max said.

"I'm on it! I'm sending a squad over to your house, asap," Erlandsen said.

"Right." I went over to my chair, and sunk into it. "I feel miserable."

"This place needs airing out. We need someone here to take samples plus I'll take that paper," Mergens stated.

I barely could manage to keep everything straight. My mind felt dull and hazy. "I need air." I stood but dropped back down right away.

"Let's get you outside." Max grabbed my arms, and stood me up. "I'm taking her out to her car to sit." He looked at the detectives. "Where's your keys?" He looked at me. "Never mind. I know." Max held me up as we walked to the workroom where my bag was, and I retrieved them.

"I can make it." I glanced around the room in search of flowers. My hand smelled slightly of bitter almond. I continued out with my keys in hand and went directly to the car. I leaned against it for a few minutes before opening it up and plunking down on the seat. I kept the door open. A short while later, Max joined me.

"Aaron was mowing and is fine. He'll be here in just a few minutes," Max said.

"Good. Now I don't have to worry about him. They're after me."

"You don't know that," Max said.

"You sound like Aaron."

We both looked at the car driving up the alley. "Perfect timing." It was Aaron, and I was so happy to see him. I tried to stand, but Max held me down. "Oh, all right." I wasn't too happy, but right after Aaron parked, he came to me.

"Honey." Aaron reached down and held me close. "What's this about?"

"Poison. Grandma's note, we think, and maybe in the workroom."

"Poison? Why?"

"That's what we all want to know and intend on finding out." We looked over as the two detectives walked toward us.

"Are you coming around, Liv, or should we call for an ambulance?"

"I'm doing fine." I forced a grin. I wanted to scream at them for not paying closer attention when the store was broken into and Edith Wilson's dollhouse trashed. I hoped they would start paying closer attention. "Did you figure it out yet?"

"You mean the source?" Erlandsen asked.

"Yes!" My spunk was returning. I glared at both. "If you'd been listening previously, then maybe this wouldn't have happened!"

"We're here now," Mergens stated, taking out his notepad. "We have someone coming and he will go through the store and check for foreign objects, and poisonous materials."

"That's mighty nice of you." I hitched myself up and out of the car, and crossed my arms. "Grandma was here yesterday morning. I didn't see the note because it'd fallen onto the floor and was almost hidden. I noticed it this morning when I looked down."

"It had to have been in plain sight for most of yesterday, honey," Aaron softly said. "Where could it have been?"

"The back door was open when I came yesterday morning." I rubbed my chin. "Customers came and went. We sold a few houses. The wind could've taken the paper. That's probably why I hadn't noticed it."

"Okay," Aaron said.

"Now that you mention it, I did see her writing something but forgot about it."

"What time is this?" Mergens said.

"Morning. Grandpa wanted Max to listen to his truck."

"Max?"

"Some clanging noise. I fixed it with a couple turns." Max shrugged. "They left about ten or a little after."

"Let's try and narrow it down." Erlandsen paged through his notes. "Let's see your receipts."

We went back inside, and I turned them over. "Simple customers."

"We just want to get some kind of timeline," Erlandsen said.

"Russ came in and tried to take away my script."

"Tell us about that," Erlandsen said.

"He did the same with Nancy." I showed him the script and the lines in question. "The woman who plays Susan B. Anthony, Joan, stated that he tried to do the same with her." The phone rang, which caused me to jump. I answered, "White House Dollhouse store. How may I help you?" After stating the store's hours, we disconnected. I looked at the detectives. "Have you checked where all the actors stood right before the performance?"

"Let us do our job." Erlandsen closed his notebook after copying down the needed information. "We'll be in touch."

The three of us watched them leave. "Now what?"

"Sooner said, and here comes the next team," Aaron stated as the next team entered.

"Detective Flypaa and Detective Smith, here to take a look at things." They wore face masks and protective suits.

"Officer Reynolds, half-owner, and my wife, the other half-owner, Liv. Our employee, Max."

"Why don't you guys go and have an early lunch? It'll take us about an hour to comb this place."

"All right."

We headed out the back door. "Max, want to come to the house? Aaron makes killer pancakes." I squeezed Aaron's hand.

"Sure."

It didn't take long before we were filled from eating too much. The hour slipped by way too fast, and we were back in the store. The two detectives were just leaving.

"It's still dangerous." Detective Smith waited a beat, and said, "Call in a professional crew to clean good. You need to get it off the surfaces. It looks like it's been sprayed all over."

"Thanks. I have a company that I've previously hired, I'll call them.""

"I'm going up and start carving." Max reached for a smoke, and winked at me. "Glad we're all in the land of the living."

"You betcha," I said. Aaron and I watched as he walked out.

"I've got a court date, then I'll return," Aaron said.

I contacted the cleaning service and they sent out a crew immediately. It took the crew about two hours before they rid the store of the poison.

The phone rang several times which kept me busy. At three, I was surprised that Aaron hadn't returned. I sent him a message, and he responded immediately, stating that the court session just started. I knew this happened frequently. There were many reasons for it. I noticed Grandma held her phone out and was texting.

"Grandpa's coming. You'll be all right, won't you?"

"Sure. I have my lines to go through."

I pulled up and chair, and that's where we were when Grandpa honked out front for her. The store felt eerie once she'd left so I closed and locked the doors. I hadn't thought of being scared, but I was. Too much had happened. I reached for the sheet of paper from earlier and read through my list. On the side where I'd written what I knew, I added: *someone tried to poison both me and Aaron.* It occurred to me that I needed to find someone who gardened.

I logged into the computer and did a search on pesticides.

Cyanide was a pesticide.

Who among the actors had dirty fingernails? Was there anyone who had talked about gardens and weeding? I didn't recall anyone. I got up and started walking around the room. I hoped that something might jog my memory. I stopped at the very first house and stared at the swamps around the Civil War house and thought about Mary Lincoln and all of her headaches, and how she almost died from the carriage accident. From what I knew, she didn't dally in a garden. Did Edith work in the garden? I doubted that, too.

I flipped back to today as I strolled down the aisles. I tried to picture Russ on his hands and knees weeding, but couldn't. It didn't seem right. The tech crew might be a possibility. How well did I know anyone in the cast?

The mailman knocked on the window, and I went to open the door. "Thanks." I took the stack from him. I locked the door and went to sit. Most of it was junk. A post card slipped out, and I picked it up. It was of the well-known picture of President Wilson in France reading his Fourteen Points. I turned it around. Besides the store address, nothing was written.

Chapter Eleven

I set it aside, wondering what to do with it. It made no sense at all to send a postcard with Wilson's picture on it and not write anything on the flipside. *Was this a message? A threat?* I decided to give Aaron a call. Pressing the speed dial, I realized I should be calling the detectives, but on the other hand, they didn't usually treat weird things with much interest.

Aaron answered almost immediately, "Hon?"

"I'm leaving in a minute and a half, can it wait?" Aaron said.

"Nope. Got a postcard with Wilson reading the Fourteen Points in France. Only the store's address is on the back."

"Set aside and don't touch it! On my way!" The squeak of the back door echoed through the phone as he disconnected.

I made an instant judgment call and went ahead and dialed Erlandsen, and left a voice mail, asking him to give me a call when he had a moment. Afterwards, I continued with tidying up the tables.

The back door opened up, and I heard, "Soup's ready!"

"I don't believe you. This is a trick." I cocked my head and smiled. "Oh, my! You brought bowls and spoons! You're not kidding." On tippy-toes, I kissed him. "When did you make soup?" I needled my brow and said, "It's summer. Who eats soup in the summer?"

"We do!" Aaron set the container down on the counter. "Now, are you gonna show me what all the ruckus was about? Why'd you call?"

"This came in the mail." I showed the postcard. "Weird, eh?" When he pursed his lips and stared at it, I said, "Already placed a call to Erlandsen."

"Good going." He held it carefully between finger and thumb on the top and bottom. "I suppose you've got your prints all over it?"

"Nope. I've been careful." I started dishing up the soup. "Soup in the summer. Never ate soup in the summertime," I muttered, and took my first spoonful. "Very good. It has to be, I haven't had homemade bean soup in years."

"Thank you. The deli at our favorite marketplace makes great food."

"I knew you were full of bologna and didn't make the soup." I grinned.

"It seemed like a good idea." Aaron nodded at the postcard. "I can take this into the precinct."

"Not on your life!" I shook my head, and reached for it, setting it aside. "They have to come and talk to me."

"That's right. I forgot."

"Did you interview the tech crew the night of the murder?" I smiled with every spoonful. "Yummy."

"What's this about?" Aaron continued eating. "You're not asking questions, are you? You'll get yourself killed. That's why the postcard!"

"I'm not that stupid," I said as Aaron stared at me. "Honestly, Aaron, give me more credit than that!"

"I'm trying here. I know you did or else you wouldn't have received the postcard."

"Well, okay. I did, but didn't pester or bug anyone too much."

"I knew it! No more Liv! Promise?"

"Maybe." I kept my own thoughts to myself about the investigation.

We finished our meal with just a few minutes to spare before I had to attend rehearsals.

"I should be right home. Probably at ten or ten-thirty."

"Okay, see you then. I want you to send messages or call at least once an hour or every half. I'm worried about you."

"I'll try. Sometimes I get too busy with lines and remembering everything that I forget to do that."

"Do your best." Aaron gathered the remains, and placed them in the bag. "Good night." He gave me a big kiss. "Be careful."

"I will." After locking up, I grabbed my belongings and headed down to the theater.

As I walked, I went over my lines and what I was to be doing on stage. When I approached the backdoor, I noticed a florist delivery truck parked across the street. I made a notation on my phone to add the name of the floral company to my list since it wasn't from Yellow Daisy Floral. The florist was named, Loon Pink Florist. The delivery person drove the van down the street, and I turned to enter the theater backdoor.

"Hey there," I said to Linda. "What's up for tonight? Anything special?"

"Nope. We'll walk you through the acts. You're doing great."

I headed back to the dressing room and stripped from my clothes after grabbing my stage costume. For this act, I was to wear a solid navy suit, skirt and matching suit coat with a white blouse under it. For performance purposes, I'd also wear a carnation.

Last night, I had learned to apply makeup easier and to wear a towel around my shoulders to protect my dress. When I'd finished dressing, Linda called, "Places!" I quickly zipped out to the stage area. I also did a once over of my props.

During break, I slipped around and checked out props and took a minute to speak with the other actors. I remembered that I hadn't sent Aaron a message, so I hurriedly did it. Afterwards, I found President Wilson's actor reciting lines, Dan O'Connor.

"Dan? You're perfect for the part. You look just like the former prez, tall and lanky, and the way you cock your head, is perfect."

"Thanks. I must admit, you don't look much like Edith. However, in costume and with the hat, you do."

"Good." I thought a moment and said, "How about I help you with your lines, if you do the same?"

"Sounds, good!"

We took turns by going in order of pages.

"I notice that someone's tried to edit your lines where you speak of the Fourteen Points?" I said.

"I won't do it. I won't change anything."

"Right you are." I stood, brushing the wrinkles away. "Why would anyone want you to do it?"

"Russ. He's been going around to everyone. Don't trust him."

"Where is he? I haven't seen him tonight." We began walking toward the stage. "Last I saw of him, he was going to speak with Linda."

"He must be up with the techies."

Once we'd made it to our assigned spot, I glanced around at my fellow actors, and saw that we were all ready to start. The props were also correctly placed. Once the stage darkened, and the actors had walked out to begin, the lights lit the stage area, and we began.

My lines were first. "*Alice Paul and all of her minions had no place to demonstrate for voting rights here at the White House! Who do they think they are?*"

I moved closer to Dan.

"*They don't belong on the street. They should be home with their husbands and children. Shame on them.*"

We continued with our monologues until the act finished and the stage lights faded.

Afterwards notes to each actor helped with our presentations. I had to look more at the audience and remember to turn toward them instead of away. When she'd finished, it was time to go home. I decided to take a look at my props again after changing into my street clothes. I wondered if my white gloves shouldn't be laundered, and held them up to the light. Linda was busy with Sylvie, the properties manager, making the stage ready for the next night's rehearsal.

"I'm taking my gloves and scarf home to clean. They look dirty," I told them, dropping them into my bag and removing my car keys.

"Go ahead."

As I started for the back door, my phone bleeped. I checked, and it was from Aaron. I replied with an *ok*. The backstage lighting was dim, and I had trouble making my way toward the door. As I walked, I thought I heard footsteps following, so I stepped aside. When stopped, I quietly listened, but didn't hear anything. I continued onward, and immediately heard quiet footsteps. I hurried to the door, and raced toward my car.

I never looked back until it was through my rearview mirror as I turned into the street. Fortunately, I didn't see anyone. My nerves jumped until I'd pressed the button to raise the garage door and drove inside. I didn't calm down until I'd entered the house.

"Aaron!" I called. "Where are you?" I found him in bed, half asleep. I decided to wait for the morning to tell him what happened. By this time, I wondered if my mind hadn't been playing tricks on me or not. I showered and crawled into bed.

Aaron slipped his arm around me, and I fell asleep. It wasn't too much later when floor squeaks woke me. I nudged Aaron, but he rolled over and continued snoring. I listened and thought footsteps were approaching so I swung my legs over the side of the bed, and grabbed my bedside book. Holding my breath, I stood behind the door and peeked out. After a few minutes, I gave up waiting and decided to take a quiet walk down the hallway toward the living room. Standing behind the wall, I peered around the corner but still didn't see anyone or anything different. I must've imagined this or was dreaming, I told myself, and went back to bed.

Grandma called early, waking us. It was decided that she'd watch the store while I worked on sewing gowns and ordering supplies. Aaron was in the kitchen toasting bagels when I entered.

"Hey you, morning!" I kissed him. "Grandma's going to watch the store while I sew and do some ordering. I'm running low because I've sold a few more houses."

"Good. It's hard keeping up. I miss Nancy's upbeat personality. Always a smile in the morning."

"There's lots to be done." I bit into my blueberry bagel. "Nummy." I remembered getting up last night, and decided to tell him. "Last night when I left the theater, I thought someone followed me. During the night, I woke and could swear that I heard someone in the house." I sipped from my glass of orange juice. "You were sleeping. I tried waking you, but you rolled over and kept snoring."

"I'll take a quick look around. Stay right here," Aaron said. "You should've woke me."

I continued eating while he was searching through the house and also checked for phone messages.

"I didn't see anything out of the ordinary," Aaron said. "Next time, make sure you wake me up. Liv? This is dangerous."

"I will and I know. Never heard back from the detectives, either."

"You should've by now."

"I'm calling the minute I get into the store," I said, and remembered the gloves. "I have to wash my white gloves and scarf."

"I can bring supper again tonight."

"Sounds like a date."

We finished and I went to the laundry area and placed the gloves and scarf in separate small pans, filling them each with mild and unscented detergent. As they soaked, I finished getting ready for work. I knew they were needed for tonight's rehearsal so I folded them inside towels and placed into a plastic bag to be air dried later.

With my bag and the plastic bags in hand, I called, "See you later!" I headed out the door. Max's truck was nowhere to be seen, and I wondered where he was. Instinctively, I glanced up to the apartment, but didn't see him. I punched in the security code and entered.

In the workroom, I set my bag before exposing the wet gloves and scarf to the air for drying. I turned lights on as I walked the short hallway into the showroom. I made my daily circle of the display tables, straightening items as I walked. Lucy Hayes needed standing. Dolley Madison's turban needed fixing since the feathers looked lopsided

I got the computer humming and took out my phone, dialing Erlandsen's number.

"Erlandsen speaking."

"Liv Reynolds, here." I waited a beat before continuing. "I'm calling about the postcard that I received yesterday."

"Oh yes. We've got the message, but have been knee-deep here."

"It's sitting here. It's weird. No writing on the back."

"It's not threatening, is it?"

"Nope. Don't you want it for prints?"

"We'll be there shortly. Anything else?"

"Maybe. I'll tell you when you get here." I disconnected. I took a look at the note I'd made of the florist delivery van, and decided to do an Internet search of the store. The phone rang, and I said, "White House Dollhouse store, how may I help you?"

"Truth will prevail."

I stared at the phone for a moment before setting it on the cradle. Puzzled, I muttered, "What truth? What are you talking about?" I looked away before picking my cell phone from my pocket and calling the precinct once again. As it rang, my store phone did also. I quit the cell phone and picked up the store phone. No one replied so I disconnected. The sound of two car doors out front closing brought a chill up and down my spine. I drew in a few deep breaths before walking to the door. I peeked out the window and noted the two detectives walking toward the door. I turned the sign to Open and unlocked the door.

"I'm glad you're here," I stated as they entered. "I just had a weird phone call."

Mergens stopped, and stared at me. "What was said?"

Both men removed their notepads.

"Go ahead," Mergens said.

"Truth will prevail." I crossed my arms. "What truth? I don't get what is happening."

"You don't need to 'get' anything. We'll figure it all out," Erlandsen said. He peered at me. "This man almost sounds desperate."

"I'm not sure if it is a man. The voice was muffled." I ran my fingers through my hair. I went behind the counter and picked up the postcard. "Here." I handed it to Erlandsen. "See? It's President Wilson speaking while reading the Fourteen Points."

"Hmm…" he replied, handing it to Mergens. "See what you think."

"We're going to have to do some research on this," Mergens prophesied. "What else has happened? You look too agitated. There must be more."

I glanced from one to the other, and wondered if they read minds. "A call came in right afterwards, and no one answered." I rubbed my chin. "Then, there's last night."

"Last night?" Erlandsen leaned against the counter, and pulled a toothpick from his pocket and poked it between his lips.

"This is just getting better and better, isn't it?" Mergens said.

"Last night, before leaving the theater after rehearsal was finished, I thought someone followed me. During the night, I thought someone was in the house but I didn't see anyone or find anything out of place."

"Where was Aaron?"

"Sleeping." I placed my hands on my hips, and said, "Then, there's the Edith Wilson dollhouse. It's an antique, you know? It once belonged to her. Why trash it?"

"Tell me what you think about the actors?" Erlandsen said.

"They're all pretty nice. The only person who really irritates me is Russ, and I'm not alone. Most everyone has been bullied by him to rewrite their stage lines."

"Know where to find him?"

"Not really," I shook my head, and continued, "if not in the theater, I don't have a clue."

"Is that all?"

"I saw a florist van leave from the vicinity when I walked down the alley."

"So?" Mergens said.

"Wasn't Nancy killed from pesticides? Cyanide?" I said. "You know? The shamrock?"

"Leave the detecting to us"

They both walked to the door, and stopped.

"If anything else should happen, let us know," Mergens said.

"Have you even looked closely at the dollhouse?"

"It's just a dollhouse, Liv. No more, no less," Mergens said.

After giving me a nod, they walked out the door. When it had closed, I took a small notepad and threw it across the room, aiming it at the door.

So much for my suspicions and worries and fears.

I went to the workroom and took a look at the unpainted doll heads. Grandma would soon arrive, allowing me the needed uninterrupted spare time. I pondered which head to first paint? Edith Wilson, Dolley Madison or Louisa Adams. I reached for the hair box, and realized that I didn't have human hair wigs for each head. I went for my order book and made a few notations. I could still paint faces, so I removed paint bottles from the shelf and set out the small bowls for dipping. The brushes were clean and ready for use, and were set alongside of them. Now I just had to wait for grandma before getting started.

I went to the computer and placed an online order for wigs.

In the workroom, I busied myself by going through furnishing inventory and made several more notations of needed items. Glancing at the clock, I was surprised to see that an hour had passed since opening the door for business. It seemed like I was pretty well set until she arrived, so I took out my play script and began running through my lines. Fortunately, I'd retained most of what I'd learned from last night session with Dan. After running through the lines, I began to wonder about Grandma when at last I heard her voice come from the back hall.

"Hey, Grandma!" I called.

"Yoohoo!" Grandma breezed into the showroom. "Sorry, but Grandpa took me out to breakfast and we met some friends."

"You can't go anywhere without meeting someone you know," I said. "Who was it this time?"

"Actually, it was Hazel from our old neighborhood."

"Really? What did she have to say?" I moved from the computer so that she could have a seat. "Haven't seen Ronnie in a long time."

"It's kind of strange, really." Grandma sat down. "Ronnie's daughter, Sharon, is getting a history degree with emphasis in the First Ladies. That's your degree, isn't it?"

"Yes. That is different." Puzzled, I asked, "Since you moved, I don't suppose you've seen her for awhile. Did she show you a picture of her?"

"Of course. She looks like Hazel, too. She's also emphasizing the Wilson years and is quite interested in the Suffragist movement."

"Oh. I'll have to make a date to meet up with her again. I haven't seen Sharon since she played the piano for our wedding." When a horn blasted, we both looked out the window. "I'm going to paint. I'll be in the workroom."

To pass the time, I played the recorder and spoke my lines while painting. It wasn't easy blending the skin tones to make it appear natural. The pink blush would come later for Dolley. I carefully began applying the base for another head when Grandma called, "Liv. Phone call!"

"Coming!" I hurried out to the showroom. "Who is it?" Grandma shrugged, and I answered, "Liv here. How may I help you?"

"Erlandsen here.

"What is it?"

"No prints."

Chapter Twelve

"That figures," I said, frowning. "No prints taken."

"Honey, you've got to let the police do their job," Grandma said. "I know it's hard to wait and see, but there's no evidence to suggest anyone as a suspect."

"If they'd brought anyone in for questioning, Aaron would've let me know. He's scared for my safety because he thinks I'm butting my nose in where it doesn't belong."

"Well, are you?" Grandma looked me square in the eye. "You are, aren't you?"

"I hate it when you do that? I can never get away with anything." I shuffled off toward the workroom. "I'm busy painting."

I continued applying the base layers on the heads before setting them aside. When the front door jingled a customer, I hurried to wash my hands and cleanse the brushes and work area. I peeked out to the showroom and watched Grandma lead a young woman around the display tables. When she glanced in my direction, I winked at her. Grandma always dazzled me with her patience and the way she was able to talk to everyone. She was the perfect spokesperson for the store. I watched them pause in front of a house, and decided to stroll towards them.

"Here's my granddaughter now. She's the store owner." Grandma looked toward me, and said, "This young lady is inquiring about First Lady Nancy Reagan."

"She was very well liked," I replied. "because of her devotion to Ronnie."

"I'll take this house," she said. The woman smiled at me. "It's for me."

"Is it a birthday present to you?" I was beginning to really like this woman.

"You betcha!"

"A woman after my own heart. Ten percent off since it's for you from you for your birthday," I said. I walked toward the check-out counter. The back door open, and I called, "Max!"

Those footsteps became louder, and suddenly stopped. "Which house?" Max said. He wore his dark sunglasses, and I wondered if he'd been out all night and was trying to cover his red eyes.

"Reagan."

"Got it." He glanced at the woman, and said, "It's a fine house. Where is your car located? I'll carry it out."

"Right out front."

While Max gathered the boxes and other items together, I rang up the sale. It wasn't long before he carried the larger items to the car, and I trailed behind him with the smaller boxes.

"There are assembly directions inside but if you need any help, make sure to give us a call," I told her. "I hope you enjoy the house."

"Thanks."

Back inside, Grandma continued with taking care of the showroom and answering the phone while I sat down to sew a couple of inaugural gowns. Max gathered needed items and went to his apartment to carve heads. As I sewed, it became clear that I really needed to place an advertisement for another assistant.

The floor squeaked above, so I knew that Max hadn't settled down with his carving tools yet. Grandma's humming grew louder, so I got up to see why. I hadn't heard the jingle of the front door opening so it surprised me to see a man circling the tables. His hunch-back and long beard reminded me of an old billy goat. He stopped right beside the Andrew Jackson White House.

"Hello, sir. How may I help you?" I stayed opposite of him, because I smelled sweat from across the room. "Does your wife like dollhouses?"

"Ain't got one." He chewed hair from his lower lip. "Want to know about this here fella called ol' Hickory."

"What would you like to know? Maybe I can help you," I said. "He let the people enter the White House whenever they wanted to."

"Why was he called ol' Hickory?"

"He was tough and aggressive. He fought duels and won. He relocated the Native Americans to Florida, the Trail of Tears." I glanced away before continuing, "His wife died three months before moving into the White House."

"Thanks for helping me out, little lady. Me wife never knew much, but I guess she won this bet."

"How's that?" I placed my hands on my hips, and cocked my head. "About the First Lady's death?"

"That, too, but why he was called ol' Hickory. I thought it was because he'd wrestled with a bear."

"Nope. You're thinking of Davy Crockett."

"By golly, I guess I am."

In an instant, the man was out the door. I turned to Grandma who still had her hand clamped over her mouth.

"I wonder how he ever learned about this place?"

"Magazine advertisements." Which reminded me of what I'd been putting off. "I need to place an ad for another employee."

"It's sad, isn't it? Nancy was a good person and trustworthy employee," Grandma said.

"Yes, she was. I miss her."

"Well, it's time for me to git!"

"Go ahead. I appreciate you helping out, Grandma." I gave her a kiss as she scooted around the counter to allow me to take her place behind the computer. "Grandpa coming soon?"

"I think he just pulled up out front." She looked out. "He's here. Talk later, honey."

Out the door she flew, and I logged onto the Internet. It didn't take long to place a Want Ad for the store. My first employee and her husband tried to kill me over a set of cufflinks once belonging to Dolley Madison, and now it was Nancy's murder. The bad luck made me wonder if I should hire another employee. I don't want a reputation of hiring only to set this person up for murder.

I realized that I hadn't had a chance to run through my memorization routine since morning, so I rewound the cassette and opened my script. First I read through the lines, and then started with cassette. With each said line, I did better at saying my part. I wanted to get the memorization down pat so that during rehearsal, all I needed to really concentrate on was my stage movements and to remember what to do with my props. It took all of my concentration to remember the script, but I did feel like I'd improved.

Aaron was due in about fifteen minutes. I logged out and shut down the computer then circled the tables and made sure that everything looked good. I locked the main door before going to the workroom where I replaced all items back to where they belonged. I'd just finished when Aaron entered with supper.

"Here with a couple burgers!" He set two bags down on the workroom bench top. "One of these nights, we should go out and eat."

"It's nicer like this. We never get to see each other."

"True. I work at eleven. Won't be home until at least seven."

"You'll be leaving about the time I get home tonight."

We took our time eating and when finished, the timing was perfect. I crumpled up our bags and threw them away before grabbing my gloves, scarf, and bag and headed out the door. Aaron walked me to the theater where he reminded me to message him several times.

The tech crew, Dave and Tom, stood right inside the door as I entered.

"Another night!" I stated. "Will it be long?"

"Hard to say," Dave answered. "You own that dollhouse store?"

"Yep," I said. "I'm nuts about the First Ladies."

"Just make sure you know the right lines," Tom replied, "and everything will go smoothly."

"What does that mean?" I said, and watched them walk away. "Jeez. I think everyone on this cast is weird, including the tech and stage personnel." I turned and walked toward the prop table. At the table, I checked out each taped section and found all of my props. The purse I held during part of the second act was opened so I closed it after checking to make sure that the long nail file was inside. The diary which had the Fourteen Points words plus her thoughts about the Suffragists were where they belonged. I opened it and found something written on the first page. My eyes opened wider as I read: *Where is it?* My heart pumped hard and I could barely breathe. I took a look around me, and fortunately, I was alone. I removed my phone and took a picture of the page before flipping through it to look for more writing but found the other pages as they should be. I sent the image with a brief note to Detective Mergens and to Aaron.

Aaron's quick response read; *I'm coming.*

I responded: *No! I'll keep you updated.*

As I began to leave the area for the dressing room, a chill swept through me.

"Hi!" Joan said. "Boy, are you jumpy."

"I know. Must be stage fright," I said. I figured she noticed that I shook from limb to limb. "I was just going to get dressed."

Single file, we paraded through the back of the stage and entered the dressing room, which was located off stage. We sat side by side and started putting on our makeup after the removal of our clothes.

"This stuff is so hard to take off."

"I know. It's also drying to the skin."

"I'm glad I have long sleeves, otherwise my arms would need coloring. I'm also wearing gloves most of the time so hopefully, my hands won't need makeup."

"If only the audience knew what we actors go through."

We both grinned, and continued applying the makeup. I slipped into a mid-length dress and swept up my hair. I realized that I should've taken care of my hairdo first. *Live and learn*. The wide feathered hat felt like a huge box on my head. Linda came into the room, and called, "Places!"

"Time to go."

"Yep." I sneaked my silent phone into a pocket, reached for my script and headed out to my opening spot, picking up the diary as I walked past. While I waited for the lights to fade, I sent Aaron a message. *OK*. No sooner had I slipped it into my pocket, when I noticed similar writing from the diary on a wall poster stapled on the door. As I began to remove my phone to take a picture, Dan came to stand nearby so I let go of the phone.

As we stood waiting to enter the stage, I mentally recited my lines. When the lights faded, we entered the stage. By the time they'd returned, we were in place.

Dan started with his first line, "*Edith! I need help here. The Cabinet is coming for a meeting. Get me seated. Put my glasses on.*"

I set the diary down beside him, and plumped up pillows and helped Dan to sit. "*Shall I bring the papers?*"

"*Yes. Put them right here.*" He patted the open space beside him. "*Bring that tray over too, will you?*"

"*Of course!*" I finished rearranging everything, and set his papers along beside him. "*I've typed them up. No one will know who wrote them.*"

"*Thanks. I knew I could trust you.*" He held my hand a moment. "*What are your thoughts on the Suffragists, especially what happened that other night.*"

"*I have enough on my mind.*"

After this scene, I left the stage. Behind the curtain, I momentarily mentally ran through my next lines while also cross-checking with the script. Each word had to be perfect because it was used as a cue for either lighting or sound, plus the next person's lines. When I heard the line before mine, I stepped back out on stage holding my diary, and I had removed my hat.

"*Alice Paul and the other picketers had no business standing outside of the White House making such a fuss. Jail suits them for that offense!*" I sat beside Dan, who had fallen back asleep now that the Cabinet had left. "*Oh dear!*" I covered him with his blanket, sat for a few more minutes, then the lights faded out and I left the stage.

We practiced curtain call and then walked back to the dressing rooms. Joan had a minimal part during the end of the act, so she'd stayed in the dressing room.

"Do you know what happened to Edith's papers?" My face felt like it cracked while I removed the top coat of makeup. "This stuff is awful."

"I know," Joan sympathized. "Edith Wilson was a rich woman, wasn't she?"

"Yes. I don't think she wanted to be bothered by the common woman. Her papers are lost. I tried researching her, but found little."

"I don't know much about her except that she was called Mrs. President, because he was so close to death for so long and the vice-prez didn't even know the extent of his illness." She hung up her dress and slipped into her street clothes. "She ruled the country during the war."

"I know. Her first husband owned a jewelry store which she inherited. Money was nothing to her. She didn't need to vote, she married the president!" I hung my outfit up and finished dressing. "I'd like to learn more about her."

"Did she have children? Maybe they have her diary?"

"Nope. No children either way." I grabbed my bag, and slipped out my phone. I sent Aaron a message stating that I was soon leaving.

"Walk you to the door?"

"You go ahead, I want to take a look at the props before I leave."

"See you tomorrow."

"Drop by the store if you ever get a chance. I'll give you a personal tour of the White Houses. Presidents and all."

"I might take you up on it."

We parted, and I quietly walked toward the area where I'd spotted the handwriting. The wall poster featured the former play, "Delicious Murder Bookstore." It was about a bookstore where a murder had happened. I heard familiar voices so I stayed in the shadows until I reached the poster. I removed my phone and quickly took a snapshot.

As I started for the backdoor, voices drifted toward me. I ducked into the shadows once again to listen and I also wanted to see who it was.

The voices were from the tech crew and they continued out the door. I wondered, as I walked outside, who had followed me the other night?

Was it one of them?

While walking to the car, I wondered why the person would write instead of pasting letters onto the diary page? I still don't know what they're talking about. What is missing? Was it Mrs. Wilson's writings? Why would they think I knew the location?

Where would they be hidden? Why was it so important to find them, if they truly were hidden?

Puzzled, I drove home.

Chapter Thirteen

I didn't expect Aaron home, so I wasn't surprised to see that his car was gone when I drove into the garage. I'd checked my rearview several times, and was pretty sure that no one followed. The overhead light still illuminated the room as I opened the kitchen door and stepped inside.

After setting my bag down and removing my shoes, I hurried into the living room and reached for my iPad. I had already transferred my "what I know and don't know" list onto the notepad. I added a notation, "what is lost?" The person who was doing this must assume that I know more—so what was I missing? I did a matching search about Edith Wilson, inquiring about her letters as First Lady. No links matched. I redirected it to family letters of Edith Wilson, and still came up empty. Every First Lady had a secretary, so I searched and, naturally, the person was deceased. I took a deep breath, and checked for messages. My friend Maggie sent me a note inquiring how the rehearsals were going and I responded by telling her that all was well, and that I hadn't broke a leg yet.

I logged out and went to bed.

My mind went in circles as I thought over all that I knew of the Wilsons. I knew he'd been married previously which produced three children. *Could one of these descendants be the killer? It didn't fit.* Edith was the seventh of eleven children, which meant she could've been close to a niece or nephew. I knew also that she was a distant relative of Pocahontas. After Woodrow's death, she lived in Washington, DC, 6101 Knollwood Dr. Falls Church, VA, where the Wilson Museum is located. I tried to recall any famous name from my university studies relating to Mrs. Wilson but was unable to. After much mind searching, I finally gave in and fell asleep.

The sun was peeking through the clouds when I woke, and I also heard kitchen noise. I slipped into my slippers and padded down the hallway. Aaron had just started the coffee brewing.

"Good morning," I said, yawning. "How was your night?"

"Boring."

We silently ate since both of us were tired. I cleaned up and went to dress for the day. After slipping into a flowered sundress, and clipping my hair back, I was ready for the day.

I kissed Aaron goodbye with the promise of spaghetti for supper.

Once I was driving and had turned on the main road, I thought of the writing last night on the diary page and then seeing it again on the wall. I knew that neither of the detectives had contacted me because I'd already checked for messages. I parked beside Max's old truck. I always wondered why he drove such an old crate because he could easily afford a newer model. I got out and went up to the door, pressed in the correct code, and entered.

The words, "Where is it?' kept rolling around in my head. I wish I knew what it was about as I set my bag in the workroom. After making my usual circle of the display tables, I stood in front of the antique dollhouse and stared down at it.

"Edith? Tell me what this is all about?" I carefully picked up individual items and inspected them before returning them to their respective place. I found no odd markings. I lightly traced my fingers along the wall seams, and was satisfied that nothing was hidden. Then I had to ask myself if I wasn't paranoid? Or, how could you possibly hide something in a dollhouse? Everything is tiny. No detectable hidden messages or secret corners. Nothing made any sense. I heaved a sigh and went to unlock the front door before going to the computer and logging in for the day.

As I checked for the store's email, the front door popped open and a young woman entered. She looked familiar, but I couldn't recall her name.

"Hello! How may I help you?"

"I'm here to apply for the job." She smiled, and continued, "I was in here a few days back with my baby and you said to apply. Here I am!"

"Sure. Now I remember." I held up one finger and said, "Just a minute." I ducked down and riffled through a few stacks of paper and found an application form. "How about filling this out for me?"

"I haven't worked in ages. Does that matter?"

"Nope. Tell me about yourself while you fill in the blanks." She stood before me, and I placed a pen in front of her. "When did you last work?"

"Before the baby? Waitress." She began filling in the spaces. "My baby's ten months old. My mother is babysitting. She doesn't mind. My husband's a fulltime student and works nights. He's studying to be a lawyer."

"Good for him. If you need to bring the baby here once in awhile, that's okay."

"Does this mean that I have the job?"

"I just placed the ad and you're the first and only to apply." I looked at her name. "Jane Hershey. That's an easily remembered name."

"I love your store." She finished filling in the form and slid it to me. "My cell phone is on there, too."

"I'll call when I know for sure," I said, and smiled. "Name's Liv."

Jane headed to the front door, and stopped, "Thanks." She opened the door and walked out, the door shut behind her.

I stared at the door for a minute and thought of how nice she seemed. Her brown eyes sparkled. Charm overflowed and her smile was bright. She stood taller than myself and had short brown hair. I also liked that she was straightforward, and she was honest about her previous work. I found that I did like her. I drew a small star in the upper right hand corner of the form using a pencil. I tucked the form inside the cash register drawer for the time being.

My cell phone buzzed. The caller was Erlandsen.

"Detective."

"Liv," he stated, matter of factly. "How can I help you?"

"I sent you that writing sample image. My diary for the play is supposed to be blank except for the Fourteen Points and her thoughts on the Suffragists. I opened it last night, and what I sent to you was written on it. I also noticed similar writing on a hung poster."

"Interesting, indeed." I listened to him sigh. "Well, I think we'll have to stop by the theater again and take a look around."

"That's a good idea." I waited a beat, then said, "I still wonder about that florist."

"We've checked into that. Flowers were delivered to a woman across the street from the theater."

"Okay." We disconnected and I slumped into the chair. Things weren't coming together at all. There still wasn't any clear known suspects, and that was bothersome. I scratched my head, and on few of my curls.

I got up and went to the workroom where I picked up a needle and thread to sew buttons and pearls on a few of the gowns. I assembled every tiny item onto a small tray and carried it out to the counter. I sat down, and began the hand sewing when the front door opened.

"Hello! Welcome. Take your time and if you have any questions, just ask," I told the perspective customer.

"Will do."

"Enjoy." I watched as the middle-aged woman ambled toward the tables. Every so often she'd stop and gawk at the settings or the items. I noticed she paused for a few minutes in front of the President Garfield White House. "Beautiful, eh?"

"This can't be Tiffany glass, can it?" The woman's eyes were wide open, and she made room for me to stand beside her. "That entire wall."

"Yep. He remodeled. Garfield wasn't in office for long because he was assassinated. Chester Arthur was his vice-president."

"No First Lady?"

"His sister eventually assisted him."

"What happened to the wall?"

"I think Teddy Roosevelt had it moved but it broke."

"Yikes." Her blue eyes opened wider. "Tiffany? Just think about that!"

"I know," I said. "Do you like any one First Lady in particular?"

"I'm just looking for now."

"Okay." I took that as my cue to move away so I went back to the sewing. After a short while later, she left. I had a strong feeling that she'd be back.

I continued with my hand sewing until finished. Holding up the gowns, I thought they looked gorgeous. The embroidery on Caroline Harrison's dress was painstaking to complete, but it looked beautiful against the Burgundy velvet. Edith Wilson's buttons were hard to attach, but they now were completed. I walked the full tray back to the workroom and began dressing the dolls. The hour slipped past quickly.

As I entered the showroom, the door opened and the two detectives entered.

"Have you been to the theater?" I asked, sitting by the computer.

"Not yet," Mergens stated. "We want to be clear on a few things."

"Such as?"

"The diary was a prop? Where had it been when you found it compromised?"

"It had been overnight on the prop table."

"So, anyone could've done that?" Mergens said.

"Yes. I saw similar writing on a nearby poster. It was centered on the photo of the First Lady, Mrs. Wilson." I glanced from one to the other. "It's like I'm supposed to know where something is hidden, but what? That's the question. Is there something important hidden by the First Lady which I'm supposed to discover? I can't imagine what it could be."

"It certainly centers around the First Lady," Mergens said.

"I agree," Erlandsen said, opening his phone. He scrolled with his thumb and held up an image. "This picture of the poster?"

"Most definitely," I responded, glancing at it.

"Thank you," Erlandsen answered, closing it up. "We'll be in touch."

I watched as they walked back out the door, and wondered if the case would ever be solved?

My foot accidentally kicked the small garbage can over, spilling the contents onto the floor. I realized that it hadn't been emptied in a long time, so after picking up the remnants, I brought it to the back door. I also grabbed the workroom garbage, which was full, and carried it to the door. Just as I'd finished dumping the garbage inside of the nearby dumpster, Max parked his truck.

I waited for him, and said, "Working?"

"Yeah, I filled in for someone at the filling station. Busy?"

"Someone filled out an application and another walked through. I've been sewing, and I've dressed a few first lady dolls in their inaugural gowns. Deliveries will come late afternoon, I suspect, then we can get more dollhouse items assembled and boxed for sale. That always makes things easier."

"It sure does," Max said.

I opened the door. "Coming?"

"In a minute," Max said.

With the garbage containers in hand, I walked inside. After leaving the one in the workroom, I carried the smaller toward the showroom. A weird feeling came over me as I walked deeper into the room. I set the container on the floor next to the counter and glanced at the partially open door.

And saw a man lying on the floor with a knife stuck in his back and blood streaming from the wound.

I stared a moment until I got my wits about me and raced over to the person. I identified him as Russ.

"Max!" I shouted, "Come quickly!"

"Coming!"

Immediately, I called the emergency services number and then sent a quick message to Aaron. I checked for the man's pulse and found that it was faint but steady.

"Over here!" Max stepped over Russ and motioned to the medics.

"How's he doing? It's Russ, right?"

"Yes, and he seems to be breathing but it's shallow."

"Hang on, Russ, help is coming."

I looked closer. I didn't see any other wounds beside the knife, which was bad enough. It didn't appear as if he'd struggled because there weren't any obvious bruises. I got up and let the medics come in and do their job.

Within minutes of them, the detectives appeared. Several squad cars also parked out front, and the detectives gave the policemen orders. I looked toward the back door. I knew that it wouldn't be long and Aaron would be here.

"I'm going into the workroom," I said, and walked away.

"I didn't see anyone around," Max said, entering through the back door. The showroom was filled with uniformed officers.

"I hope he'll make it."

Max followed me into the workroom where we stared at each other from opposite ends of the room.

"What's your theory?" Max finally broke the silence.

"Edith Wilson hid something. That's all I can figure out."

"Any clue about it?"

"No." I shook my head. "Why would someone want to stab Russ?"

"He was a fool, admit it," Max said.

"That's not reason enough to try to kill him." I felt chilled, and ran my hands up and down my arms. "I feel like going home and crawling into bed."

"But you won't."

"Nope," I said. "I aim to figure out who is doing this even if it kills me, which it might."

"Don't say that."

Mergens stood right inside the doorframe. "What can you tell me?"

"Nothing," I said. I looked at Max. "I'd just brought out the garbage and we talked for a few minutes. I went inside and found Russ on the floor with a knife in his back." I wiped my moist eyes and blew my nose.

"This is so convoluted." Mergens looked at Max and asked, "Where were you?"

"I'd worked a short shift at a filling station. The one down on the corner, next block. You know the one?"

"Anyone creepy in the store? Anyone different in the last few days?"

"A man who looked like a billy goat was here yesterday asking about Andrew Jackson. An older woman, but she seemed okay. A young woman applied for a job this morning. Someone else was here and looked at the Garfield house, and left. I've been alone ever since. No one really stands out. Sorry."

"Any names?"

"Nope, except for the applicant and she'd been in here with her baby a few days ago. Right after Nancy's murder," I said. "The application is right here." She showed it to them.

"Okay. If you think of anything, you know how to reach us."

"Will Russ live?"

"That remains to be seen," he said. "Anything else?"

"Did you find my prop diary?"

"Yes, and the poster."

Chapter Fourteen

"This ought to make ya feel better. Just brewed a pot so I filled cups as soon as the message came," Aaron said, setting the box and cups down on the countertop. "Tell me what happened."

"It was Russ." I burst into tears, and Aaron gave me a hug. After regaining my composure, I asked, "Why did it happen? Why him? What are we missing?"

"I wonder why he chose to come into the store and not stay in the theater?" Aaron frowned. "Unless he thought he'd be safer getting away? This whole thing is confusing. The pieces don't fit."

"I think someone finally had enough of his bullying, and killed him," I said, more to myself than anyone.

"It's definitely centered around the Wilsons, that's for sure," Max interjected. He drank his coffee. "Just what I needed."

"Do you both think that?" Aaron said.

"I really do," I said. "We'd just been discussing the case when this happened." I took a chocolate and bit into it. "Now I feel better."

"Did you take pictures?" Aaron said.

"No." I frowned. "Are there any leads on Nancy's murder?"

"Nope. Not at all," Aaron said. To Max, he said, "Did you get a chance to look around outside?"

"I did, but didn't see anyone lurking out of the ordinary. I've been with Liv since I arrived this morning."

"I wonder about rehearsals?" I pressed the call button for Linda. When she answered, I said, "Have you heard?" When she hadn't, I went ahead and told her of what happened to Russ. "Will we have rehearsal?"

"Yes. We need to continue with the production and he wasn't part of the cast."

"You're taking it quite well. I would've thought the production would be canceled."

"Nope. The show must go on, as they say."

"Okay. I'll be there." We disconnected. "Still on."

"That's odd. You'd think it'd be cancelled for tonight, at least." Aaron rubbed his temples.

"You know what I wonder?" Max said, and we both stared at him. "I wonder who the mastermind is behind the play? Besides the playwright? Who stands to make out the better, not just in dollars but in publicity? Or purchasing the scripts, all the productions. How old is it?"

"It's newly licensed," I said. "Russ stood to make the most or lose the most since he owns the theater and is the producer and Wilson's biographer."

"Why murder Russ if he's only the money-man?" Aaron said.

"They're all good questions, but maybe it's more; if finally the real story is told?" I thought a moment, and said, "Could be. Maybe that's the motive. All the notes say, 'where is it?' Or 'the truth will prevail'. Someone wants something."

"Yes. They want the world to know."

One of the uniformed officers knocked on the doorframe and said, "I'm to tell you that the room is cleared for now. Don't touch anything."

"Great." I glanced at the clock. It was time to get ready for rehearsal.

"We'll take care of closing. The detectives said that they know how to reach you if they need you." He gave a slight nod. "I'm to tell Officer Reynolds that he's to report to them once he reports in tonight."

"Will do." We watched the policeman leave before Aaron said, "I guess they want me early. Better leave."

"See you and be careful," I said. Aaron gave me a kiss before leaving.

"I'll stay home all night, Liv. If you need anything. Anything should happen, call or text. I'll leave the phone on and it'll be right beside me all night."

"Thanks."

I watched as Max left, and heard the back door close. The silence in the room engulfed me like a dark night, and I shuddered. Aaron and Max had left before either of us thought to walk back into the showroom. I knew I shouldn't go alone, but there wasn't any choice in the matter at least the police were still investigating.

After picking up the empty paper cups and throwing the debris away, I took the last candy piece and placed it in my mouth. I imagined fields of flowers and tried to keep the pleasant imagery in my mind as I slowly walked into the showroom.

Taking care of the business had to come first and I might forget to log out and shut down the computer if I went straight to the area where Russ had lain. After taking care of business related things, I stood beside the marked area and wiped the tears from my eyes.

I was late for rehearsal and hurried.

I slipped inside the theater and hurried to the dressing room, hoping that I wouldn't be missed. Joan had finished applying makeup just as I entered.

"We wondered if you'd come," she said. She checked her makeup in the mirror, and touched up her hair. "It must've been awful."

"It was, but what have you been told? How did you even know?"

"Linda told us that something happened to Russ and that you found him in your store." She reached for her costume. "She didn't know how badly he was wounded."

"I didn't know when I called." I sat and began applying the makeup. "Had he been here earlier, do you know?"

"Don't know," Joan said. She buttoned her dress since there weren't zippers at the time of her character. "But, he's always here."

"Like all afternoon?" I said. I finished and began undressing.

"Guess what I found out?" She still wasn't finished buttoning. "You'll never believe it."

"Well?" I said, and started dressing into the navy blue suit. "You're leaving me dangling here in midair."

"Russ was having an affair, and you'll never guess who with," Joan said. "Sylvie."

"Sylvie? She stays out of everyone's way unless you don't return your props to the correct place." I shivered. "Her and Russ? They don't seem like a couple."

"I wonder. Maybe there's a jealous party around?"

"As in a threesome?"

"Hard to say."

Linda walked into the room, and called, "Places!"

"Dang. So soon." I swore and quickly slipped on my shoes and buckled them. "I'm late."

I grabbed my script to have handy for easy reference, and chased to the back of the theater and got in place. Linda peeked around the corner, and nodded. I watched her speak into her mic, and the lights slowly faded. I presumed that she gave the message to raise the lights too, once we were on stage and ready. When the lights were up, I began my dialogue just as the detectives entered through the audience door. My heart sunk, knowing they were here for questioning. I kept speaking as they approached Linda. Instinctively, I knew what would happen next.

"Let's take a breather," Linda called.

"Figures," I said, eyeing them. "Couldn't you have waited until I was finished?"

"Nope. Not this time," Erlandsen said.

"Okay," I said. I got a knot in my chest, and left the stage. I found a quiet place and sent a message to Aaron which read: *Russ? D or A?* Almost instantly, he responded: *D as in doornail.* I dropped the phone back into my pocket. It dinged, and I checked the message. Once again, Aaron warned me of my safety. Rumbling voices echoed from the auditorium, so I went to join the other actors. The tech crew had also joined the cast and were seated behind the actors, making a total of eight. I wondered where Sylvie was as I sat down beside Joan. "Where's Sylvie? She's the only the one missing," I whispered to her. "Any idea?"

"I haven't seen her." Joan nervously tucked her hairpins back in place. "No clue." She opened her script and looked down at it. "Let's talk through our lines."

"Give me a second. I have to hit the bathroom," I said. I rushed inside and sent Aaron a message about the affair between Russ and Sylvie and her missing. I flushed to make it sound authentic and rushed to my seat.

Mergens came onto the stage, and said, "Sorry for the inconvenience, but we're going to have to ask each of you questions. Stay in your seats, and we'll try to make this go as peaceful and swiftly as possible. There's myself and my partner." He looked behind, and Erlandsen walked toward him. "He'll go to the back, and I'll take my questions on the other side of the auditorium doors."

Aaron came from behind them and said, "I'm here to make sure no one leaves their seats. Officer Reynolds."

Mergens motioned for Tom. Aaron stood at the base of the stage with his arms crossed, and glanced around the room and then at the rest of the crew and cast. I removed my phone and sent him another message: *Why didn't you tell me?* His phone dinged, but he held his head high and avoided looking in my direction. I knew he was on duty, but thought he would've at least checked his message.

Frowning, I opened my script and followed Joan's lead. "We should do this. You're right. You go first."

"Page four," Joan replied, flipping her script to the right page. She pointed her finger on the spot. "Right here." She closed her script.

"Alice Paul says that---" I read the before line and she jumped in with her own. We went through the first act and just started the second when we heard her name called. "Erlandsen summons you. Good luck."

"Thanks," Joan softly said.

I watched her walk out. I wondered why she'd been so fidgety earlier, and I also questioned what news the interviews would bring forth that I wouldn't be privy to? I took a deep breath and walked over to Aaron.

"I'm going to the bathroom. Be right back."

"Don't get into trouble," he shot back.

"Don't worry." I quickly walked away, heading towards the muffled voices. I found Joan and

Erlandsen together. The lights weren't lowered so I crouched behind the nearest prop flats and listened.

"What time did you arrive?"

"Five."

"What's the call time?"

"Five."

"Who else was here?"

"Don't know."

"What can you tell me about Russ?"

"Is he dead?"

"Now, why would you think that?"

"I figured that's why you're here."

"Who would want him dead? Know any enemies?"

"Don't know."

It looked to me as if Joan was shaking. I thought she might collapse. It didn't appear as if she was going to tell them about the affair. I wanted to wait to find out, but the need to peek inside of Sylvie's office was greater.

I walked toward the restroom door which was right beside Sylvie's office. My plan was to take a quick look and then dash into the restroom. No light stream came through the bottom of the closed door, so I twisted the knob and opened the door. It appeared as if no one had entered the small room for a couple of days, then I recalled that she hadn't been around for very long at the previous nights' rehearsal. I went to her desk and turned the lamp on, which exposed Russ's biography on Wilson. I picked it up and looked through the Table of Contents. I immediately went to the pages for the famous Fourteen Points. They were torn out. After a glance around the room, I swiftly shut off the lamp and exited. I made my stop next door and as I headed to my awaiting seat, I noticed that Bev had returned.

Joan was in her seat when I sat down. "Went to the bathroom," I explained. Aaron frowned when I looked at him. *The man read my mind.* I glanced around me and noticed that Tom was absent. I was next.

"Let's start reading lines again," I stated. We picked up from where we'd left off and soon we'd finished hers, and started on mine. We'd barely made it through the first few pages when my name was called. "My turn." I took my script, and followed Erlandsen. Mergens called for Linda as we walked away.

"What can you tell me that we don't already know?" he asked once we'd come to an out of the way area. "I saw you wander around, by the way."

"Dang!" I said. "I have learned a couple of things."

"Let's hear it, Miss Snoop," he said with a grin.

"Joan told me that Sylvie and Russ had been having an affair. Did you know that?"

"Can't say as I did. What else?"

"Now it's your turn. You tell me something." I crossed my arms. "No good deed goes without another, you know."

"Russ was here from about one o'clock on. Linda saw him come in at that time. That's all I can tell you." He shifted his legs. "Now, what else are you withholding?"

"Have you looked on Sylvie's desk?"

"Why?" Erlandsen narrowed his eyes. "Liv, you're going to get yourself into trouble and we won't be able to get you out of it." He shook his head. "What is it?"

"Russ's book is open and two pages have been ripped out."

"We'll take a closer look." He leaned closer, and whispered, "Stay out of police business. It's not conducive for living a long life."

"I'll try and remember that," I whispered.

Together we walked toward the stage, and I curved around to the audience chairs, and sat down.

"I wish she'd cancel rehearsal," Joan whispered. "I'm having trouble focusing."

"I would guess that we all are. I really am."

No sooner had we opened our scripts when Linda and the detectives walked out onto the stage. Aaron wasn't in his usual place, and I wondered where he'd slipped out to. The cast members became instantly quiet as Linda stood in the stage center.

"I think we'll cancel the rest of the evening's rehearsal, but tomorrow night we're going to run through the entire play. Top to bottom, and have stage notes right after. Liv, make sure you start speaking about a half-beat before the lights are completely up. Otherwise, you're great."

"Okay." My face became hot from being singled out.

"Go home. Get a good night's rest." She nodded to the detectives. "Finished?"

"Just want to say, thank you, to all of you. Good luck with the play."

The three walked off the stage, and I matched Joan, step to step, back to the dressing room. Soon, we'd shed our costumes and were dressed in our street clothes.

"Have a good evening," I said.

"You, too."

I made sure she'd left.

Chapter Fifteen

Curious, I slid my bag over my shoulder, made sure my phone was in my pocket, then walked toward the back door. I heard voices from off stage, and noticed Linda speaking with Bev. Ducking down behind a flat, I listened to what they said.

"Where was Sylvie?" Linda asked.

"Don't know," Bev replied.

"I saw you out the other night with him, down at the bar and grill. Pracna on Main."

I sucked in my breath, and covered my heart, knocking a table.

"Did you hear that?"

"Someone's listening."

I sneaked away as fast as possible, and stay hidden by the back door. I didn't want to rush out for fear that they'd follow and recognize me. I counted to one hundred and when no one came, I slipped out the door and raced to the car.

As I drove home, I glanced at the mentioned saloon. It was within a short distance from my house, and it caused me to wonder if it hadn't been Russ who'd followed me the night? Or was it Bev? It could've been Sylvie. A full love triangle. One of the women could've easily thrust the knife into Russ's back. Jealousy and envy was a perfect and workable motive for murder.

How did Nancy work into the circle or was her murder completely separate?

I tended to believe it was and went on the premise that her murder had all to do with the script and nothing to do with a love triangle. She refused to edit her lines. Nancy was principled, and believed in the truth prevailing overall. There were those words—truth will prevail. It led me back to—where is what?

Nancy's contact numbers were easily available in the store, so I gave her parents a phone call. I called Yellow Daisy Floral and asked to have an arrangement made ready for me.

I climbed into my car and headed toward Nancy's parents' house after picking up the flowers. At the knock on the door, her mother greeted me.

"Please accept my condolences," I said. I handed her the spray of fresh summer flowers. I'm so sorry."

"Come in and have a seat, Liv. My husband isn't here at the moment."

"I sure miss Nancy. She was loyal and trustworthy."

"Thank you. She liked working for you."

"I haven't seen any notifications in the paper for a funeral. What are your plans?"

"The paper has the information today. The funeral is day after tomorrow."

"Thank you," I said. I wondered how to continue, but decided that full-speed ahead was the best way.

"What can you tell me about her friends or theater people, boyfriends? I'm taking her place on stage."

"Not much to tell. She got along with everyone. There was one person who annoyed her, and that was the guy who wanted to change her lines. That's all that comes to mind."

"Thank you. You've been helpful."

I gave her a hug goodbye and condolences.

In the car, as I drove toward home, my thoughts were about Nancy. She was such a pleasant person and wasn't easily annoyed. Who else had Russ annoyed to their limit?

I grabbed a bottle of soda from the refrigerator and nuked a couple pieces of cold pizza. As I ate, I checked for messages. Aaron sent one saying that he wouldn't be home until morning. I knew that, but sent a reply telling him to be careful. Grandma sent a goofy message that went like this: Should we be a twosome and get our hair styled together? A) Yes. B) Maybe C) Don't care. D) No. I answered: A.

Her second message read: Should we wait until after the play is done? A) Yes B) No C) Yes and No. D) Get out of my face.

I answered: C.

My reply will make her wonder what it meant.

Another read: Should I make an appointment at A) Jeanette's Hairnet or B) Marilyn's House of Curl?

I responded with A.

That ended the messages.

Before rehearsing lines, I read Nancy's obituary. I sent another message to grandma to see if she'd sit in for me so I could go. Next I ordered flowers for Nancy from the store. My thoughts went to the evening's rehearsal and all that happened. I sent a message to Aaron which read. *Bev was the third member of the triangle.* I sent the same to Detective Erlandsen. When finished, I took care of my mess and went out to the living room, and turned on the television.

I made myself comfy in my jammies, and padded back to the couch. As an old movie played on Turner Classic Movies station, I reached for my iPad. Now that I had quiet time, I decided to do a search on Russ Lippmann. Several sites popped onto the screen. I clicked onto the first and read through it, taking notes of where he was born and how many siblings plus current personal life. He was divorced and without children. Two books were listed under his name. Wilson and the other was a biography on some obscure individual I'd never heard of. I clicked from the site and did a different search about the play's author, Ann Michel.

I found that she had several published plays, and most sounded political with two comedies. She was a celebrated author. Off Broadway, her play, "Oh Please? Really, Eleanor?" had played for one year. The other celebrated play was this one, "Meet Presidentress Edith Wilson," by Michel. The feedback comments were all positive. One comment stated, "Yes, now the truth is out about Wilson's presidency. She was the Presidentress, wasn't she?" Another commented about knowing, "the Fourteen Points was a speech which was designed from a secret series of inquiries, called Inquiry and was full of Wilson's idealism. Because of his belief in neutrality, he chose to focus as president on the matters of war and peace instead of women's right to vote." I wondered if he wasn't one of the men who believed that a women's place was in the home? Why did the United Nations have to end up in New York City?

"Interesting," I stated out loud. "He did have a way of talking forever, and I've never heard of anyone who likes having the foreign diplomats in this country."

Another comment read: "He encouraged a climate of secrecy and bullied the African-Americans. He was anti-women's rights."

I closed from the site, and set the iPad on the table. It gave me an awful lot to consider as I finished watching a program on tv.

As I climbed into bed, my thoughts still spun in circles.

During the night, I sat straight up in bed. I glanced at the clock and it read 2:00. Aaron wasn't in bed, and I hadn't expected him home. His shift ended at seven. I rolled over and dragged the blankets up over my shoulders and closed my eyes. I wondered what caused me to sit up when I saw bright lights flash into the windows. Getting up, I looked across the street and realized that the noise and lights were from our neighbor girl who had obviously come home too late. Her boyfriend's car backfired as he drove from view, but I watched her sway with each step up to the front door and enter.

I crawled back under the covers and fell asleep, not waking until morning and the wonderful smell and sound of fresh coffee perking. I checked for messages before climbing out of bed. Sure enough, Grandma responded. It read: Jeanette sounds good. The following message read: Another dead body? Who did it? A) Stage manager. B) Prop person. C) Costume person. D) Tech crew. E) None of the above. F) Someone off the street?

I replied, E) don't have a clue.

It was time to get up. I dressed and hurried down to give Aaron his morning kiss. He was busy pouring us our coffee as I entered.

"How'd it go last night?"

"We brought in both Sylvie and Bev for further questioning."

"Where'd you find Sylvie?"

"In Pracna on Main," he said. "Thanks for the tips."

"Anytime." I finished my breakfast before asking, "Did you search Sylvie's office?"

"Can't do that without a search warrant. We need positive evidence."

"Good grief." I reached for my cell phone and placed a call to Temporary Services, and lined up two cleaning ladies for today. "I think I'm going to get Bonnie and Ruth again. Just a feeling. I shouldn't need chemical remover cleaners like I did with the cyanide."

"In spite of that fact that they drink while on the job and look like they came from some backwoods farm and haven't seen the light of day for at least a year and a half, they do a good job, don't they?"

"Yes, actually. I almost hope that it'll be them." I got up from the table and went over to give Aaron a kiss. "I miss you."

"When is opening night?" Aaron asked.

"Next Thursday and it runs two weekends. Thursday, Friday and Saturday nights, and one Sunday matinee. That's it." I tried to remember the last time we'd been out with Aaron's buddy Tim and my girlfriend, Maggie. "We should see if Maggie and Tim want to see it and then go out after the first performance."

"I'll see Tim at work and talk to him about it."

"Maggie's busy with starting a new job. We've sent a few messages, but it'd be fun for them to see the play and the four of us go out afterwards."

"I'll figure it out."

We kissed goodbye and I left. I hated leaving. I hoped to never be in a play again. All the rehearsals took me away from precious time with Aaron plus it left me with little time to keep up with store business.

In the short distance to work, I considered what he said about a search warrant and Sylvie's office. It made me wonder what else was hidden. Then there was Bev. I knew so little about any cast or tech crew, that led me to believe that I needed to know more. It was obvious, that any one person could know more about me than them, simply because of being a store proprietor.

As I turned down the alley, my thoughts went to Russ and the sad situation surrounding his death. The idea of entering the showroom and inspecting the area where he lay was depressing, but it had to be done. I parked, turned off the car, and swiftly walked to the store's back door. Knowing Max's truck was parked beside mine gave me a nice, comfy feel as I punched in the code, and opened the door.

A slight smell of metallic wafted toward me, and I figured it was because of the store being closed for several hours. I set my bag down in the workroom, and headed into the showroom. The phone rung just as I entered, and I went to answer it.

"White House Dollhouse Store, how may I help you?"

"I'm from the Nordeast paper-,"

I slammed down the phone. It rang again. I was sure it was the same person who'd called after Nancy was murdered. He left a message for me to call back. *Not on your life!* The phone started ringing off the hook. *Thank heavens no one knows my cellphone number.* Suddenly, my cellphone chimed. I stared at the phone before answering.

"Grandma."

"Good morning!" It was Grandma, which brought a smile to my lips. "You alone?"

"Yup!" I knew exactly what she was going to say, and stopped her. "I'm fine, Grandma. Max is here. Not here-here, but upstairs here, if there's any problem down here-here. Okay?"

"Olivia, we'll bring chicken soup for lunch." She disconnected before I could object.

Chicken soup? More soup in the summertime? It's going to be ninety degrees today. Geez. I massaged my forehead, and said, "What next?"

I got the computer started and went over to the showroom, and stopped. Yep, there it was. Blood stains and all. I knelt down, and studied the area, and realized that it wasn't so terribly bad. Most of the blood must've pooled on his shirt where it dried and prevented it from making too much of a mess on the floor. Last night, I'd been able to get most of it washed out. I heard the backdoor open, and stood up.

I saw the two cleaning ladies walking in, each carrying a pail and mop. Ruth had a bulge near her pocket. I knew what it was because of the last few times she'd cleaned for me, a flask filled with her favorite liquor. She liked taking long lunches.

"I'm in here," I called, walking toward the hallway. "Oh. We meet again."

"You betcha!" Bonnie said, giving me a thumbs up sign.

"Gots our cleaning buckets with. They're all out yonder in the bathroom ready for a scrubbin'," Ruth told me. "Just tell us where to clean."

"Looks mighty spotless to me." Bonnie glanced around the room.

"Ja, uff-da!" Ruth looked downward. "Oh vell, Bonnie, not again."

"Oops. Another one bit the dust, eh?"

"Can you two get this cleaned for me? I got out a lot last night, but as you can see, there's still some remnants left."

"Okie dokie," Bonnie said. "Well, we'll git started."

I watched them give each other a look, and turn toward the back. I was sure I saw a flask being past between them, too. Trying to hide my amusement, I went to the chair and sat down. I waited until the two women returned with their buckets and started cleaning the floor before I logged into the store's website and e-mail.

A message from Linda was sent to all cast members: *Rehearsals at four. Be prompt.*

I'd have to ask Grandma to sit in for me. One other person sent a message inquiring about the job, but the prospective employee had horrible spelling and never wrote a complete sentence. I deleted it.

I heard a loud burp, and glanced up to see the two women giggle. Bonnie placed the cover on the flask, and slipped it into her pants. I shook my head and pretended that I didn't see anything. I knew they should be reported, but I really didn't have any complaint. They'd cleaned the showroom after a horrible murder a few years ago, and I fell in love with them at that time because of their skills.

I went ahead and did a Google search on the makeup person, Bev, but came up empty. The next person on the agenda was Sylvie, and the results were the same. Sighing, I got up and started my daily routine of circling the display tables to make sure that all was set right before I opened for the day.

The recent White House dollhouse needed a bit of straightening. Laura Bush's gown was a bit rumpled, so I fixed it. Barbara Bush's hair was out of place, so that also needed tending.

My Penny Dolls needed tending, as a couple had tipped over. The First Lady pictures needed looking after, also. It seemed to me that the police must've made plenty of commotion while they took care of the situation yesterday.

I went over to the cleaning ladies, and asked, "How's it going?"

"Ja. Almost done, you know?" Bonnie said, "Right, Ruthie?"

"You betcha!"

"Good." I said. The floor looked better than it had a mere half hour ago.

After they'd finished scrubbing, I opened the main front door and the back one to allow fresh air to breeze through. About a half hour later, I went to close them, but Inga rushed inside.

"Hey, you." Her eyes opened wide. "What's this I hear about another murder and him found in your store?"

"I should've called. Sorry," I said, and stared into her eyes. "It's been tough. The cleaning ladies just left. It was Russ, the biographer."

"You still getting those weird messages?" Inga said.

"Yep. Last night the police questioned everyone from the cast," I said.

"Did they ever really look at Edith's dollhouse?" Inga said.

"Not very well. I'm not any closer to figuring out who killed Nancy, and I firmly believe that the dollhouse holds the key because of Russ lying here in the store. However, but what is the missing clue?" I said.

"That's something we may never know," Inga said. She looked on the floor. "I see where he fell. Almost the same place as the other one." She started for the door. "I was checking in. If you need anything…"

"I know."

I watched her leave. Inga was a good friend, and I felt guilty for not contacting her to relay the news about Russ. As if on cue, Max entered.

"Hey, you. How was rehearsal?"

"Horrid. The police spent most of the time interviewing people, including me," I said. "I found out a few things."

"I knew you'd never be able to stay out of trouble. Let's hear it." Max stood beside the counter and cocked his head.

"I sneaked into Sylvie's office, the prop manager, and on her desk the biography was open, but two pages were missing. Can you guess which ones?"

"His little black book list?"

"Don't be coy. The two pages featuring the Fourteen Points. Odd, eh?"

"What else, Miss Nosy?"

"I found out that Sylvie and Russ were having an affair, and there's a possibility that he was having one with Bev, also. A perfect triangle. However, it's a rumor. Joan told me."

"How do you do it?"

"Just a natural," I said. "Guess what else?"

"What?"

"Flowers are personal."

Chapter Sixteen

After a short while, Grandma hollered from the back hallway, "Anybody home?"

Max and I turned toward her, and he asked, "What are you carrying?" In an instant he was beside her, and grabbed the large covered cooking pot. "Smells good. Can I have some, too?"

"You betcha!" Grandma smiled. "It's chicken soup, still in the pot!"

"Where's the bowls, Grandma?"

"The car, hon."

"Let's eat in the workroom rather than the showroom, please?" I hurried out the door to fetch the bowls and spoons. Back inside, they had made an open space on the worktable. "Here." I removed the bags' contents. "Thanks Grandma, but soup in the summer?"

"Nothing wrong with that," Max answered, before grinning. "Marie's soups always hit the spot."

"I know they do. I love them," I said. Really, I did.

As we ate, I related the news about Nancy's funeral tomorrow. Grandma will watch the store while Max and I attend the service. When Grandma packed up and left, Max offered to watch the store after his return from taking care of personal business. Aaron sent a message, stating that he was sleeping.

I took the cassette player and quietly sat reviewing all of my lines. When finished, I retrieved the window cleaner and went outside to give the front a good cleaning. All the dust from the streets made it hard to see out of it. I left the front door open in case the phone should ring. While wiping it down, I noticed Linda walking toward the theater with a stranger, or at least, someone that I'd never met. It appeared as if Linda tried to keep her distance from this woman. I wondered who it was as I finished my job and went back inside.

At three-thirty, Max arrived and I left for the theater. I hoped for a peaceful evening, and that we'd be able to run through the play without a hitch. Sylvie climbed from her car as I approached.

"Hi! Another night, eh?" I greeted her. "I hope it doesn't end up being real late." I walked by her side. "What do you think?"

"I don't think anything, anymore," she grumbled.

I noticed that she had puffy cheeks and red rimmed eyes. "Heard anything about services for Nancy or Russ?"

"As if it mattered to you." She opened the door, and it almost slammed in my face.

"Watch out!" I said. I caught it soon enough. "What's with you?"

"Me? Listen, honey, keep out of my business."

I stood for a minute and stared after her. *Grouchie lady.* I hurried to the dressing room and found that my area was a mess. "What the heck?" I grumbled, and began to straighten it. "I'm sure I left it clean and neat."

"It's not now," Joan said. She applied lipstick. "Can you button my back for me? The collar isn't quite right."

"Sure." I did as requested. "Did you see anyone else in here?" I stripped my clothes off and dropped my outfit down over my head, then buttoned myself up. "How about Sylvie?" I frowned when I realized that I'd skipped one and had to re-button two. "Any idea what's going on with Sylvie?" *I must learn better tactics of eavesdropping.*

"Not a clue. You'd better hurry."

Fortunately, I'd applied makeup in the morning, and it was still visible so the amount for the rehearsal wasn't as extensive to apply. It didn't take too long before I was ready. Just as I began styling my hair, Linda called her usual word, "Places!"

I finished my hairdo and followed Joan out to the stage area. I picked up the diary prop and set my script down on the floor as the lights began dimming. Silently, I walked to my opening spot and as the lights began to brighten, I mentally counted to ten before beginning my monologue.

Dan entered right on cue and began his dialogue about the Fourteen Points and discussing their attributes with me.

"The United States must be in control. We must have the final say on all international matters," I said.

"You're right. The United States must also have the League of Nations housed right here in this country. The rest of world will know that we mean business," Dan said.

The lights lowered and we exited from the stage.

Joan entered from stage left. *"We must have voting privileges. It's our right as Americans!"*

I left the stage area and went for a drink of water as Joan completed her script. When I returned, I picked up my script only to find that someone scribbled all over it. I almost screamed when I saw it. *Who hates me so much?* Furious, I dropped it, and stared straight ahead.

I hadn't seen Carol all evening, and now that I thought about it, neither Sylvie or Bev were around. All three ladies had access to my script. As I stood waiting for my entering cue, I looked around me. Everything seemed as it should. However, Sylvie should've been by the tables or in sight because of getting ready for set changes. Now I spotted her and she was over by Dan. That didn't make any sense since the side I stood on was easier to access for carrying the lamp. I heard my cue, and went on stage and sat in my designated spot.

When the act was over we had only a few minutes to make our costume change. Fortunately, mine went without a hitch, as did Joan's. I left the dressing room and went to the stage area. Since I wasn't first on stage, I wanted to hide out a little and see what happened when I wasn't there. Linda stood to the side, and spoke into her headset, presumably to the tech crew. I did hear Tom's name. I glanced around for Sylvie, and saw her moving the chair and desk and then setting the lamp back in position.

Linda looked ready to bite a dog. She sat in the front row with a notepad in hand. I hoped she wasn't making future notes for me. I barely had time to make the needed changes as it was. I still didn't see Carol or Bev. I would think she'd want to make sure that our makeup was on correctly.

I slowly came out from behind my hiding place, and went to stand next to the prop table. I picked up my hat, and the feathers fell from it.

"Yikes!" I loudly said. "Linda, come here!"

"Oh, no. We're staying right on schedule."

"If you insist." I poked the feathers back into the hat the best that I could, and hoped it didn't look too funny before placing it on my head.

Joan came up behind me, and said, "Let me help." She straightened it. "Whatever is happening to your stuff? It's like you're being targeted."

"Don't have a clue."

I was extremely happy when the rehearsal ended and we made our final curtain call. I joined the cast as we sat for notes.

Linda strode to center stage and said, "First off, everyone was great. It'll be wonderful. The audiences will love you." When the clapping ended, she continued, "That brings me to the individual stage notes. These are picky so be ready."

"Start with me, would you?" Dan said, clearing his throat. "I have to get going."

"Sure." She said to us all, "Make sure you jot this all down on your scripts so that you'll remember."

I thought of mine and how messy it was from someone's purposeful scribbling, and anger surged through me. I gritted my teeth and studied each and every one seated. Since Sylvie still hadn't made an entrance, she was towards the bottom of my list. However, the tech crew continued disregarding suggestions, making sure that the lights weren't quite shone where I stood. I always had to step forward into the light. It was as if they were trying to sabotage me. I forced myself to listen.

"You need to turn on the ball of your foot toward Liv. It's more natural." Linda nodded. "I think that's it for you."

"Thanks," Dan said. He stood and walked from the auditorium.

I made a mental note of where I'd placed all of my makeup and costumes plus props. I wished that I could've followed him out to make sure that he hadn't been the culprit to mess with my area.

"Liv, we'll go with you next." Linda gave me a grin. "Thanks again for joining us on such short and horrible circumstances. You're doing great. Go through your lines. You need to be a little tighter. Don't forget to face the audience and summon that voice up from your belly. Very good."

"Thanks!" Joan squeezed my hand, and I whispered, "What a relief."

"But, I'm curious about your hat and why there's a problem getting you into the stage light? Can you enlighten me?"

"I step into the light, then it immediately shifts. My hat. That's another dilemma which is unexplainable. It was fine before we started. Someone messed with it. The prop person, Sylvie, should've watched over the table. Where is she, anyway? Carol and Bev? I've needed help."

"Leave that to me. I see that you're not reviewing your script," Linda said.

"It's been scribbled all over it. I've tried to tell you," I said. "It happened when rehearsal began, sometime when I was onstage. I left it near where my next entrance was supposed to be."

"Someone from outside must be coming in and damaging the items. I bet that's the cause of it. I'll make sure that all is right by tomorrow night's rehearsal," Linda said.

"I doubt it!" *There's more to this than what meets the eye!*

"I'm next!" Joan called.

"Yes, and you're right on top of it all. Don't worry." Linda flipped through her notes. "You two can leave, and I'll speak to the tech crew now."

I watched as Joan stood, and I followed right behind her. I wanted to stay and hear what Linda had to say them, but decided the timing wasn't right. I wasn't sure if I should've said anything or not, but by bringing the prop situation out into the open might help the investigation into the two murders. The detectives didn't seem to be any closer, and I didn't feel safe.

Once in the dressing room, we removed our costumes and dressed for leaving.

"Why do you think someone would single me out like that?"

"No idea," Joan replied. "I too, would like to know where the other managers are. How can we have a play without them? We need the stage crew for it to run smoothly."

"Someone needs to guard that prop table plus be around for sets. Where is she? Where are the both of them?" I fumed, and wondered if I saw a form of mischief in Joan's eye. "It isn't right especially with opening night just four nights away."

"I know what you're saying. I don't believe Wilson wrote the Fourteen Points for the nation's benefit, he wrote it for himself. He didn't believe in women's rights," Joan shook her head.

"The Fourteen Points were considered nothing but propaganda. He was a pacifist, through and through. It wasn't until he saw that the United States had to redeem themselves and get involved, that he started putting together an army." I hesitated, and asked, "What do you think about a love triangle between Bev, Sylvie and Russ?"

"I think it's very plausible." Joan straightened her area and wiped it clean. "Time for me to go."

"Me, too." I did the same with my area, and headed to the door. "I forgot something."

"See you."

I turned and sneaked to the back, finding my way inside the office area. Bev's door was locked, so I took out a hairpin. My thoughts went to those old tv movies and how the detectives gained easy entrance into houses by picking locks. Luck was on my side and I managed to enter. I waited a beat for my eyes to adjust and then went to her desk, turning on a lamp. I gazed down on the contents on top but didn't see anything out of the ordinary. Opening the top drawer, I found two numbers scribbled on a post-it, and took a picture of it. At the sound of voices, I shut off the light, and went to stand behind the door. The voices drifted away, and I recognized them as Tom's and Dave's. *Why would they be in this area?* When I no longer heard them, I slipped out from the office, making sure it was locked.

Quickly, I went to the back door and left.

I hurried to my car and started the engine, and soon was headed home. I sort of knew which cars belonged to the missing stage crew, so I gave into my curiosity and decided to drive through Pracna on Main's parking lot. Slowly I drove up and down the rows of parked cars. I didn't see either familiar car, so I continued driving home.

Aaron was at work, of course, so I took my time getting ready for bed. In the shower, I let my mind churn over all the known facts about Russ's demise. I was certain that it wasn't connected to Nancy, otherwise, they would've been at the theater tonight.

I toweled dry and put on my jammies. I picked up my phone, and iPad, and went to bed. I opened the file for Nancy, and read through it. I added the dollhouse and the received cryptic messages, and the sabotage of props and my script, but had nothing to add to solving the case. I opened another file on Russ. Under what I knew, I typed in death by stabbing. He annoyed Nancy. Was it true what Joan said? That Bev and Sylvie had an ongoing affair with Russ? I questioned why he came to my store. After, I wrote, because he wanted to get away from both? My next step was to find evidence. So far, all I had was hearsay. I closed the files, checked for messages, and tucked the iPad on top of my dresser. I bookmarked the addresses for both Bev and Sylvie on my phone.

I shut my eyes and fell asleep.

The sun drenched room woke me. I put on a little sundress, sandals, and grabbed my bag and phone on the way out the kitchen door. I did stop long enough to leave Aaron a love note.

Once in the car, I pressed on the button telling me where Bev lived. She was closer than Sylvie. I began my drive to the nearest drive thru where I ordered a raspberry, white chocolate chip scone and a medium sized cup of Irish cream latte' I continued to drive toward University Avenue. I stayed on the roadway until I saw the hospital and knew it was time to turn. I slowly drove down Madison Avenue, until coming to the right street, which brought me behind the Barnes and Noble bookstore. At this early hour, I hadn't expected to see Bev's garage door open, but it was. Sylvie's car was parked right beside it.

I turned around and drove toward the store.

Chapter Seventeen

When I entered my store, I dropped my bag and went to the showroom. As I flicked on the lights and looked out the front window, Mikal was passing by. I opened the door, and called, "Mikal! Come on in for a minute!"

"Oh. Olivia." He briskly turned around and came on inside. "Haven't seen you in ages."

"It's been a long time." His blue eyes sparkled, red bowtie looked crisp and neatly tied and his blue checked-summer shirt was neatly pressed. I deemed him dapper looking. "What brings you here at this hour?"

"I've had to do a lot of thinking because of the latest murders, you know, plus they circle around Edith Wilson, or so it seems," I said.

"Oh, dear. Another First Lady puzzle," Mikal said. He frowned, and crossed his arms. "I bet you want a handwriting reading, don't you?"

"It might help." I stepped closer to the counter and reached for a pad and pencil, and began to scribble.

I wrote:

This is all crazy. I don't have any idea yet who killed Nancy and neither do the police. I think I know what happened with Russ, but am not sure. I also wonder who killed him? I worry about my safety because of all the stuff that happened at last night's rehearsal. I was definitely singled out. Something evil is happening, and I hope that it doesn't happen to me.

Olivia Reynolds

"Here," I said, passing it to him. "I know you don't have your spyglass, but is it okay?"

"I'll do my best," Mikal said. His white hair gleamed from the sunlight when he tilted his head upward. "Very nice."

I glanced out the window while he studied it.

"Hmm." He scratched his head. "Well, it appears as if you've got yourself in a pickle and you're right in the middle, too." His eyes twinkled.

"I don't like your grin."

"The end is coming. I have to tell you that you'd better beware with all your snooping. Stay undercover. Fool them. Use your knowledge to figure all things out."

"That's just what Grandma said. Use your knowledge. What does that mean?"

"You have a great perception of people. Use your gut instincts, and be careful."

"Stay undercover, though? That's what you're telling me?"

"Yes. Let them wonder who it is snooping around. Keep them guessing." Mikal stood and moved around to my side. "Hope that helps."

"Too late, Sylvie already knows," I gave him a hug. "Thanks. I'll buy you coffee."

"Glad to help."

Mikal let himself out the front door, and I sat down and thought about what he'd told me. Stay in costume. Let them wonder who it is.

Since I hadn't had time to walk through my morning routine, I went ahead and did that. I found a few pieces tipped over, and I put them in place. Stopping by the Edith dollhouse, I found it in alarming disarray. I stared at it and scratched my head. I was certain that when I left yesterday, it was in perfect order. I was about to contact the detectives when Grandma entered.

"This house is a mess. Someone's been in here. I'll contact Aaron and the detectives. Is Grandpa with you?"

"He's parking and will be right in," Grandma said. She walked over beside me. "That's awful. Why?"

"Good question!" I left a voice mail on either phone and also relayed that I was going to Nancy's funeral. Grandma and Grandpa would be in charge of the store.

I text Max a message: going to N funeral.

I sent it, and hoped for an instant reply. I slipped my phone into my pocket as it chimed. Max texted that he couldn't make it. I'd go without him. The phone dinged once again, I looked at the caller ID and it was from Detective Erlandsen.

"I'm on my way to the funeral," I said, "but I've got more news for you."

"Go ahead. I'm listening. Mind if I record this?"

"Why?"

"So my partner can hear this. I have a funny feeling that he won't believe this any more than me."

"Oh, for god's sake. I don't care." I clamped my jaw and stared at the ceiling.

"Okay, go ahead."

"At rehearsal last night, my hat was sabotaged. All the feathers were messed up." I heard a bit of a chuckle in the background, but wasn't sure. "You'd better not laugh."

"I'm not, but is this all?"

"What do you think?" I scratched my head. "There's more. The tech crew kept moving the spotlight away from me. My script is all scribbled on."

"All this means is that someone is not happy. They're playing kid games. Nothing else."

"There's more. This morning, I saw Sylvie's car in Bev's driveway. I think they're a couple, and Russ was too conservative to accept it. Neither were at rehearsal nor was Carol. Isn't that odd?"

"It only means that they had a sleepover. Girls do that."

"Not adults." I silently fumed. "Lastly, this Edith Wilson house is a big mess. I know that it wasn't like this when I left yesterday."

"Back to that again, eh?"

"Yes. I swear, it has to hold the key."

"Key to which murder?"

"They're separate. I swear, Nancy's has to do with the Fourteen Points, and Russ with some sort of love triangle." I frowned. "Someone else must have a key to the theater and know my password."

"I'll discuss it with my partner."

"I would think that you would."

"I'm going to Nancy's funeral." I disconnected first. I wondered if the detectives would attend the funeral.

I turned to see that grandma was busy attending to other matters.

"I'm leaving Grandma. I'll be back as soon as I can. Grandpa's in the workroom. I can hear him humming a tune."

"Say a prayer in my name too, honey. Nancy was a sweet girl."

"Yes."

I hiked out the door and went straight to the car. I didn't want to be late and the church was a distance away. Soon I was on the Interstate and in south Minneapolis. The funeral was at Minnehaha Lutheran. I parked a block away and hurried inside.

The service was just beginning. During the service and at the cemetery, I had a chance to look around at the participants, but saw few that I recognized. Linda and Sylvie were off to the side but Joan stood apart. I went to stand near her.

"So sad," I said.

"Yes."

We both shed a few tears. Afterward, I offered condolences to Nancy's parents before leaving.

Grandma had the store in tip-top shape when I entered.

"I'm back."

"I see that."

I was about to ask how things went and where grandpa was when a customer entered. Grandma took care of the customer and I sat down in front of the computer.

Sitting by the computer, I logged into the webmail, and found several messages. One caught my eye, and I wished that I'd seen this before contacting the detective. The unknown sender wrote: *Where is Mrs. Wilson's papers? Where are they?* I responded, *No clue what you're talking about. Who are you?* I closed the site and looked through the website pages to make sure that all was okay, and it seemed like it was. Posted pictures of the houses were in order as well as the descriptions. A hacker may have been able to rearrange things, but it didn't appear like this person was interested in that sort of harm.

At least now I know what the person was after: Edith Wilson's papers. As far as I knew, all correspondence available of hers and Mr. Wilson are in the Wilson library. All papers were turned over so this struck me as puzzling. Did it contain notes of the Fourteen Points plus the Suffragists in her writing? What is so darned important?

I went ahead and made another search of the author, but found little of value. The papers had to be found, and soon. This person had already murdered once and would do it again, I was positive.

"I've sold a house, Livvie dear. Please move so I can have room to ring up the sale."

"Yes, Grandma. I'll get the house together in the back since Max isn't here. Which is it?"

"The Barbara Bush house."

"Okay." I looked at the woman, and said, "Thank you for the sale."

No sooner had I entered the backroom to piece together the correct dollhouse furnishings, my phone chirruped, and it was from Max. It read, *b rt dwn*

"You must've sent it while walking down the stairs," I said as he entered the room. "Help me get the Barbara Bush house together. Grandma's with the customer."

"Sure."

As we worked I filled him in on the news, such as the house being totally messed up.

"This is ridiculous, isn't it?"

"It wasn't trashed like before, it just looks as if someone checked it over for hidden rooms." We carried the boxes of the house and furnishings out to the main showroom. "Where's your car?" I asked the customer.

"Right outside."

"Okay."

Max and I followed her out and deposited the boxes into the woman's car trunk.

"Thank you again."

Max and I reentered the store.

"I'm leaving. Grandpa's waiting for me in the car. He'd went for the paper, earlier."

"Thanks, Grandma." I watched her leave then turned back to Max. "What a day. Linda, Sylivie and Joan were at the funeral. I didn't see the detectives, but maybe someone else took their place." Back at the antique dollhouse, I said, "It looked as if someone was searching for something."

"Grandma must've straightened it up." Max rubbed his chin and rubbed his palm across his whiskers. "Have you done the same? You know, look for hidden rooms?"

"I wonder why the First Lady desk isn't in the dollhouse?"

"I didn't think there was one."

"President's have desks, so do the First Ladies. Who knows? There could be one that they write personal letters to the next First Lady and all are stored in it. It's possible. Anything is." I looked at him as I continued, "Of course, I've looked for hidden rooms in the house which had belonged to Edith Wilson. Remember? I bought it earlier. I moved it down below the countertop." Crossing my arms, I nodded affirmatively. "I also received another message inquiring where Mrs. Wilson's papers are. What on earth are they talking about?"

"Have you told the detectives?"

"Yup. I've told the professionals about everything except the message. I didn't know about that when I contacted them about this house, and I told them about last night's rehearsal and all the sabotage against my stuff and me. It was treated like a joke."

"I don't like the sound of this, Liv. Not at all," Max said. "You need to take more precautions. Does Aaron know about all of this?"

"Nope. He just keeps telling me to text him all the time."

"I see that our warriors really know what they're doing once again," Max sarcastically answered. "What next? Got any kind of a plan, Miss Snoop?"

"Not sure. I'll keep you up to date." I smiled at him. "Thanks. I knew you'd be on my side." I squeezed his hand, and he gave me a big hug. "I feel better now. You don't think I'm nuts about any of this, do you?"

"Nope. Not at all." He smiled. "I'm going to organize the houses to have ready for sale, and replacement."

"Okay."

My cell phone buzzed, and it was from Grandma. "Hi, Grandma!"

"Busy?"

"Sort of. Why?"

"You alone?"

"Nope. Max's here."

"Okie dokie. I won't worry." She disconnected, and I stared at my phone for a minute before returning it inside of my pocket.

I removed the script and erased most of the scribbling, and was very thankful that a pencil was used and not a pen. Afterwards, I ran through my lines, and felt much better about them. I studied the stage directions to make sure that I remembered to do everything that was expected.

Chapter Eighteen

For the next hour, Max and I took out every piece and inspected it. Carefully, we ran our fingers over each item, and set it aside on another table. When finished, I said, "Nothing. Just as expected."

"Want help putting them all back?"

"I can do it. Thanks."

"I'm going now. If you need anything, just holler."

"Yup." I watched him leave, and by the time he'd reached the hallway he already had out a smoke. "You need to quit!"

"Never!"

The backdoor closed, and I was left to my own devices. Carefully, I replaced the pieces to their original spot. After, I took out an old magazine featuring America's Castles, and began to skim through it. As I did, my mind wandered to the dollhouse, then to the Wilson museum in Washington where Mrs. Wilson lived until her death. I searched for a picture of it in the magazine, but it wasn't a featured house. As I continued skimming the many articles, the front door opened and two customers entered. I said my usual line and stayed seated. The two women circled the tables and spoke with each other, pointing out various things. One lady called out, "Do you know anything about Nellie Taft? Something that no one else knows about?"

"She visited the White House at an early age of seventeen as a guest of President and Mrs. Hayes."

"Really?" the customer said.

"It's true."

"You know your stuff," the customer said. "In that case, I'll buy the house!"

"Wow! Thank you." My eyes opened wide. I wished every house was this easy to sell. "I'll get the papers ready." I texted Max, and he responded immediately.

After the sale was completed and Max carried out the items, I spent the rest of the afternoon setting up new houses and furnishing them. When I glanced at the clock, it was already three. I hadn't heard from Aaron so I called him on the cell phone.

"What have you been doing?"

"I'm at work. I was called in. There's been a rash of burglaries all across the metro area, and they needed extra officers."

"When will your shift end? Aren't you supposed to have time off?"

"Tomorrow, honey, and I've taken off opening night and took the liberty of asking Tim and Maggie to join me. The three of us will be in the audience and we can go afterwards for a pizza."

"That sounds wonderful. Be careful and I love you."

"I know, and you too."

We disconnected, and I got ready for rehearsal. As I was leaving, Grandma sent a text message. It read: A) Need company? B) Don't need company? C) Aaron with you? D) Max with you? E) none of the above. I replied, E) Rehearsal. I pressed the send button and continued out the door. As I walked to the theater, I thought of Mikal's advice. Stay in costume. Don't let people know who you are. I began to think that it might be the means of finding out much needed information.

Once inside, I made my way to the dressing room and was pleasantly surprised to find all of the back stage crew present.

"Hey, Sylvie. Missed you last night."

"I'll be here from now on." Sylvie straightened the props on the table. "Hear someone messed with yours last night."

"Who told you?"

"Linda." She plugged the feathers into the hat, and set it where it belonged. She picked up the lamp, and brushed a cloth over it. "There. Now it'll shine."

"Good to see you." I continued to the dressing room where I found Joan busy with applying makeup. I sat down in my chair checking the sheet.

"Sylvie's here. Did you see her?" Joan asked. "So's Bev and Carol."

"Yes. Anyone say anything about where they were or what they were up to?"

"No." She leaned into the mirror and began applying eyeliner. "Bev looks a little rattled, though, and so does Sylvie."

"We're all out of sorts," I said.

"I hope it runs smoothly tonight," Joan said. "I'm tired of wondering how it's all going to go. I have my thoughts on it, but I'm keeping it to myself."

"What are they?"

"Never mind," Joan said.

A thread of darkness shone in her eyes, but it diminished just as quickly as I saw it. Shivering, I wondered what was going on with Joan.

I set to applying makeup and getting into costume. I glanced over at some of the dresses and other outfits laying around, and wigs. An idea began to take shape. It wasn't but a few minutes before our stage call came, and we went together to our places.

As I stood waiting for the light cue, I studied where each actor stood, and realized that although every performance was virtually the same, the actors behaved differently beforehand. Either they stood silently, presumably mentally preparing themselves, or else they peeked out through the curtain. Sylvie usually sat by the table, and between scene changes, she'd be up and running about. Bev was never around and neither was Carol. I didn't recall really witnessing them doing anything other than assisting before a rehearsal.

On cue, I walked out to my spot, and within a few seconds, the lights were up and zeroed on me. I began my monologue: *"My dear husband did not want us to enter the war. He was a pacifist and did everything he could to prevent it so he signed pacts with the Kaiser. Some people wanted to impeach him for it."*

Dan entered in a wheelchair, and I exited.

I wasn't due back onstage for about five minutes.

"I'm going to the restroom," I whispered to Sylvie. Quickly I set out. The bathrooms were in the direction of the dressing rooms. I hoped to catch a glimpse of Carol or Bev, and it turned out that I was lucky.

As I entered the dark hallway, I saw movement on the side and heard their voices. I took a moment to hide to the side and listen.

"The cops better not call me in again for questioning," Bev said. "It's your fault. You'd best learn to keep your mouth shut."

"Me? What about you?" Carol answered. "That Russ. He should've minded his own business. He never should've threatened to expose us."

"He thought he was some kind of God. That's what his problem was."

My eyes opened wider, and I sucked in my breath. I tiptoed backward, and hoped they didn't see or hear me. When I could, I raced to my designated place for the next scene, and it was just on time.

At first, I stumbled with my lines but then I focused and the scene sailed by. It wasn't long before the evening came to a close. We all gathered in the audience to hear what Linda had to tell us.

"Everything went well. Liv, don't worry. We all stumble once in a while, but you're doing great considering that you just came on board." She waited a beat, then continued, "Tomorrow night, a handful of people will be in the audience. It'll be just like opening night. Remember, that's day after tomorrow."

"Finally," Joan exclaimed, sitting beside me.

"I'll let you all go. Get a good nights' sleep."

In the dressing room Joan and helped each other by unbuttoning our large collars. Removing nylons was always a tricky business too when they were worn under a girdle. I felt like I'd been released from a month's worth of laundry when all had been removed.

"Going home?" I asked Joan.

"Yep. I'm pooped. My husband is waiting for me," Joan said.

"Ever find out where Carol was yesterday?" I said.

At the very same time, she entered the room. "If you want to know, just ask," Carol said. "I was home sick with the flu."

"Okay. I'm glad that's that it was and I see you're feeling better." I glanced in the mirror and noted that my neck, and entire face were beet red from embarrassment. I grabbed my bag and swept right past her and out into the hallway. I flipped on the light so that it wouldn't be so dark and kept walking until reaching the backdoor. Behind me I heard footsteps, so I glanced back and it was Joan.

"What a grouch," she said, following me outside.

"I agree." We stopped for a minute. "It was odd last night that no one back stage was there to help, wasn't it?"

"Yes. See you tomorrow."

Joan continued to her car and I headed down to mine. After hopping inside, I turned on the oldies station after starting the engine, and put it in drive.

Soon I was on the main street and heading toward home.

I decided to take a detour and drive through Pracna on Main's parking lot. As I slowly entered and began driving up and down the rows, I spotted a familiar car and the lights just blackened. I stayed where I was and watched Bev and Sylvie climb from the car. They held hands all the way to the door.

After turning, I drove out onto the street and finished my drive home. As I opened the garage door and entered, my thoughts were on the two of them. My gut told me that they'd had something on Russ. What I needed to discover is where the knife came from because I hadn't seen anything resembling a kitchen utensil in the theater. *That doesn't mean that it's not possible.* I shut the car off, and went into the kitchen, locking the door behind me.

I sat down and immediately sent Aaron a message telling him to call me. I grabbed a beverage from the refrigerator and went into the living room where I turned on the television. To my surprise, C-Span had a program going about the presidents. It was about Wilson and how he'd called the British "boobs", before we became involved in the war. Then he made an about face after he saw that there was no way out of entering the war. We were close to war with Britain because of him. I shut the set off and got ready for bed. As I climbed into bed, my phone rang. It was Aaron so I answered it.

"Hey, babe," he said. "What can I do for you?"

"How much have Bev and Sylvie been questioned?"

"A few times. We're making headway with Russ's murder but not Nancy's. Is that what you're asking?"

"Sort of. I overheard a conversation tonight that might be of interest."

"Let's hear it."

"Bev and Sylvie argued about the police, and both admitted that Russ had no business poking his nose in their business. I also saw those two walk hand in hand into Pracna on Main tonight after rehearsal."

"Why were you there?"

"I noticed them walking on my way home. What do you think about Bev and Sylvie?"

"Not enough for a motive."

"I would say so," I said. "Did I do good?"

"Yep. I'll let the detectives know about it."

We disconnected, and I thought, Detectives? What do they know?

I pulled out a book and read for a few minutes before shutting off the light. As I fell asleep, my thoughts turned over what Bev grouched about, and what I'd heard backstage. Sylvie was an angry woman. Would she be angry to kill? It made me wonder. I rolled over and fell asleep.

During the night, I woke and found Aaron snoring softly beside me. I got up and looked out at the full moon, and thought about how lovely it was. I climbed back to bed and tried falling back asleep, but had trouble. Joan mentioned her husband, which struck me as odd at the time because she'd never mentioned him in the past. I decided that it was worth investigating. It hadn't sounded to me like he supported her, on the contrary. I thought it sounded like he belittled her.

Finally, morning came and I pulled myself out of bed.

After dressing, I went to the kitchen and made myself something to eat. I left Aaron a note. A) Bring hamburger. B) onions. C) ketchup. D) fries (warm). E) all of the above. Love you.

I grabbed the needed items and went out to the car, and started it right up. As I drove the few miles, I grinned. Aaron enjoyed those goofy notes, and Grandma taught me how to do them. What a legacy! Goofy notes! I put on my blinker and drove down the alley, parking beside Max's truck.

I logged into the webmail and found several new messages. Not one appeared cryptic, much to my relief. Two asked questions about certain First Ladies, such as the size of foot they had or how many buttons were on the dresses, that type of question. I answered as many as possible. It surprised how many people were interested in our First Ladies. I heard the back door open, and called out, "Max!"

"Yep it's me." He walked into the showroom.

"What houses do you think we'll sell today?"

"Let's gather the furnishings for the Ford White House, Kennedy and which other one?" He flipped his baseball cap off and on. "I bet I know what you'll say."

"We always have to have Dolley's house ready to go. At least two. That's a given." I gazed out at the houses. "You might be onto something there about the Kennedys. I also think that we should be ready for few more Wilsons since the play opens tomorrow night."

"Okay. I'll get started."

"I'm going to give you a raise. You deserve it."

"Thanks."

I reached under the counter and came up with the want ad and also Jane Hershey's application. I gave her a phone call.

"Jane?"

"Yes."

"You've got the job if you still want it." I swear I heard her smile over the phone wires. "You can start today or tomorrow. Whichever suits you the best."

"How about in an hour?"

"Great." We disconnected, and I went in search of the needed tax forms for her to fill in. I was very pleased. She could begin by helping Max gather some of the furnishings because it would be a wonderful means for her to acquaint herself with what belonged with which house.

A customer entered and I waited on the side after telling her my usual speech. I noticed how she bypassed several houses but studied the antique Wilson house. Something about her back was familiar, but I couldn't tell who it was. I went back to straightening papers when the front door opened once again.

A deliveryman entered bearing a beautiful spray of roses.

"For me?"

"You Liv Reynolds?"

"Then, they're for you!"

"Who sent them?" I searched for a card, but came up empty. "I don't see a card."

"Don't know, I was just told to deliver it here."

The pink flowers were beautiful. "Thank you." I offered him a tip, and he strode out the door. I hurried to the window to try and catch the type of car he drove but was unable.

I noticed the woman left right at the same time.

Chapter Nineteen

I called Erlandsen, but his line was busy so I gave the other one a buzz. He answered. "Liv Reynolds here. Someone just delivered a spray of pink roses."

"Yeah. So?"

"Don't you think that's a little suspicious considering what's all been happening around here?"

"Any card?"

"Nope. I asked, and he didn't know."

"Who delivered it?"

"Loon Pink Florist." I could almost see him looking up to the ceiling and rolling his eyes. "How about someone coming and taking it? I'm the next target."

"I'll send a squad car and have it picked up as evidence and contact poison control."

Afterwards, I gave Minnesota Nice a call to have someone come and look at my alarm system to make sure it's working properly. I called out to Max and when he didn't respond, I texted him. Almost instantly, he responded by saying he'd return in an instant.

Narrowing my eyes, I stared at the roses.

I brought the vase over to a shelf, right beside the back door. It could stay there, and any scent shouldn't harm me. Again, my thoughts went back to that woman and wondered who she reminded me of.

Another customer entered, and the shortish young woman asked a few questions about Dolley Madison and within a few minutes, she'd purchased the historical house. Fortunately, we had all needed pieces already boxed and it wasn't troublesome to load them for her. Afterwards, Jane entered.

"Hi! It's me, Jane." She smiled from head to foot. "Am I right on time?"

"Yes, as a matter of fact." I returned her smile. "You're very much needed. Later, Max will show you the list in the workroom of what's needed per house, and how to put it all together."

"I'm excited." Jane's fluffy brown hair and pretty one-piece navy blue cotton dress made her look charming. She didn't look as if she'd just had a child. "My mom's got little Ellie. Her name's Eleanor after the First Lady."

"Oh, my goodness. You're as much of a nut about the First Ladies as I am. We'll get along famously." I stepped around the counter and stood beside her. "Do you want to acquaint yourself with houses on your own, or do you want me cluttering up your mind right away with little obscure facts?"

"I'd like to meander around. You have them labeled, so that'll help. Do you mind?"

"Go ahead. I'll check on Max."

I watched as she slowly circled the houses and stopped to read the little signs posted beside each one. I texted Max, telling him that Jane was here. He'd left for a run to the store for a bottle of pop and water for me. My next purchase was going to be a decent small refrigerator and microwave. He responded: soon there.

"Tell me about this one?" Jane called. She stood near the Wilson house. "The upstairs rooms are weird. So is the Cabinet. Why?"

"He had that debilitating stroke and was laid up for many months and his wife, Edith, ran the country. She kept everyone out except the doctor."

"How could that happen?"

"It happens. There were rumors around President Reagan plus Trump's erratic behavior," I said. The more I learned about this Mrs. Wilson and the president, the less I liked or felt like I knew. "She decided what was important and that's what he saw."

"But if he couldn't speak or write for those many weeks or months--?"

"See? Which leaves me to wonder, are there other hidden unknown papers?"

"Stands to reason. In her position, I bet that she did." Jane gave me a quizzical look. "Where would they be? Has it ever come to light?"

"Not that I'm aware of. There's the drafted Fourteen Points. Did she write them and have him copy them? What about the Suffragists and the picketing of the White House? Why were they jailed? They fought for voting rights, and what's wrong with that?"

"I thought the Wilsons were for Women's Rights?" Jane faced me, and said, "What are you talking about?"

"The Night of Terror, a night we can't forget. Not as women." I dropped my arms and sighed. "Alice Paul almost died in jail. Many women were sent to jail and left there. Families didn't know where their loved ones were. Several women went on a starvation diet to try and draw attention to their plight. They were beaten by guards, and who knows what else? Maybe raped."

"All that for the Right to Vote?" Her mouth dropped open. "Really?"

"Yes, November 14, 1917. Once they'd been rebuked and jailed, it was the last any were heard of until news leaked out and a reporter got wind of it. A judge released them."

"Oh, for heaven's sake." She shook her head. "I wonder if any of Alice Paul's or one of the other women's families ever tried to seek justice for it?"

"In those days, they wouldn't have gotten far. He had the Espionage Act going on, too. Anyone could've been sent to jail for speaking out about the war."

"I see." She frowned. "I wonder where Alice Paul's personal papers are?"

"That's the question of the hour."

I started to go into a diatribe about the president when the back door opened. "I bet Max is here."

"I'm home," he said, walking into the showroom. "Hi! I'm Max. I hope it's all good things that she's said about me." He narrowed his eyes and looked at us both. When we smiled, he said, "Good! I brought you a nice cold water, also. Our refrigerator broke and our fearless employer hasn't bought a new one to replace the old, yet." He winked at me as he handed us our bottles.

"Thanks," we said in unison.

"I'm going to like working here," she said, opening her bottle. "I'm Jane."

"We haven't talked about hours or salary yet."

"I'll be in the back room," Max said. "Send her back when you're ready. I'll get started."

"By the way, I sold another Dolley right after you left."

"Fine. I'll set up another straight away." He turned and walked away.

"He's my right hand. He probably knows more about the business than I do. I know he can take over in heartbeat if anything should happen." I steered her to the counter. "Let's talk about these things."

"Is ten a good time to begin? I'd work until my little girl wakes from her afternoon nap. My mom is happy to see me come at that time."

"What time is that? I suppose about two or three?"

"Is it okay if we go day by day? It'll always be around that time."

"Sure. For now, we'll say three. We can play it by ear." I slid a W-2 form in front of her, and said, "Fill this out. Then you can look around as much as you'd like before assisting Max or whatever you care to do. I'd like you to become acquainted with the houses before you help customers."

"You want me in tomorrow at the same time?"

"Oh! Right! Let's make it ten."

"Ten to three. That's sounds good. We'll go by my baby's nap time." She took the pen and filled in the blank spaces. "Here." She set the pen down. "I think I'll continue with my walk around the tables before going to the workroom."

"Enjoy, and take your time." I turned back to business matters and retrieved my financial book, and copied down needed numbers, and took care of getting her on the payroll. Since I only had two employees, I took care of payroll. In the future, I hoped to hire someone to handle payroll. Afterwards, I glanced up toward the tables, and found that Jane had already walked down to the workroom.

I thought over what Jane said about the payback for all of the Suffragists, and I wondered about that. Would someone seek vengeance after all of this time? I turned to the computer and punched in a search for the Night of Terror, and printed out the names of the women.

At that moment, I saw a police car parked out front. "Finally!" I said aloud to myself. I looked over to the back and went to retrieve the roses.

By the time, the patrolman entered, I greeted him mid-way across the room. "I believe you're here for these?" I held them out. "Better be careful."

"Yes, ma'am." The first officer took the vase in hand.

"We'll get back to you, and poison control will be out."

"Oh!" Figures, I thought. "Over here. Got some kind of container?"

"You bet."

My phone chimed and knew it was from Aaron. "Just a minute." I set the vase on the counter.

"How do you like the roses?" Aaron asked.

'They're from you? I thought they might be poison," I said. "I'll call you back in a minute."

The officer and I stared at each other, and I wanted to sink into the floor. "I think I just cried wolf!"

"I'll take the sample anyway. You can't be too careful these days," he said, and poured the small water sample into a container. "You must have a good reason for requesting this to be analyzed, so we'll go ahead." He gave a quick call to the station to cancel the poison control team.

"Thank you. You're very kind."

"No problem."

Within a few minutes, he left with a sample, and I sunk into my chair and felt like a complete idiot. I took a moment to compose myself and gave Aaron a call back.

"Got them, but didn't know who sent them."

"I wrote up a card. There should've been one. They were a mixture of flowers, weren't they?"

"Nope. It was a spray of pink roses."

"That's not right." He waited a minute before continuing. "Did you call the detectives about this?"

"I did because of no card. I'm jumpy."

"I'm glad that you did. Was someone just there for the sample and that's why you didn't answer?"

"Yes. You must've just gotten a text?"

"I did. They both keep me informed since the investigation is quirky." I heard him blow out a long breath. "I'd better get busy. Let me know when you get your flowers. You should've received them by now."

"All right, honey."

Puzzled, we disconnected. I was anxious to learn the results of the water test. I wish that I'd thought to ask how long it would be to find out. I went to the workroom, and found that Max was busy explaining where everything was.

"I hope it's not too complicated," I said, stepping into the room. "If you can think a better method of organization, let me know."

"I see how you've done it. By the years and also the names are on the drawers."

"You understand the filing system?"

"Yes." She nodded.

"I was just about to show her the houses and how they're labeled," Max said.

"Good." I had wanted to speak to Max alone about the flowers, but decided to wait. "I'll be in the showroom."

I sat by the computer, and finally opened my water bottle to take a drink. The raspberry flavor tasted good, and my spirits slightly brightened. I started to think about the idea of descendants taking revenge, but thought it sounded ridiculous, but nothing else panned out. I went ahead and began a fresh search of the Suffragist descendants from the Night of Terror on an ancestry website.

One by one, I went down the list. Most individuals went on to lead decent lives and mother several children and good marriages. A reporter interviewed one of the Suffragists. She was quoted as saying she'd like to seek revenge on the Wilson's. However, the Suffragists name was withheld. I took a picture of the woman so that I'd have it in case of accidentally coming across a name.

Something about the picture struck my interest, but I wasn't sure what it was. The eyes? Nose? Mouth? I didn't know. Certain traits are passed down through the ages, and I wondered what it was that reminded me of someone else.

I went for my duster, and slowly went around the room, dusting my dolls and other memorabilia, and at last, the houses. With each one, I picked up the individual pieces and dusted them. The woman reminded me the jailed woman. I wish her name was printed under the photo.

Another customer entered, which fractured my thoughts. "If you need anything, just let me know," I greeted the man. "Are you here for a gift for your wife?"

"Of course! She's been begging for one for ages."

"That's wonderful." I walked over to the counter and set the duster underneath on a shelf. "Who is her favorite?"

"Jackie Kennedy. My wife is a master gardener and loved the Rose Garden when we visited Washington last year."

"She was so beautiful and did so much for our country. The rose garden was actually started by George Washington, did you know that?"

"Really?" He stared at me through his stylish lenses. "I never heard that one before. Tell me more."

"He wanted the world to know that we're a peaceful nation and stated that he'd like a garden to reflect it."

"Serious?"

"Serious."

"You know what? I've changed my mind. I want the historical house. Actually, the one Abigail Adams lived in and James Monroe."

"It'll be my pleasure. Finish looking around and let me get my assistant." I hurried to the workroom, and held up a finger for Max's attention. "Two houses. Historical and Jackie Kennedy."

"Okay." Jane glanced at me and then at him, and started right in to locating the items. I went back to the showroom, and over to the computer. "I'll begin the paperwork. How do you plan to pay?"

"Credit card." He walked over and took his card from his wallet. "Here you are."

By the time that I'd finished, the two entered with boxes. "Where's your car?"

"Right this way." He signed his name, and led them out the door.

As soon as they left the room, my phone chirruped. I saw it was from the police station so I immediately answered. It was from Mergens.

"Well, Liv, there's cyanide in the water."

Chapter Twenty

After Max and Jane left for the day, Aaron popped in with burger baskets and the spray of flowers. I kissed him.

"Thanks. They're lovely," I said. The flowers were irises, and tiger lilies. They brightened my mood. "Poison was found in the water."

"I know. They've already been around questioning the place where it was bought. Evidently, the person who delivered them is suspect," Aaron said. "I want you to quit the play, Liv. This is getting too dangerous. I can't change my shift right now because of too many on vacation. You have to either quit asking questions or the play. I mean it, too!"

"Oh dear!" I jumped in my seat. "Please Aaron, I'm careful. I really am. If I quit acting, the show would close. It wouldn't be fair to the other actors."

"It wouldn't be fair to me to have a dead wife!"

"I'll quit asking questions and text you all the time. Is that all right?"

"I don't like this at all Liv. I don't trust you at all about any of this. No! No questions."

We finished our meal and zipped through my play lines. Afterwards, he left and it was time for me to go to rehearsal. I felt guilty all the way to the theater. I couldn't possibly walk out on the performance. What was he thinking? It would be terrible. The production is ready to close, anyway.

I was first in the dressing room, surprising me. I hurried and was applying makeup as Joan entered.

"What a day," she said, plopping into her chair. "I went for a musical audition, over at the Guthrie."

"I didn't know you could sing," I said.

"I've had voice lessons," Joan said. She began dressing. "Guess who else was there?"

"Not a clue," I said. I finished with the blush and began putting on lipstick. "Who?"

"Carol. She wants better pay and more of a say in matters."

"What does that mean? Doesn't she pick out the costumes which we wear?"

"That's her ballgame, costumes. And as you say, not a clue," Joan said. "I do think she's pretty upset over something, but I am not sure what it is. I heard her grumbling the other night."

"I'm all ears," I said, and touched my right ear. "About what?"

"She said that she wants the world to know what happened with those poor women and how the presidentress dealt with the matter."

"When did you hear all of this?" I said.

"She said it one night to Tom."

"I'm going around in circles about all of this, aren't you?" I sighed. "First one person says one thing, and then another says something else. However, we do have two murders."

"Yes, and I wish the cops would figure out who dunnit!" I wasn't sure what to believe from Joan. Was she just feeding me information to keep me from asking questions about her? *I better not ask any questions.*

We finished preparing and Linda entered, calling our beginning cue.

"All right," we both said.

I got up and said, "Meet you out there."

By the prop table, I made sure that all of my stuff was in position before going to my spot. I took a moment to peek out at the audience, and saw a handful of people, just as Linda had described the night before. Then I recalled that once again I didn't see anyone near the table, nor had I seen Sylvie or Bev. It made me angry because of the production plus curious. Just as my mind started to think of different scenarios, Carol sat down, and I smiled at her. I still speculated over the other two as the cue lights began to change and I walked out to my spot.

Everything went smoothly until right before the intermission. I accidentally skipped a line, but Dan picked it up and I recovered, ending the act magnificently.

"Thanks for getting me out of that mess."

"Not a problem. Everyone drops lines once in a while." When we walked to our dressing room, Dan said, "You did great. You're a natural."

"Thanks." I felt like jumping for joy as I turned the knob to enter the room. As I did someone came up behind me, and covered my eyes, and cranked my neck around. "Ouch. You're hurting me."

"Listen, missy. I'm not going to jail. Mind your own business, and stay out of mine," a woman snarled.

She dropped her hand, and by the time I turned around, I saw no one. It was as if it hadn't happened. I wasn't sure of the voice, but it sounded a great deal like Bev. I didn't like where this was going, and so I took a u-turn and slipped into the bathroom and sent a text message to Aaron and Detective Erlandsen. I left the room, and went to the dressing room.

"What took so long?" Joan inquired, changing her outfit.

"I talked a minute with Dan, and went to the bathroom. He told me that I'm a natural. Wasn't that nice?" With shaky fingers, I unbuttoned my outfit and poured the next dress down over my head and figure. "He's a nice guy."

"You do really well out there. You don't seem nervous, that's for sure," Joan said. "Not like now, where you're shaking and can barely get out of your dress."

"I don't know what got into me." I barely was able to button up. I did a last minute check on my makeup, and deemed it all right. "I think we need to get back stage."

"Certainly. It won't be long."

I tried running lines in my head, but drew a blank. It felt like the room was closing in on me. I checked my phone. Aaron hadn't responded which left me more nervous. I was ready to scream and run when the door opened, and Linda called, "Places!"

The second and third act went by just as successfully as the first, but without a mishap from me. I figured that because of my nervousness my memory of the learned lines tripped into action. Linda deemed us as perfect and the audience clapped, and we did an encore of two lines before we completely finished.

After changing and going out to my car, I could've sworn that someone watched me from between the buildings. I was certain that a cigarette was snuffed out the minute I came close to the edge of my store. If not for the late night and the earlier incident, I may have walked over to the area and looked. I didn't feel the least bit brave. I hadn't wanted to ask someone to escort me, but who is trustworthy?

Once I'd jumped into my car and started the engine, my phone rang.

"Hey."

"Liv, I told you not to ask questions. I didn't respond but a patrol car was commissioned to stay nearby in case of any further incidents. Geez, you get my goat with all of your snooping."

"I'm sorry. I'll try to not get caught next time."

"There isn't going to be a next time," Aaron said. "Now, come down to the station and tell us what happened."

"Okay, if you won't bite."

"I won't."

Instead of turning the car toward home, I went in the opposite direction. In five minutes, I parked outside of the precinct. Aaron stood by the door as I entered, and he let me inside, and led me back to the detectives' offices.

"It was all weird like," I said, sitting on the chair beside Aaron's desk. "Neither Bev or Sylvie were there again. I don't trust anyone. I'm scared that one of them is the murderer and I'm next in line."

"Since you insist on performing, I want you to just pay attention to yourself, honey, and don't worry about them," Aaron said, reassuringly. "Tell me what happened."

"Neither were there, not that I saw." I reached for a tissue and blew my nose. "It was scary. I walked off stage after the first act and during intermission, I spoke with Dan." I watched him write it all down. "Then, he went into his dressing room and I turned to reach for my doorknob when I was accosted from behind." I snapped my fingers. "It was that quick."

"What did this person say?" Aaron said.

"'Listen, missy. I'm not going to jail.'" I thought a minute. "'Stay out of my business and I'll stay out of yours.' Or something like that."

"Any indication if they meant your personal business or the store?"

"I took it as personal," I said.

"Why?" He studied me. "You seem to be doing okay, baby girl."

"I am as long as I don't think about it." I bit back tears. "It seemed like it. That's the way I took it."

"And you think it was female?" I nodded and he asked, "Could you identify the voice?"

"I thought of Bev. The voice sounded real deep and mean, almost like a man's, though. Hmm, now I wonder." I rubbed my chin. "Maybe it wasn't a woman. 'Listen, missy' sounds more like something a man would say, or not?"

"We'll just have to continue our investigations." Aaron finished filling out the sheet of paper. "We've questioned those two a few times, and now we're comparing notes. It won't be long and we'll have an arrest."

"Yeah, but for which murder? Does someone want to kill me?" I frowned. "I'm still right smack dab in the middle."

"Leave it to us." Aaron stood, and pulled me up. "I'll follow you home and wait until you're inside before I leave."

"I appreciate that. When I went to the car, I could've sworn someone put out a cigarette between the two buildings."

"Liv. I want this play done. I want you out of it."

"I know. I'll try to be careful."

"I'm going to have someone in the audience every night," Aaron said. "We'll line up your grandparents, and Maggie and Tim and I will be there opening night, tomorrow night. I don't want something to happen to you."

"Good." I yawned. "Follow me out?"

"I'll have an officer follow so I can drive you home."

Aaron walked me out to the front desk, and arranged for a squad car to pick him up at home.

"I wish that you didn't have to work." I stared out of the window. "It'll be nice when this is done. Two weeks and it will be."

"Not soon enough." Aaron turned onto Main Street. "Do you have rehearsals next week?"

"Not sure."

"The squad car is right behind me, so I won't be able to go inside. You'll be all right though, won't you?"

"Yes." He parked the car into the garage, and came around to my side. "Good night." He stayed in the shadows and watched me continue inside, flicking the lights on as I went. I wasn't sure whether or not I'd closed the garage door, so I checked. I hadn't, so I shut it down. Back inside, I turned lights on as I entered the rooms. A horrible, eerie feeling seemed to follow me everywhere. I showered, and brought a load of dirty towels down to the washing machine and started the wash. I checked the dryer for a load, but it was empty.

I went upstairs and jumped into bed. I wished for Aaron, and hoped he'd find some way of getting off duty early, but I didn't expect for it to happen. The voice rolled over and over in my mind, causing me to toss and turn until sleep found me. I woke to my man sound asleep beside me. I kissed him before crawling out of bed.

In the kitchen, I found the toaster laid out for me as well as butter and raspberry jelly. The coffee was already brewed. I made myself breakfast and then hurried to dress. I wanted to stop by an appliance store on the way to work.

After dashing downstairs and throwing the towels into the dryer, I went to the bedroom and dressed. I slipped into a colorful top and navy capris. My shoes were bright red. I kissed Aaron on the cheek after applying red lipstick, and smiled.

On the way to University Avenue, I dug into my bag to make sure that I had the store's credit card with me, and I did. In another ten minutes, I parked in front of the small store.

"Hey, Bill!" I said, going up to the salesman. "I need a couple items."

"Well, pretty lady. How can I help?" He grinned. "Whatcha need?"

"A fridge for the store and a microwave."

It didn't take long before the business transaction was complete, and I was in the car driving to work. I looked forward to surprising Max with the purchases.

Once I'd parked, and opened the back door, I went to fetch the microwave. I figured that Max could carry the refrigerator for me.

I set the appliance up in a back corner and made room for the new refrigerator. Now I wished that I'd brought a bowl of leftover soup with for lunch. I removed the bottle of water from my bag, ready for the refrigerator.

Today was the appointed date for the Minnesota Nice company to send their employee to work on my alarm system. I had hoped for an earlier date due to the break-in, but they were booked solid. A knock on the back door alerted me to a visitor, so I went to open it. The man before me wore a Minnesota Nice badge.

"Hi! I'm Liv. You're not Kenny."

"Nope. Jim. I'll take a look at your system and let you know if there's a problem and why the alarm never sounded."

"Thanks."

It was perfect time for me to take a look at the gathered items and boxes that Max worked on yesterday with Jane. I wanted to make sure that all the pieces were ready for individual houses. This was almost the easy part. Making sure the right dolls are boxed and placed inside the correct box is the tricky part. I glanced up to make sure that the timeline with the names, dates, house numbers, was still where it belonged. I also checked on the item list for each house. That list was also still easily read and found.

Afterward, I went out to the showroom and strolled up and down the aisles. A couple dolls had tipped over and a lamp or two were off the tables. They were all taken care of before I stopped in front of the Edith house. It still puzzled me. What is it about this house that makes people want to break into my store at night, and trash it? Max and I had methodically gone through it. I'd also searched it alone. We'd checked the walls, and even tried to open the minute desks and dresser drawers. We'd also looked for hidden compartments but without success. No hollow books with hidden papers. The house was an enigma.

I went to the hallway, and stopped for a small plastic bag before going out the back door. I wanted to see for myself if someone had hid between the narrow building walls. I bumped into Jim as I opened the door.

"Found anything?"

"Yes. Someone knew how to trip the wires. I'm going to reprogram it so that won't happen again."

"How is it possible that the person could do it?"

"People can find out anything on the computer nowadays."

"I'll let you do your job." I moved away just as someone tapped my shoulder from behind, startling me.

"Liv," Max chuckled. "You jumped to the moon."

"Max! Oh, my gosh!" I caught my breath.

"Liv," he said. "You're like a freight train sometimes."

"I have a surprise, but you have to carry it in." I kept going to the car. "Bet you can't guess what it is." I unlocked the door. "It's too heavy for me."

"It's got to be a refrigerator." Max came up behind me. "Let me at it."

I stepped aside for him to pull it out, and hoist it up.

"Excuse us," I said to Jim. He stepped aside for us. Max carried it through into the workroom.

"Right here, don't you think?"

"Looks good." He set it down, and removed the box. "Didn't expect this, and I see you have a microwave. Good."

"Let's get it plugged in." He did that and I opened the door to adjust the settings. I closed the door after putting my water bottle inside. "Let's see how long it'll take to cool it down."

"Five minutes." He snapped his fingers.

"I'll be right back."

I chased out the door and marched down to where I thought the snuffed cigarette butt should be. Staring down at the area, I didn't notice it at first because it was slightly under a broken piece of brick. There was no way for me to know if it truly was from last night, but I thought it was since it wasn't like Max's remnants. Carefully, I lifted the butt and placed it inside the plastic bag. I sealed it, and slid it into my pocket.

Chapter Twenty-One

I wasn't quite sure what to do with the butt end, so I sent a message to Aaron. It read: Found cig butt, but what to do with it? A) Throw away. B) Save. C) Contact detective. D) None of the above.

Max busied himself in the workroom, and Jane came promptly at ten.

"Morning," I greeted her. "How's Ellie?"

"She's great and so am I," Jane said. Her smiled was like the sunshine. "What do you want me to do today?"

"Tell you what. I want to walk with you around the houses, and see what you can tell me about them and the First Ladies," I said.

"All right," Jane said. "I spent last night after putting Ellie to bed researching the First Ladies. I know that I'll never be as smart as you--"

"Don't even think that."

We started with the historical houses.

"Jefferson put in the indoor privies," Jane said.

"Right. What else?" I said.

"He called Dolley his First Lady because she sometimes stepped in as his hostess." Jane took a breath and smiled. "He also didn't believe in dressing up."

"Nope. So he's in this house. What other prez's?"

"Martha never lived here. The land was given by Washington."

"Very good." I placed my arm around her shoulder, and said, "Who started the rose garden?"

"Don't know." Jane's eyes opened wider. "I failed the test."

"Nope. Not a test." I chuckled. "Washington wanted a garden of peace, to show that we're a peaceful people. Abigail Adams, our second First Lady, planted it."

"I'll remember that."

We finished with the historicals and continued onward. After a little while, I said, "Time for a break. Go ahead and help Max. He's in the back."

"I'd like to observe you with a customer."

"Good. I'll fetch you when the next one enters."

Two customers entered simultaneously, and I fetched Jane from the room. She stood to my side and followed along as I answered all questions. At the check-out, I let her begin to learn about processing a bill of sale. She and Max carried out the needed boxes.

Afterwards, my phone chirruped and I checked the message. Aaron replied, and he answered with B and C. I responded with an ok.

My phone rang shortly afterwards. It was from my friend Maggie and fellow cop-wife in ages so I answered happily.

"Hi! Long time since we've gone out," Maggie said.

"I know," I said. "Tonight we'll go out after the performance. Be in your seat about 7:20. Curtain rises at 7:30."

"What to wear? Casual?" Maggie said.

"Whatever you'd like."

"All right. See you later." She giggled. "Break a leg."

"I hope not." I logged out and went in the workroom to see how Max and Jane were doing.

"Oh. We're just about finished here getting together another Wilson house," Jane said. "Wow! This takes a lot of time. It's a good thing that I have this list to follow. Max has been a big help."

"Where is he?" I wondered because it was unlike him to leave a new employee alone like that. "Having a smoke?"

"He got a call and said he'd be back in a few minutes." Jane shrugged. "It just happened. No problem."

"Any questions?" When she shook her head, I said, "I'm going back out front to sew on buttons." I took the needed pearl-like buttons for the dress I was presently working on, and left the room.

Before cozying up to the needle and thread, I texted Max to find out what he was doing. I played the cassette while sewing, and recited my lines but it took longer than usual. Memories of Nancy onstage came to mind and hindered my ability to focus properly. I couldn't wait for tonight's performance to be over.

About an hour later, Max entered. "I had to run an errand for a friend. I'll show Jane how to take care of order intake, if you'd like."

"It's almost time for her to leave," I said. "Let's do it another time."

Just then, Jane joined us, and said, "Time for me to go and get my little Ellie."

"All right. See you tomorrow. Have a nice evening."

I was left to my own devices after a few short minutes. I glanced at my watch, and it was only 3:15. Plenty of time left before I needed to check-in and begin dressing. I decided to take the duster around, even though I was sure it wasn't needed. Afterwards, the clock read ten minutes later. I took out an old historical magazine of president's and first ladies, and flipped through the pages. The pictures were of the inside of the Wilson library, and in one corner there were a few images of gifts for the First Lady. The dollhouse was featured as it was a gift from the Kaiser. I read closer, and found that the original dollhouse had vanished in the closing days of the First World War. *How did it get on the open market? Is this why my store has been broken into? There must be something hidden in the house which I purchased online.*

That made no sense at all.

Further reading shown that the original was once given to the First Lady from the Kaiser. *Was the dollhouse a peace gesture? Do I own the stolen house?* I closed the magazine and set it aside, and went over to the house. *What a mystery.*

Staring down into the house, I crossed my arms and wondered what on earth could be so important about this house? I was going to have to find out if this house was the house in question.

With only an hour left until I was needed in the theater, I sent Aaron a message updating him on the new learned fact about the dollhouse. I also told him when I was going to leave for the theater. We'd already made plans to meet in the theater's foyer after the performance was over, and then we'd decide where to meet. They were arriving together.

I grabbed my things, locked up, and headed out the back door. As I walked the block, I saw Joan parking across the street. I waved to her when I became closer.

"Finally, eh?" I said. "I'm nervous. How about you?"

"You bet."

Silently, we walked into the building, and she went straight to the dressing room. I checked in with Linda, and made sure that all of my props were ready. The table looked wonderful. The stage set looked marvelous. It almost seemed to sparkle. An image of Nancy standing on stage came to mind. In costume she looked so beautiful, poised, and confident. I prayed that I would be half as good of an actress that she was. I turned and went to the dressing room.

"I'm excited." I flipped my clothes on the floor, and flicked them up high with my heels, and they landed right on the couch. I picked them up and smoothed them before slipping my stage costume on over my head. The nylons felt a bit sticky. I hated them.

Soon I sat before the mirror and began applying makeup. Almost instantaneously, Bev entered, then Sylvie.

"Let's make sure you two gals look terrific." Sylvie marched over and held out her hand. "Stand! Both!"

We glanced at each other and stood.

"No, you don't. I want to see that makeup. They look fine." Bev plunked her hands on her hips. "Put the makeup on."

"Oh no," Sylvie glared at her. "I'm in charge here."

"I think Joan and I are doing just fine," I said, sweetly. "Don't you two worry now. We'll make sure that we're fine."

"Exactly." Joan smiled.

"We've got it all under control!" I turned back to the matters at hand and worked at applying the makeup. Slowly, I methodically smeared on the heavy, cake base. I wondered if the makeup was tainted. I decided to use my own eye liner and mascara. The two women stared each other down. I grit my teeth and kept my mouth shut.

"Well..." Sylvie stomped out of the room.

"You haven't heard the end of it." Bev glared at me. "Watch out."

After both had left, I asked, "What was that all about?"

"Beats me." Joan finished her chore. "Ready?"

"Give me a minute." My mind whirled as I finished with my job. I set the tube of lipstick down, touched up my blush, and said, "Done."

Together we walked into the darkened hallway, just as Linda was opening the men's dressing room.

"Places!" she called. She looked at us, and asked, "Ready?"

"Yes. We're on our way."

"Full house. Remember to wait for responses to begin fading before continuing with your lines," Linda said.

"Will try to remember."

Only glow tape lit our way to the stage area. I stopped beside the prop table and took my hat and gloves plus the purse. Inside was a gold compact, which I was to pretend to use whenever I had a down time. With the items in hand, I went to stand in my spot. I peeked out and looked row by row for Aaron but didn't spot him or the other two. I stepped back, and mentally began rehearsing when the music switched to songs from the turn of the century. I tiptoed forward and had another look, and found them sitting in the center section, and almost in the middle of the auditorium. I moved back. The jitters overcame me, and I was happy when the music faded, lights, and my cue for walking on stage happened.

The feathers from my hat fell off, scattering across the floor. I ignored that, and kept right up with my lines. Dan did an excellent job of making light of it. My glove fingertips were cut off. I curled my hands inside the gloves so as not to expose them. Someone had deliberately sabotaged my props. I was very happy when the first act finished, and I had a short break. With my hands on my hips, I marched over to Bev.

"What's the meaning behind all of this?" I wagged the gloves under her nose. "Huh? It's opening night."

"Best keep a closer eye on your props." Sylvie turned away and got busy with the set changes.

"You're in charge of costumes. Get me another pair, asap!"

I hiked back to the dressing room, and sent Aaron a message about the situation.

"Anything happen with your props?" I asked Joan.

"Nope." She was busy touching up her makeup. "Why?"

"You didn't see what happened?" I looked incredulously at her. "Sylvie—it had to have been her—snipped the tips of my gloves off. My fingers almost went through when I pulled them on."

"Really? Why would she do that?" Joan said.

"I know. The feathers kept falling from my hat also." Suddenly, my phone chirruped, and it was from Aaron. I read it aloud, "Aaron said it's great and that I'm doing excellent. He said I'm another Meryl Streep," I flushed, grinning. "I've got him fooled."

"You're lucky."

Her response made me wonder more about her and her relationship. "Is your hubby here tonight?"

"He won't come. He's a descendant of one of those women that was imprisoned, and is upset over the way she was treated by the president."

"That was so long ago. Who was it?"

"Alice Paul's niece or nephew. Something like that." She stood and started for the door. "Meet ya over there."

That revelation sent shivers up and down my spine. I finished touching up my makeup and changing my outfit. I knew I was running late, but I tried making up time by not brushing through my hair and repinning the hairpins.

"Places!" Linda called from the door opening.

"Yep!"

I stood in my spot to wait and took a moment to peek out. I smiled at Aaron, Tim, and Maggie. The set looked great from the back, if only I could appreciate it. My mind buzzed. Was this where it ended for Nancy? Am I standing where she was? I couldn't wait for the final two set changes to be done, and then the performance would end. I looked forward to meeting with Maggie and Tim and going out for a little while. An after performance pizza sounded good.

Towards the center of the back stage, behind the curtains, I noticed Bev and Sylvie nose to nose. I wondered what all the fuss was about when Linda came over and shooed them both away, pointing to opposite ends. Sylvie went to the left and Bev, the right. I hoped for the other way around. Bev growled as she passed me by and sat in her chair, which wasn't far from where I stood.

On cue, the lights faded and the second act began. My lines flowed naturally, and I was relieved that nothing more happened to my props. I almost felt like a pro by the end of curtain call, and then we came back out twice for a standing ovation. At the very end, Aaron strode to the front and handed me a dozen roses.

"Meet you by the car," he said.

"I'll hurry."

With the long stemmed rose box in hand, I walked to the back of the stage, when voices grew louder and louder. My eyes became wider as I watched Bev and Sylvie face off. I folded my arm around the box, found my phone inside a hidden pocket, and slipped it out. I quickly rang Aaron.

"Get back here. Both you and Tim," I said, moving back on stage for better reception. "Now!"

They must've still been in the theater because within a minute, they were racing up the aisle toward the stage. In swift move, they climbed up on the stage. The voices by now echoed ever louder.

"It's your fault! Don't tell me it's mine," Sylvie said.

"If you'd only left him alone, like I asked you to," Bev said.

"Maybe he liked both of us! Ever thought of that?" Sylvie said.

I watched Aaron nod to his right, and he pointed to the left. At me, he raised his finger to his lips, telling me to be quiet. He also held up his hand to tell me to stay. *Fortunately, I can hear what's being said!*

By now, there were more voices, and I recognized one as Dan's. I inched closer. At the very same moment they went behind the curtain, Bev flung a small lamp at Sylvie. Sylvie, who had been clutching a pillow, threw it at Bev. Instantly, they were on top of each other.

Tim grabbed Bev. Aaron grabbed Sylvie. At this time, Maggie came from the stage and stood beside me. I had out my phone and took a video with sound.

I sent them to the detectives.

I looked at Maggie, and said, "Let's get me out of these clothes, and you and I go for a pizza."

Chapter Twenty-Two

Aaron and Tim each texted us once the squad car came for the two women. Maggie and I had left, and I called Aaron since she drove.

"What are they booked with?"

"Disturbing the peace."

"That's it! I don't believe it. They all but confessed to murdering Russ."

"They're going to be questioned."

"I sent a video to the detectives. That should help identify my assailant. Maybe they'll pay attention."

"Where are you two goddesses?"

"At the Corner Pizza Shack." We disconnected. "Do you believe those two? The detectives? Good grief."

"What's it going to take for them to believe you? Another murder?" Maggie parked the car.

"It might be."

We walked side by side after climbing from the car and locking it.

"Men! They're so hard-headed sometimes."

We stood for a minute to let our eyes adjust to the dark room before going to the back to sit in a booth.

"Tell me what this is all about? Why'd the two start fighting in the first place?"

"I think they murdered Russ. He was the financier, theater owner, and biographer. He may have tried to come between them. That's what I was told. I believe from Joan who plays Susan B. Anthony."

"Sounds like it's solved. Why don't the boys see it?"

"Because there's no evidence. This fighting only adds up to two people who don't get along." I shrugged. "I hope they'll put more pressure on them now, and one of them will tell the truth."

"It sounds like they're on the verge."

The waitress walked over with menus and asked, "Drinks?"

"How about a pitcher of cola with four glasses? Our husbands will soon join us."

"Okay."

I watched her walk away before turning back to Maggie. "I sent pictures to the detectives, also."

"It's too bad you didn't record their voices."

"I did." I pulled out my phone, and pressed a couple buttons. "Let's find out."

As we watched and listened to the loud voices from the video I said, "Oh my gosh, this sure has my attention."

"If that's what you sent, it'll be enough to question them."

"Good. Then we're finally getting to the end of that murder, but who killed Nancy?"

"Any ideas? Clues?"

"Not at the moment. I'm starting to wonder about a few things, people, but nothing really has taken shape. No ideas."

"By now, you usually have an inclination."

"Not this time." I looked up and noticed the waitress carrying a tray and I presumed it was our drinks. Right behind her were the men. "They're here."

"Right on cue. I'm starved."

After Aaron slid in beside me, he kissed me as did Tim with Maggie. We went ahead and ordered a large pepperoni and sausage pizza.

"Well?" I asked. "What's happening now?"

"Detective Mergens is with Bev, and Erlandsen with Sylvie. They'll crack it open."

"About time," I chimed. "Should've listened to me in the first place."

We talked and I filled them in about the play and how the rehearsals had gone and how hard it was to keep everything straight plus remember it all. I concluded with how pleased I was to have learned the lines before having to remember all the scene blocking. It hadn't been easy remembering where I was to be and which way to turn and who to do what with. All very confusing at times.

Once our pizza came, we dived into it. We ate and laughed and soon on our separate ways home. I was happy to crawl in beside my hubby.

I had trouble sleeping. My mind kept going around and around over the altercation between the women. I wondered who would replace them, and decided that Linda would probably be doing the extra jobs. I rolled over and thought about Nancy. I tried to understand how her death could have such a chain reaction.

I fell asleep, and didn't wake until after my usual time. It was nine-thirty, which meant I'd be late for opening the door if I didn't hurry. I gave Aaron a kiss and told him the time before jumping from the bed. My closet was almost void of clean clothes. I was happy that tomorrow was Saturday, and we'd close early afternoon. I planned to wash clothes and clean house.

After slipping into another summer shift, this one full of wild animals, I pulled back the side of my hair and placed a huge clip which featured a lion. In the kitchen, I picked up a roll and poured a cup of coffee before heading out the door.

Ten minutes later, I parked behind the store and stuffed the remnants of the roll inside my mouth. With my bag and coffee cup in hand, I hiked up to the backdoor and opened it. The cool air enveloped me, and was refreshing. It reminded me of why I loved the fall of the year. The crisp early morning air and the withered leaves falling like a symphony. Summer was full of sunshine and was supposed to be a time of picnics and fun, but this year wasn't because of the two murders.

I scowled to myself as I set my cup and bag down on the counter. I glanced around the room and saw the quilt strips that needed tending. I hadn't thought about my Dolley Madison star quilt in ages. The investigation and play had kept my mind buzzing. I looked forward to picking it up soon and sewing. Grandma would be upset if she found it lying around, so I folded up the sewn together strips and set inside a large basket.

As I began walking into the showroom, Jane entered.

"Morning!" she said, smiling. "Just get here?"

"Yes. I overslept, which something that almost never happens." I noticed that today she wore dangly earrings and a matching bracelet, which fit the turquoise color of her tanktop and white capris. "You look great today."

"Thanks!"

"You caught me just ready to do my morning routine. It's perfect timing. Come on, and I'll show you what I do." I nodded toward the tables. "I make sure that everything is upright. That's the main thing. It all has to be neat and tidy. There's times when customers from the day before move furniture, and I've missed the change at the end of the day."

"Which row would you like to test me on?"

"That one. The furniture near the presidential desk and also the bookcase." I pointed to the center aisle where there always were a few tipped over items for some unknown reason. "Have you touched any of these items?"

"No," Jane said. She shook her head.

"Was the door locked when you entered?"

"Yes."

"Hmm. I'll have to check into this later," I said. "Let's get started. I'll try not to make you nervous."

I walked down my aisle, noting that it looked fine, and continued to the outer row near the front. The phone rang just at the minute I opened the front door for business.

"You get it," I instructed Jane.

"I hoped I could." Jane raced to the phone and answered it by saying, "White House Dollhouse Store, how may I help you?" Her eyes opened wider, and she held out the phone and said, "They want to speak to the owner."

"Really?" I took it from her and into the receiver, I said, "Liv Reynolds, the owner speaking. Can I help you?"

"The dollhouse and diary belong to me," the garbled voice stated, and the phone became dead…

I held the phone for a few more beats, and stared at it before replacing it on the holder. My heart beat furiously, and I glanced at Jane. "Be right back!"

Briskly, I went to the workroom and found my phone inside my bag, and pressed the emergency number, which rang Aaron's cell.

"Come on," I urged, "answer!" I chased right outside the backdoor, and he answered right as the door closed. "I just got a crank phone call. It wasn't a crank, really. It was all garbled. A cloth or something was over the mouthpiece and came on the store's phone."

"Slow down. Tell me about it?"

I counted to ten. "Something about wanting the dollhouse and something else."

"Think, Liv. You can do better than this. Take a few deep breaths."

I did as told, and then said, "Now I remember. The voice said, 'the dollhouse and diary belong to me.'" I looked over and saw Max approach. "Jane answered and they asked to speak to the owner." Max nodded to the door when he heard me speak, and continued inside. "She handed me the phone, and I stated my name and then that is what was said."

"At least we know it's not Bev or Sylvie. Any clues?"

"Nope, but why kill Nancy over it when they know I own the dollhouse?"

"Maybe they tried to find out where the diary is, and she couldn't tell them?"

"Sure, and they worried that she'd be able to identify them." I smiled, because now her death made sense. "She was a casualty and murdered by the same person?"

"Unfortunately. I'll let the detectives know. They have your video of last night, and it's useful in the investigation. However, Liv, I swear, that if you ever snoop, ask question or blatantly go against my wishes- there WILL be hell to pay!"

"Yes, Sir!" My eyes opened wide. "I can't help it sometimes, Aaron. I did stay back and out of sight."

"I don't want to lose you." Aaron disconnected.

"Yikes!" I felt a flush creeping up from my chest to the top of my head as I stared at the silent phone. *He was right, I didn't follow his wishes. I rarely do when it's a case that I'm involved in, but I'm trying to help.* I walked to the opposite end of the alley, near the theater to calm myself before reentering the store.

I found the two staring out the front window. "What's up?" I asked, striding towards them and noticed the blinking red and blue lights presumably from a squad car. "Accident?"

"I wonder if it wasn't drug related?" Max looked at me. "All taken care of?"

"Yes. Aaron's going to handle it."

Jane looked across at me, and asked, "Why? What's happening?"

"I'm not really sure, to tell you the truth. When I'm here, from now on, I'll answer the phone. I think it's better that way."

The day slipped by with three sales: FDR, TR, and Wilson. It made me wonder if people favored the war White House over any other time period because the historical White House loomed large and also featured Dolley who was First Lady during the War of 1812.

Jane took care of making sure that the sold items were replaced inside boxes for future sales.

"See you." Jane left, leaving a void. Max had already left for his apartment where he planned to do head carvings. By working in his apartment, he was able to smoke and play his music loudly, which made me crazy.

I took out the cassette and began running through my lines. I did it twice before Aaron arrived with a burger basket, and dressed in his uniform.

We sat by the workroom counter since I'd already locked the front door for the day. I took a big bite, and thought over how lucky I truly was as I chewed.

"I'll be in the theater tonight."

"The two aren't going to be there, are they?" I wondered. "Didn't you get a confession?"

"I'm not going to be in uniform. I'll be in the audience. I've asked to be assigned there for the performance. Both detectives think it's a good idea."

"Nancy and Russ are dead. I barely knew Russ. Nancy was an employee and now I'm playing her part and have been assaulted and threatened. Now they're finally paying attention," I said. "I'm impressed."

"Don't get smart. I'll be all over, just pretend like you don't know me. Okay?"

"All right." We finished eating, and he left.

I packed and locked up and walked down to the theater, arriving in the dressing room before Joan. I took the extra time to think deeper about something she had said. It had to do with Alice Paul, and that made me curious. I left the room to look for Linda. I found her onstage.

"Hello, Linda. Did you have a good day?"

"Not really," she said, shaking her head. The stem from the headset wiggled. "I suppose that you already know the big news. No one to do the set changes."

"Not my fault."

"Oh yes! Your husband and your video!"

"How did you know about the video?"

"I saw you." She glared at me, crossing her arms. "Let's hope no slip ups tonight." She tapped her foot.

"The performance will go just fine." I turned and walked away, stopping by the prop table. I studied it to make sure that everything was where it should be, and then held my hat. The feathers were attached. My gloves were replaced. I felt good as I walked back to the dressing room. I stopped in the bathroom and sent Aaron a text, which read: *a o k.* Then went to get ready for the night.

While dressing, Joan walked in carrying a box of chocolates and offered me a piece.

"No thankyou. I get too nervous." I smiled, and went after a bottle of water.

"Your choice. Bev and Sylvie won't be here," Joan said.

"How do you know?" I said.

"After last night? It only stands to reason," Joan said.

We finished dressing and getting prepared for the night, and were almost finished when Linda called, "Places!"

Surprisingly enough, the night's performance went without a hitch. I saw Aaron in the back of the auditorium, once backstage, and that was all. I thought I saw him in the wings after the performance but wasn't sure.

After changing and heading out the door, my phone chirruped. I read the message once I'd locked myself inside of the car. It read: *done good.* I replied: *thanks.*

In ten minutes, I'd locked the garage and entered the kitchen. I felt so lost now that I was alone. I missed

Aaron. I also hadn't had time to speak to Grandma lately. It was good last night to connect again with Maggie, and I thought of her. I sent her message, telling her that tonight went well.

I went to the back bedroom of our house, and realized that I hadn't cleaned in here for a while, either. I opened the small closet door, revealing a stack of books that needed to be brought to the library for donation purposes. I did plan to keep my collection of *Nancy Drew*, however, and *Little House on the Prairie* books. A love story fit my fancy. I flipped through the stack and came across an old one from Phyllis Whitney. It was one that I'd read when I was a little girl.

I set it on my bedstand, and made myself ready for bed before jumping under the covers. I no sooner opened the front page and read the first twenty pages when the yawns overcame me. I set it back down, turned off the light and went asleep.

I awoke with Aaron beside me, and the book knocked to the floor. So was the Bible which always sat centered on my dresser. The dried rose given to my mom from me, and held in her hands while in the coffin, was beside it.

Chapter Twenty-Three

I nudged Aaron. "Honey, wake up!" he grumbled, and I nudged him again. "Shh! Honey. This is important. Wake up." I shook his shoulders before removing the blankets.

"What?" He wiggled and opened one eye.

"My book's on the floor and so is the Bible and the rose is all crumpled, too. Something's not right. You need to get up," I whispered.

He'd shut his eyes. I pulled his ear.

"Ouch! What is the matter with you?"

"Quiet! Sit up, now!" I whispered. I stood, arms crossed, and stared at him. "Look!" I pointed to the floor. "Did you do this?"

"What?" He scratched his head and leaned over the edge of the bed. "How'd that get there?"

"Good question, Sherlock. Now let's find out the answer, shall we?" I stared at the floor. "This really hurts. Last thing of my mom's."

"You didn't touch anything, did you?"

"Of course not!"

"I'm calling it in. We need fingerprints." He placed a call to the precinct. To me, he said, "You stay right here, and don't move. For the life of me! Can you follow my orders this time?"

"Yes." Tears sprang into my eyes.

He swung his legs over the edge and sat up. A hidden handgun was in the closet. With it in hand, he slipped from the room.

I pulled on my clothes and listened to him quietly open hallway doors.

"Honey," he called.

We stood at the room doorway where my books were stored.

All of my books were heaped on the floor or spare bed. The dresser drawers were opened and clearly searched. I wanted to cry, but knew it wouldn't do any good.

Aaron glanced outside. "I see a squad car parking.

"Whoever it is wants something and will kill for it. They could've taken the dollhouse by now, but haven't because they want me to search for the darn thing. That's what I think. The person is trying to lead me onward," I said.

"It's like playing a game of chess."

"I'll wait for the patrolmen to continue the search," Aaron said. "There's bars on the windows, so they couldn't have come in from downstairs."

I opened the door with Aaron right beside me.

"Officer Ingalls."

"Officer Brockton."

Both shown badges.

"The detectives will be here shortly," Officer Brocton informed.

"The lower level needs clearance," Aaron said. "I'm Officer Reynolds, by the way. Obviously, I need to fetch mine. My wife will lead the way so I can get dressed!"

"This way." I steered them to the kitchen area and toward the basement stairs. I turned my attention to my morning duty.

No sooner had the coffee pot started rumbling when Aaron returned.

"How'd they enter? I asked.

"No clue," Aaron said. He focused on the patrolmen as they reentered the room. "See anything amiss?"

"No." They each made a notation inside of a notebook.

"Who would know our pass code besides Grandma and Grandpa?"

"Good question. I just heard the doorbell," Aaron said. "It must be the detectives."

I picked up my phone in the living room and headed toward the bedroom to call Max. I asked if he would open the store and stay until Jane arrived for work and went to finish getting ready for work.

In the living room, I went to stand beside Aaron as he spoke to the same detectives. The patrolmen had just left.

"Right when we were sleeping," I joined the conversation. "The guy's got guts."

"Or gal," Detective Mergens stated. "You never know."

"Lead the way," Detective Erlandsen said to Aaron.

"Right this way." I directed them to the living room mess. "See? Not much. Just a couple of books opened and upside down."

They stared at the books for a minute.

"Show us the rest."

"The back room is where most of the mess occurred." I led them onward and stopped at the doorway. "Go ahead and look."

"The book beside Liv in the bedroom, her Bible and the pressed flower on the floor in our room."

"The flower had been in my mother's coffin. I'm not happy."

"Yes, ma'am," Mergens said.

"Oh! I've forgotten about this," I said. "Hold on a minute." I searched my bag for the cigarette butt and turned it over to Mergens. "This was outside of my backdoor the other night. It may have belonged to the person who assaulted me and messed up my dollhouse."

"Or your house during the night," Mergens said. He took the plastic baggy in hand. "I'll look into it."

I left them to their own devices and returned a moment later with a full mug of coffee. "What's the scoop?" I asked, standing in the doorway. They stood over the pile of books and near the bed. "Should I stay or go into work?"

"You can go ahead, Liv," Aaron answered. "I can answer since I was with you. If they need anything else, they know where to find you."

"That's just what I wanted to hear."

I turned and headed out to the kitchen. I grabbed my belongings and made for the door and out to the garage. The store's clock read 10:10 when I walked inside.

"I'm here," I called, dropping everything on the counter.

In the showroom I found Max sitting by the computer and Jane walking down the first aisle of tables.

"How does it look?" I asked, sidling up along beside her. "Straightened much?"

"It's okay. Not much, but I see why you have to do this." Jane glanced over to me. "It's like the dolls try to walk during the night, and tip over."

"Gotta be it!" I heard a snort coming from Max's direction, and I looked over at him. "The guy dolls asked the girl dolls to dance, and they told the guys to step on someone else's toes."

"We still have a cobble-stone street out here and once in awhile there's carriage rides plus buses and normal traffic," Max said.

"That might be the answer," Jane said.

"You're late, because?" He gave me a cock-eyed grin.

"I'll tell you later." I nodded toward Jane.

"All right. Doesn't sound the best." He pressed a few buttons on the computer, and said, "You're all logged in for the day."

"Thanks." To Jane, I said, "Keep on with the tables, I must speak to Max for a minute."

I started for the workroom with Max following. Once in the room, I made sure that Jane couldn't hear by partially closing the door.

"What happened?" Max asked, sitting on a stool. "For you to close the door, plus call me at the last minute to come in early—something's up."

"Last night," I gulped, "something dreadful happened. For starters, we need to call Minnesota Nice out here once more."

"I'll get right on that, but what happened?"

"Our house was broken into during the night. We must have the security code changed for the store and home?"

"Someone broke in?" Max reached for his smokes and removed one from the package. "Let's go out."

"All right. Meet you there." He left to go out, and I went to the showroom to tell Jane where I'd be. "I'm standing out back with Max while he has a smoke. Come get me if you need me."

"Sure."

I hiked straight out the back door and stopped beside Max. "If not for never smoking in my life, I'd ask for one right now. I'm ready to jump out of my skin." Max continued smoking while I took a moment to glance around the perimeter before continuing, "Someone broke in last night while we slept. They were searching, I believe, for Edith Wilson's diary. There must be one hidden. That's what this is all about. I haven't told you about the e-mails, because I thought it wouldn't amount to much, but I'd contacted the detectives."

"I see where that got you, being patient." Grumbling, he shook his head. "What else?"

"The book beside my bed, the Bible from the dresser, were turned over on the floor beside our bed this morning." I looked at him, and noticed the back of his neck turned red. "There's more. The books in the back room plus the dresser drawers were all overturned. The few in the living room were also." I sighed. "Nothing with the kitchen, that we could see."

"That all?" Max stomped out his cigarette butt.

"For now. What's your thoughts?"

"I take it that the police are at your house now, and Aaron is there to answer questions?"

"That's the gist of it," I said. "I believe that Bev and Sylvie, from the theater, will be eventually charged with Russ's murder and hopefully, Nancy's. It's all about this darn dollhouse."

"I say that we lock the dollhouse up in the workroom at night from now on." Max reached for another smoke, and lit it. "In fact, let's put it in hiding, like up in the apartment."

"You were almost killed once because of someone wanting a document, I won't let that happen again." The killer who was after President Lincoln's Lost Speech had tried to kill Max. "I don't want it over at my grandparent's house, either. Any ideas?"

"No." He shook his head. "That was my second choice."

"I don't want anyone getting hurt and the fewer people involved, the better." I stared down the alleyway and into the street beyond. "I'll give Aaron a buzz."

"I'll go back in and make sure that Jane is okay." He briefly smiled. "I'll call Minnesota Nice right away, too."

I removed my phone and pressed speed dial while Max put out his smoke and went back inside to join Jane. Aaron answered almost immediately.

"What's happening now?" I asked.

"They're still here. Forensics is taking a few prints from the book and Bible. They'll be leaving soon."

"We need our house code changed. Max is calling Minnesota Nice for the store. It has to be someone who would know the code. Know us. But, who?"

"You've told a million people that Dolley Madison is your favorite. Look how Mikal sneaked in that time? We've changed the store, but never felt a need for the house." Aaron covered the phone and mumbled something. "Sorry, I had to tell the guy there's nothing here in the kitchen, but he wants prints from the door."

"Oh! That's good." I waited a minute, and said, "I think you should come and remove the dollhouse. It needs to be hidden somewhere but I don't want anyone else put in jeopardy. Let's put it in the basement for now. I know it's damp, but it shouldn't be much longer before this comes to a head and Nancy's killer is found."

"All right, I'll come when they're done here."

"Should I call Minnesota Nice or do you want to? It's an emergency. The house code needs changing ASAP."

"I'll call. What should we change it to?"

"My mother's birthdate. It's--"

"Let me get a pen and paper." I heard him rustling through a drawer. "Back. Let's hear it."

"February 1956."

"Okay, we'll go with that!"

"Right." I disconnected, and slipped my phone back in my pocket. I still had a bit of pent up energy and briskly walked to the other end of the alley. At the theater door, I found it open. I looked around, but didn't see any familiar cars. Should I or shouldn't I enter, I wondered.

As I reached for the door, I realized that I hadn't a flashlight and I didn't want to turn on a light. How did Linda get around at times? There had to be a flashlight somewhere. I remembered seeing one on the floor near where Carol sat, next to the prop table.

After opening the door, I held it wide open for a brief moment so that I could place where everything was located before entering. I stepped inside and made sure that the door quietly shut. I held my breath as I waited and listened for voices or footsteps, and time for my eyes to adjust. It seemed like an eternity until I took my first step forward. Walking around the larger chairs, desk and table, I almost made it to the correct place when I walked right into a curtain. I almost screamed, then realized how stupid and funny it was. I moved it aside, and walked around it, which brought me to where I intended. The chair was right where it belonged, and I sat on it, and eventually found it.

With the beam on dim, I used it to light the floor as I advanced to the back offices. I wasn't sure what to look for, but I knew that I must begin and hope that whatever I need would become apparent.

It was very possible that one of the backstage ladies held the key to hidden diaries whereabouts. If not, then whom? I intended to find out.

Chapter Twenty-Four

Carol's office door was locked. I jiggled it and tried slipping a lone piece of paper into it, but gave up. Sylvie's and Bev's were also locked, and I wasn't able to enter either. I wasn't about to give up and go back to the store, so I made my way up to the tech loft. I'd crossed through the auditorium, and climbed a narrow but winding staircase near the entrance lobby. Once in the loft, I shown the flashlight across the area, and discovered the light board and two scripts open for tonight's performance. Both Tom and Dave had markings on certain cue lines. I flipped through various piles of papers and letters, found nothing worth noting. As I was about to give up, I noticed a note from Joan, which stated: I'm certain.

What does that mean? Why send a note to Tom? What's the connection?

I slipped the note into my pocket and flashlight, zipped out of the loft and down the stairs.

I never stopped until I stood next to the back door of my store. That's when I realized that Aaron was inside. I was certain he'd be upset. I smoothed down my clothes, patted my hair into place, put a smile on my face, and entered the building.

"I'm back," I called, going into the workroom, where I found Max and Aaron. "I found a note."

"I was just about to go in after you," Aaron grouched. He took the offered note. "No more investigating. That's final!"

"Have you loaded the dollhouse yet?"

"I just got here." He eyed me. "I don't want anything happening to you."

"I know. It's just that, I'm scared. I don't want to lose anybody else. I feel for Nancy's parents and family as well as Russ's. I worry about who is next?"

"Let the police and me do our jobs."

"I will. But now, I'm checking on Jane."

I walked out to the showroom, and found Jane with the duster and holding up Edith Wilson's doll as if she could talk. "Do they say anything to you?"

"They are so real looking, aren't they?"

"Yes. Sometimes, I imagine conversations between the couples. Anyway, sorry about this morning."

"I hope you get it all figured out. Mind telling me what it's all about?"

"I'm not really sure myself. The less you know, the better." I smiled and went to sit by the computer. "I'll be happy when the play is done. We have tonight, tomorrow's matinee and then next Thursday, Friday and Saturday. Five left."

"At least you can count them on one hand."

"Yes. Don't forget that we close early today. By the way, has anyone called or come in?"

"Someone called with questions about Abigail Adams and her daughter-in-law, Louisa. I think I answered them just fine." She finished with the house, and walked over to me. "Someone came in who looked like they wore stage makeup. Their face looked smudged or thick or weird like."

"Tall? Thin? Can you tell me anything?"

"It seems like she should've been tall, but was hunched over and walking with a cane. It didn't appear as if she needed help because of never leaning on the cane."

"What house?"

"That's the other thing." She rubbed her chin. "The person stopped at the house you have that was Mrs. Wilson's dollhouse and stared at it. When I asked if she needed any help, that's when she shook her head and said, 'No'. She placed her hand on the top of her head as if to prevent the wig from slipping around."

"Interesting." I pulled on a few curls and chewed on the ends. "I think it's a good thing that we're going to move it out for now." I stood, and told her, "Be right back!"

Aaron bumped into me as I started to walk into the room. "Slow down, baby girl!" He caught me in his arms, and kissed me. "What's up?"

"Someone's been here, dressed in costume, looking at the antique dollhouse. I know darn well it's the same person that was in here earlier this week and broke in during the night. Have you read the note?" I nodded toward it. "See? Someone in the cast is behind all of this and won't stop until the diary is found."

"I'll look into it. The dollhouse is loaded up, and I'll put it in the basement."

"Minnesota Nice?"

"Called," both Max and Aaron stated.

"Use the code which I gave you, right?" I frowned. "This person must've realized I'd be using the First Ladies birthdates." I scribbled down a different code. "This one should work for the store. It'll never be figured out." I handed it over.

"Looks good," Max said, reaching for a sheet of paper. "They'll be here anytime." He shoved the paper into his pocket. "I'll need this just to get inside."

"Catcha later," Aaron said, walking out the door.

"I'm in the showroom."

"After I take care of the code, I'll leave. I have a few errands that need running."

I went back to sit behind the counter.

"I studied up on the First Ladies last night," Jane volunteered. "I learned that Abigail Adams was a feminist. I learned Betty Ford was a dancer, and she brought breast cancer awareness to a whole new level."

"She was fascinating." I was about to say something else when a customer entered. "Take your time and if you have any questions, let us one of us know."

Jane leaned forward and whispered, "What should I do?"

"Pretend to straighten dollhouse items or else you can go to the workroom and start collecting items for another box."

"I forgot."

I watched as she went over to the recent houses and began moving around items. I smiled, knowing that Jane fit well within the framework of my expectations of an employee. I got into the website and checked it over to make sure that it still looked good before logging into the webmail. Three messages greeted me, and all were fine. I went ahead and answered them all.

Afterwards, I did a search on Joan Mitchell, and it showcased several of the former plays she'd had a role in. There were many productions which I was unaware of. I scrolled through the list of cast names, and came across Tom's and Dave's. Both had been in productions with her many times. I wondered why she'd never mentioned that before, so I went ahead and did a new search, first of Tom. He'd majored in theater at Bemidji State University, as had Joan. My next search brought me to Dave, who had also attended BSU during the same time as the other two, receiving a degree in theater. I found Joan's website and began studying it. The one odd item that stood out was that Joan was from out East, and had transferred here at the end of her sophomore year. I wondered what had interested her in Bemidji? I further read that she'd also minored in history and the presidents. This confused me since she'd never let on that she was interested in history.

I closed out of the account just as the customer spoke out loud. "Could you come here, ma'am? I have a question to ask."

"Of course." I got up from the chair and walked over. Jane must've heard the person, and also came from the back to join me. "Why don't I let Jane, here, answer your questions? If she has a problem, I'm nearby." I backed over to the side to let Jane take over. It was a great time to listen in and observe how she handled customers.

"Hello. How may I help you?" Jane clasped her hands together, then dropped them to her side. "This house is from the Kennedy era. Look at the beautiful rose garden!"

"That's just what I was wondering. She was so beautiful, wasn't she?"

"Oh my, yes. Such a good mother, too. She redesigned the garden, and she formed a Fine Arts Committee to advise her on acquiring historical furnishings that formerly belonged to the White House."

"Well, thank you dear. Because you're so kind and sweet, I think I must purchase this house." She smiled sweetly at Jane.

"Thank you. Right over here, if you don't mind?" Jane led her to the counter, and I walked toward her. The woman was right beside Jane.

"The sales receipt is right here under the counter." I removed it, and told her how to take care of the sale. "This is her first sale."

"How special," the woman said, removing her credit card and handing it over. "She's a very smart young woman."

When it was all rung up, I asked, "Where are you parked? I can carry the boxes out to your car."

"Right outside the door, but don't you have someone to help you?" She stuck her wallet back into her purse, and pushed up her glasses. "They might be too heavy."

"My helper just stepped out. It's not a bother. Don't you worry." I finished business matters, and looked at Jane. "Mind helping?"

She followed me into the workroom, where we retrieved the needed boxes and each carried them out to the woman's car. When finished, I gave her a big hug. "You were great!"

"Thanks. It was super." Jane grinned.

"It's almost time to close for the day, so you can take off and we'll see you on Monday morning."

"All right." I watched her leave before picking up my phone and dialing Aaron. "Did you contact Minnesota Nice?"

"Yes. They just left. Everything's been recoded. I was just about to call and tell you."

"Martha's birthdate, right?"

"Right. Next time, if there is one, I get to pick the dates."

"Okay. If you stay presidential."

We disconnected, and I called the company to see why no one had come by yet. I learned that since it was Saturday, they were on skeleton crew and would be out on Monday. I said, "Thank you," and disconnected.

I took out the cassette and ran through my lines. When finished, I locked up the store and went home.

As soon as I drove into the garage, I found Aaron outside mowing. He shut the power down when he noticed me walking toward him.

"What did you find out about the note? Did it help at all?" I cocked my head. "I'm going a little crazy here. I'm afraid to spend the night here after last night."

"It should be safe. I work tonight, and then have two nights off."

"Good! Then I'll have you home to protect me and snore through the night."

"At least I know you have some faith in my skills as a peace officer. The detectives are working on it, too. Don't worry."

"We can always hope." Tears filled my eyes, and I wiped them with the back of my hand. "What about Bev and Sylvie? Were they booked this morning?"

"Not that I know of. I'm not on duty to hear what all happens."

I turned on my heels, and went into the house. I went into the backroom and stared at the pile of upended books and the mess on top of the bed.

"When will this end?" I mumbled, and began the chore of turning the drawers upright and sliding them into the dresser. After the drawers were in place, I began sorting through the items and placing them into their original spots. It took the rest of the afternoon.

Silently, I went downstairs to check on the dollhouse, and found it in the back corner with a sheet over it. At least it was out of public viewing, I thought. In the bedroom, I grabbed items for tonight's performance. Aaron was in the kitchen. "I'm leaving. When can I expect you home?"

"About one. I have to work a few extra hours. I want you to text me all the time. Will you do that for me?"

"I'll try, if you'll at least find out the status of Bev and Sylvie."

"I planned on it."

With my bag in hand and other articles, I left for the theater. It wasn't long and I turned onto Main Street. A crowd of people stood in front of Pracna on Main, which caused me to remember seeing Bev and Sylvie enter it a few nights ago. Tonight I parked on the street across from the theater's backdoor. It was six-thirty when I checked-in and walked over to the prop table.

Inside the right glove, a small piece of paper scratched me, and I pulled it out. With shaky fingers, I held it to the light to read. *Watch it! It'll all soon belong to me.* I trembled.

"Whatcha got there?" Carol asked, coming up behind me.

"What?" I dropped the slip of paper, and reached over for it. "Piece of paper, nothing else," I said. "Why?"

"You looked a little nervous. Everything all right?"

"Of course!" I set the gloves back on the table, slid the note in my pocket, and walked away. Carol acted as if she knew what was on the note, and it scared me. I hurried to the dressing room. The door creaked as I entered.

"Joan? You here?" I asked, going to the costumes. Her purse was on the dressing table so I figured that she was some place nearby. "How was your day?" I began peeling off my clothes and stepping into the costume. When there still wasn't an answer, I began to get a little nervous. A small event book had fallen from Joan's purse. I took it as an opportunity to take a quick look inside of it. I tip-toed through the area to make sure that no one else was around. I slid my bag so it hid what I was about to attempt to do. Quickly I began to flip through it.

The door opened, Linda entered, scaring me half-to-death. "Ready for tonight? It's looking like a full house."

My heart felt like it would jump out of my chest as I watched her through the mirror. "Wow! Yep. I'm good to go." After she walked away, I clutched my chest and tried to prevent it from beating so hard. I knew there wasn't much more time. It had dates scribbled all over it and numbers beside them. One date was starred, which said, "book launch. I slid it back into the purse. It was just in time because Joan entered right then. I took my brush and began first with styling my hair.

"Where were you?" I asked, sticking in hairpins to hold my curls into the French roll. "I looked all over and thought you were lost."

"I had things to do." She reached for her purse and set it on her other side. In a few minutes, she'd undone her hair style and swept her hair up into a tight bun. "These buns are horrible. How did the women do this?"

"I know. Thank heavens we don't have to dress up in all of these things. Crinolines and bodices and the list is endless."

"Any more news about Bev and Sylvie?"

"Nope. What do you know about Tom and Dave?"

"Not much. Just met them this year. Why?"

"Curious."

"Don't forget that curiosity killed the cat."

"So do lies."

Chapter Twenty-Five

I finished getting ready and looked over to Joan. "Ready?"

"I was just thinking about what someone said to me earlier, and it had to do with a First Lady."

"The First Ladies aren't what they're cracked up to be."

"What do you mean by that?"

"Nothing. Let's go."

We walked to our places and met Linda. I said, "Beat you to it!" Either I was paranoid or Linda really did give me a dirty look as we passed by.

"Good luck," I said, at my designated spot.

"Break a leg!" Joan fervently stated as she past.

As I studied all the heavy ropes holding the curtains, I wondered about Joan's remark. First Ladies are a great asset to the President. They do marvelous things for this country. Usually people love them. I had to focus on tonight's performance so I shoved it from my mind to return later. I peeked into the audience, and thought I saw Aaron in the audience but couldn't be sure. I was upset with him. The slow investigation process made me crazy. Did either Sylvie or Bev murder Russ or Nancy?

My thoughts went to Joan. Why did she feel the need to lie when it's easily proved that she knows the tech crew? Frowning, I focused on the matters at hand and opened my script.

Until the light and music cue started, I read my lines and focused on the opening act. At the chosen time, I entered the stage, took a cleansing breath and began speaking. The entire first act sped right by, and soon it was intermission. I hurried to the rest room, before going into the dressing room to spruce myself up and make a costume change. The rest of the performance went just as quickly. I hurried to undress and leave.

I called Aaron, and left a voice message saying I was going home.

By the time I drove into the garage and shut down the door, I thought I was over being scared, but found I was wrong. A rush of fear sent a wave throughout my system as I reached the kitchen door.

I set my stuff down and waited, forcing myself to listen but found it difficult to hear anything over the hard pumping of my heart. Silently, I moved to the living room but found nothing askance. Aaron had picked it up, which restored my faith in everything being all right. I continued to the back room and found it completely picked up. In place of Mom's flower, a fresh long stem red rose took its place. The card read: *To my wife. I love you, my darling.* I called him and left another message telling him that I loved him, too.

Aaron returned the call with little time to talk. All he said was, "They're booked. One for conspiracy and the other for murder. Got to run. Now you can sleep in peace."

"Not completely." We disconnected.

I got ready for bed, and climbed in, falling asleep immediately. I woke to the sun shining through the blinds. I hadn't heard from my grandparents for a while, so I gave them a call. The rest of the morning I spent at their house and later I had the afternoon performance.

The performance went just as quickly as the night before. I was very happy to have the play almost finished. I also was pleased that there wouldn't be rehearsal all week, and I wouldn't have to see any of these people until the following Thursday.

Monday morning lifted my spirits. Aaron planned to spend time with me after he woke. I kissed him goodbye and headed out for the store. Max's truck was where it should be, which made me happy. Even though he was my employee and I depended on him, I hadn't a clue what he did with his life. I knew he had girlfriends that came and went. I knew he helped out his friend who managed a filling station. At one time, he gambled, but I didn't see evidence of that anymore. In many ways, he was a loner. He was a great renter. I charged him very little because it was important to me to have someone trustworthy living above the store. I looked up at his bedroom window and thought I saw movement, but wasn't sure. I grabbed my stuff and went to the store, punching in the new code.

I set my bag down and picked up the duster, then set it down realizing this could be one of Jane's jobs. Aaron and Max arrived at the same time, only Aaron brought with him donuts and coffee. Jane soon arrived and the morning opened up to new beginnings.

"Bev's being arraigned for murder today and Sylvie tomorrow for conspiracy." Aaron sipped his coffee. "The detectives pitted each other against one another and eventually, they both confessed. There was little evidence and that's what took so long. Your video gave us ideas of where evidence was hidden and helpful at getting a warrant. Good work!"

"Thanks!" I chewed my chocolate covered donut. "Now we just have to find out who killed Nancy. I'm starting to lean toward a cast member. The tech crew and Joan all went to Bemidji State, did you know that?" Aaron shook his head. "She denied knowing them last night."

"Why would she do that?" Max asked, scratching his chin.

"Aren't you scared being around those people?" Jane asked.

"Yes, but I try not to let it bug me." I frowned.

A customer strolled into the shop and inquired about the post-Civil War house, and I let Jane show her which one it was. She did great answering a few questions. I listened nearby, pretending that I was busy dusting. When it appeared like Jane had everything under control, I went to the computer. I could still hear Aaron and Max in the back, talking and laughing. I opened the webmail and read through the messages. Someone asked once again where the diary was hidden and that it belonged to them. I didn't bother to respond, but forwarded it to the detectives. I got up and went for Aaron.

"Come here," I told him, motioning for him to follow. "Look at this." I showed it to him. "Can't your computer geek put a tracer on these? They're annoying and creepy."

"Someone should be with you, Liv. I worry about you constantly. You get these messages, strangers coming into the store. Fortunately, so far, the flow of people are customers. Go about your everyday life and hopefully nothing horrible will happen."

"Not until I'm murdered."

"Honey, the detectives have an extra patrol car cruising nearby." Aaron hugged me. "I'm going to go and get started on laundry. I'll be home when you get there. Supper is all taken care of."

"I'm so lucky."

I switched gears and watched Jane slowly stroll up and down the aisles with the customer. The woman appeared to be in her fifties, but I wasn't sure. She was probably close to what would've been my mother's age. Not for a long time had I thought about my mom, but this woman reminded me of her. I decided that it was from the way she carried her purse. It's funny what a person remembers. It seemed like just minutes, and the two stood before me.

"I'll take the Civil War house. I always felt sorry for Mrs. Lincoln

"What a rush," Jane said, back inside. "I enjoyed that."

"You're a great salesperson."

"I'm going in the back and boxing up another house."

"I need one to replace this one!" I called out.

Jane followed Max to the back, and I went for the duster to wipe down the table before they returned with another house.

The rest of the morning we rearranged the new house, and filling it with the appropriate furnishings. In the afternoon, two couples entered but we didn't sell another house. Jane left at three and Max—was Max!

I was left to my own devices and with the script in hand, locked up the main front door, and went to the back room. I sent Max and Aaron a message saying that I was leaving for home.

The evening and the rest of the week sped by way too quickly, but I was happy for the last few performances to be done. I noticed that there were a lot more different cars and people milling about near the theater's entrance. Wednesday afternoon, I decided to find out the reason.

Jane was busy dusting and straightening the houses, and we'd just sold two: one Wilson and the other Lincoln. She rung up the sales.

"I'm going for a short walk," I told Jane. "I'm curious as to why there's so many cars and people around the theater. I won't be gone for very long."

"I can manage." Jane flipped her hair behind her ear, and gave me a smile before saying, "Don't you worry about a thing. I've got you covered."

"I believe you." I did, too, so I slipped out the backdoor and stood, looking down the alley toward the building. I saw three unknown people walk to the door, with Linda following. I wondered if it wasn't another play rehearsal. When they were inside, I walked down there and entered.

Several voices echoed throughout the area, from up front. I meandered backstage until coming to where all the voices were from, and saw Linda with her headset on and standing to the side. Another person, who I assumed was the director for the next play, stood center stage. She read from her notes, and spoke while pointing to items. They were in the process of blocking certain scenes, so I backed away.

As I went to the exit, I changed my mind and decided to take a look through the dressing room once again. Joan's dress hung next to mine, and I looked through the pockets. I searched her makeup. I ran my fingers through the hat in case of a hidden message. I'd found messages hid inside of Victorian hats when I searched for the Lost Speech of Abraham Lincoln, and found needed clues which Mrs. Lincoln had squirreled away. I hoped for the same results, but feared I wouldn't be that lucky again.

Edith Wilson's diary was what that person kept reminding me about. Where would it be hidden even if there was one? Was it a full diary or only a few pages hidden away? I didn't know what to think, when I opened up Joan's script and saw how she'd scribbled all over it. Large circles went around her lines, big 'X's' over mine. For the first time, I wondered if she hadn't been the culprit who'd scribbled all over the inside of mine. I flipped through it further but found nothing else catching. I returned it the same way found.

I wanted to leave before seen. Three performances left, and I wondered how I'd make it through them as I walked back to the store. It was as if a dark cloud had passed over when I entered the store. I shivered.

I got up and went to the showroom. Jane sat by the computer. "I'm back." She was ready to stand, and I motioned for her to stay.

"The phone rang twice, and that's about it." She glanced up at the clock. "Mind if I leave a little early?"

"Go ahead."

"Thanks!"

Jane reached for her belongings and walked out the door. I checked my webmail, and found two messages. One was from Linda, who called for a line run-through this evening at six. "Shoot!" I murmured to myself. I pressed speed dial for Aaron's number.

"Hey, babe," he answered. "What's up?"

"Line run-through tonight at six. I'll be home right afterwards."

"Okay."

We disconnected, and I slumped in my chair. I so wanted to leave. My mind spun in circles and I decided to renew my search on the Wilsons. I wondered if Nancy's death wasn't about the death of his first wife? The first First Lady Mrs. Wilson?

I typed in Ellen Axson Wilson, the first Mrs. Wilson. She was a descendant of slave owners and from Georgia, where she was buried with her family.

However, as First Lady, she helped to improve the slums of Washington. D. C. There wasn't anything that captured my interest, so I clicked from the site. Once again, I was stuck.

I logged out of the computer for the day, and shut it down. After locking up for the night, I walked to the theater.

Fortunately, the read-through rehearsal went fast. Everyone was present except Joan.

Where is she?

Chapter Twenty-Six

Aaron and I watched a bit of television before climbing into bed. I was exhausted, and hadn't much time to think about the identical scribbling of my script. There also wasn't a motive. *Or was there?*

I fell asleep with this on my mind, and woke with it still churning. There was a few minutes to spare before I had to leave. I fired up the laptop and did a search on Joan Mitchell. The link for the script author Ann Michel, popped up. I clicked on it. The only new piece of news I learned for Ann Michel was that she was a descendant of one of the jailed women from the Night of Terror. I clicked from the site after reaching a dead end.

After slipping a small flowered clip in my hair, I kissed Aaron goodbye, and went to work. The drive took its usual route, and when the old Stone Arch Bridge came into view, I thought of how nice it was to live in such a wonderful city. I turned into the alley and parked beside Max's truck. As I got out, I wondered if he'd thought of anyone who could help him out with the carving. At the door, I pressed the correct numbers and entered.

I placed my bag down onto the workbench and took a long study of the room. There weren't any new heads ready for painting, but I knew that one head took hours. Max did such an excellent job, I worried how well someone else would do. I needed to order a number of supplies, and decided that after Jane arrived, that's what I would do.

In the showroom, I turned the lights on and circled the room. Standing by the door, I glanced up at the Penny dolls and grinned. They were so cute to look at because each had their own personality. Smiles, dimples, winks, and so on—they were adorable. The First Lady pictures were lopsided, and needed straightening. I opened the door for business before setting the pictures aright.

No sooner had I sat by the computer when Mikal appeared, looking like a Popsicle in his lime green pants and shirt with a black bowtie. I chuckled in spite of trying to hold it back. "You look so springy!"

"I had to stop in. First the good news. Grandma is bringing you a pie," Mikal said. "I got the hee-bee-gee-bees last night about you."

"Oh, dear God! About what?" My eyes opened wider and I held my breath. He usually was right about things, so I tried to listen closely. "Really?"

"Don't go out tonight."

"I have my play. It's the last week, and it'll be done." I cocked my head and said, "Why? What's bugging you?"

"Don't go home tonight. I have a horrible feeling in my gut."

"Mikal? I have to go home. I live there." I frowned, and turned on the computer. "What's got into you?"

At the same time, Inga from the antique store entered. "What's up? Just passing by and here's you two looking like you've seen a ghost. I'm all ears."

"Mikal just told me not to go home tonight." I frowned. "Not possible."

"Just be careful. There's bad people out there and they're moving closer."

"Who?" I stared at him. "Can you tell me who murdered Nancy? Then I'll call the police and this whole mess will be settled."

"Is this about the diary?" Inga asked, grabbing my arm. "A new diary was just found that once belonged to Edith Wilson."

"Where? How? By whom?"

"One of my contacts sent me a message last night," Inga said.

"Interesting. What a find," I said. "Thank heavens for that!" I heaved a sigh of relief. "Maybe this person will quit sending me cryptic messages."

"It's not a diary this person is after," Mikal stated, "it's a few sheets of paper."

"That's it! Out with the both of you!" I reached over and took their arms, pulling them along. "This way. Don't come back unless you have something positive to tell me. I'm already paranoid and ready to jump out of my skin." I opened the door, and said, "Scoot!"

"I'll keep in touch," Inga said, giving me hug. "Don't work so hard, you look a little flushed." She felt my forehead. "Take an aspirin." She hurried out the door.

"You are kind of blotchy, Liv. I think you should sit down for a few minutes, then you'll feel better. Get a nice cold drink, too." Mikal hugged me. "Want me to bring you a cup of hot tea?"

"I'm fine." I held the door open. "Have a good day."

When he was out the door, I shut it tight and almost locked it. I leaned into it, and shook my head. My heart beat hard, when all of a sudden, I broke out into a cold sweat. *Why am I so hot?*

It had been some time since I'd worked on my quilt. I brought the pieces out to the front of the store and began piecing the squares together. After pinning several blocks together, I spread it out on an empty table. I smiled. The patriotic stars blended so nicely, I loved it and couldn't wait until it covered our bed.

The back door opened and Max called, "I've got two new heads here for painting!"

"Oh! Good!" I walked out to meet him. "They look all sanded down, too." I watched as he placed them on the stand, and then moved closer. "Smooth, too. They look so human like."

"They should."

The back door opened, and Grandma called, "Got your favorite chocolate pie here, girl." She entered the room and handed it to me. "Enjoy! Gotta run!"

"Thanks!" I stood with my mouth dropped open. *How could Mikal have known about the pie?* I scratched my head.

"Set it down before you drop it," Max advised.

"Right." I did as told. "Help yourself." I reached for paper plates and plastic utensils. "Mikal just told me that this would happen."

"Don't listen to that old coot. She probably e-mailed or called him to say that she was going to do this."

"I bet that you're right!"

I dished up a slice for each of us, and cut one for Jane for her arrival. Back at the computer, I called Grandma and thanked her once again. I sent a message to Mikal and Inga to tell them about the pie. Afterwards, I checked the webmail and found five messages. Four were legitimate, and asked certain questions about either a president or a First Lady. The fifth read: *Two sheets.* I forwarded the message to the detectives even thought I was sure it didn't advance the investigation. I also did the same to Aaron, and wrote: *Another one. This time, no diary is mentioned.*

Jane came a little later, blaming it on the baby being up half the night. She got to work dusting and I left her to handle the customers while I worked on orders in the workroom. Between the three of us, we gobbled the pie down in record time. The day whizzed by and soon I was left alone at the close of the day.

I wanted to be in the dressing room before Joan arrived because of my puzzlement over why she didn't have her script. I had dressed and was applying makeup when she strolled through the door.

"How was your last few days?" I asked.

"It was nice to not have to think about this place, wasn't it?" She quickly undressed and began to dress in costume. "I loved not having to rush in the late afternoon."

"I know, but I thought I heard you were a theater major?"

"I am, but once you have a family — well — it makes it so much harder to break away. This time of the day is supper time!"

"True. Do you have children? Aaron wants some and so do I but we haven't been blessed yet. I hope for one in the near future."

"It'll happen," Joan said. "No, we don't. My husband doesn't want any."

"How well did your husband know of Alice Paul?"

"His relatives still speak about her and the way she was treated by the First Lady and President which is why I accepted the role of Susan B. Anthony."

"I thought you might've been a descendant to Mrs. Wilson."

"Nope. Not at all."

"Thanks for telling me," I said. "You didn't bring your script home last night." I held up mine. "I have to review my lines constantly."

"What is this? Twenty questions?"

"Nope. Just saw it sitting here." I finished by applying my lipstick. "I'm going out. Break a leg!"

As I walked to my assigned place, I made sure that Linda knew of my arrival and that I was ready. I noticed two new people backstage while I stood waiting. The background music played, *Oh You Beautiful Doll* and *Me and My Gal*. The audience seating was slowly filling, and it made me nervous.

Dan soon stood and glanced at me, giving me a nod. Joan did, also. I'd recited my lines, and as the lights dimmed, I took a few deep breaths before walking out onto the stage. The evening's performance went by without a hitch. We all knew our parts well by now, so neither of us had a problem except for a few minor things such as coming in a little too soon or dropped a word, here and there.

Joan beat me to the dressing room after curtain call.

"Great night!" I said.

"You betcha!" She giggled. "We're going out tonight, my man and I. Can't wait."

"Have fun!"

We walked out the door together, but parted after stepping outside. I briskly walked to my car, but stopped in my tracks.

All four tires were flat as a pancake. I tried to scream only no sound came out. I made two fists and pounded on the hood. Once I pulled myself together, I speed dialed Aaron. "I've got four flat tires."

"What?"

"Four flats! I'm too mad to do anything."

"Go lock yourself inside the store. I'll let you know when I get there."

As I punched in the code, I got the creeps. It felt as if the hair on the back of my neck stood on end. The door squeaked as I slowly opened it. I flipped on the light and went into the workroom, turning on that light. As I sat on the stool, I looked around. The refrigerator noise scared me, and I almost fell from the stool. I pumped my crossed leg up and down, and then got up and stared at the sewing table. Footsteps from above made me jittery, even though I knew it was only Max. When the backdoor squeaked open, I went to stand behind the workroom door.

"Liv?"

"Aaron." I stepped out and he gave me a big hug. "The garage fix-it man is here and putting on tires. Any idea?"

"No, not really. No one comes to mind. Maybe Joan? There's never any free time." I wiped my moist eyes. "I'm scared."

"I'll follow you home."

"And, you'll walk me through the house. Right?"

"Yes."

Aaron was in uniform, and it was nice knowing that he'd be able to walk me through the house before he returned to work.

Once the car was safe in the garage, he led the way inside.

"I don't like this at all, Liv." He flicked on the kitchen light. "We need to be extra vigilant. We've checked out everyone, including Joan, and there's nothing in her background to warrant an investigation or questioning. The other two are safe behind bars. Then you got another message just today." He shook his head. "Well, we'll get it figured out. I've already asked to be dismissed earlier than my scheduled hours for tonight. Look for me in another two hours."

"That's if all is well." I sighed. "Oh! Actually, there's something else. Both point to Joan, but it could also the tech crew."

"Okay. Those two are off the radar. I'll do what I can tonight to look into them, but what were you going to tell me?"

"Joan. I think she's the one who scribbled all over my script. The three went to BSU together, and she denies knowing them."

"That doesn't sound right." He crossed his arms. "That's Bemidji State?"

"Yes. They have a great theater department. Her husband is a descendant of one of the women who was jailed during the Night of Terror."

"Which is?"

"Women picketed the White House for voting rights. They were jailed. A few left to die. Many tortured. A couple women went on a hunger strike. This all during the Wilson years. Edith never stepped forward to help the women. Wilson didn't do a thing, either. Maybe someone wants revenge?"

"On you? Revenge you? Explain?"

"Not revenge on me. They want actual writing to see exactly what they had in mind during that time. They might just want to set the record straight."

"What about the Fourteen Points? Isn't that what Russ tried to edit your lines about?" Aaron placed his hands on hips and said, "Then why try to poison you? Why the tires? Why murder Nancy?"

"To keep us out of the way so that the President and First Lady are exposed for their treatment of the Suffragists," I said. "That's what I think."

"I'm starting to think otherwise. With Russ gone, nothing else has happened. I think that subject has fallen away." I waited a beat, and continued, "There's something else. Joan made a remark about the First Ladies aren't what they're cracked up to be. Isn't that odd?"

"This all sounds far-fetched."

"I know." I reached up and pulled his mouth down to meet mine. "Murder isn't."

After a goodbye kiss, Aaron left. I popped up a bag of popcorn and went into the living room. I knew that I wouldn't be able to sleep because of the night's events. After showering, I turned on an old movie, and fell asleep watching it.

Three in the morning I woke to the TV still blaring, and a crook in my neck. I shut the dang thing off and went up to bed.

Aaron was beside me when I woke. I dressed and went downstairs.

In the kitchen he left me a note: *Sorry. Too many calls tonight. I've tried to put in for tonight off. Don't know yet. Love you.*

I responded with: *I hope so. You, too.*

Continuing with my morning routine, I ate a bagel and had a glass of juice before going into the store.

I jumped into the car and a short detour brought me through an out-of-the-way section of northeast Minneapolis. It was the area full of Catholic churches, and once settled by Germans, Polish, and Slovakians.

Soon I was back on Main Street and stopped at the light near Lowry Avenue, which crossed over the Mississippi River. The light turned green and before long, and I drove past the old Hamm's Brewery, which is now in use as a library. I crossed over and turned down the alley toward where I park.

Something seemed odd as I climbed from the car. I had such an eerie feeling surrounding me, that I felt chilled to the bone and it was seventy degrees. An attached white sheet of paper to the back door scared the life out of me.

It looked as if drawn in a child's hand of women standing behind a fence. The eyes were reminiscent of a cartoon witch. The text used was cut-out magazine letters.

It read: *Where is it?*

Chapter Twenty-Seven

I took a picture of it with my phone, and sent it to the detectives plus I called the emergency number, and was advised that a squad car would arrive within a few minutes. I called Aaron, and left a message. Next, I called Max, who answered.

"Get down here."

"Huh? Why?"

"Never mind. Just get down here—pronto." I disconnected, and dialed up Aaron again only this time he answered.

I no sooner disconnected and slipped the phone inside of my pocket, when the squad car drove up and parked beside my car. Max was still buttoning his shirt upon arrival. I stood back and pointed at the paper. "Look."

"Officer Sherman." He showed his badge, and was alone.

"Liv Reynolds, the proprietor." I was sure he was a rookie because he had too many pimples across his nose. "This is Max, my employee and he lives upstairs in the apartment."

"Howdy-do," Max said in typical fashion.

"Any idea?"

"I've plenty, but no one seems to pay attention. Maybe you will?" I gave him a once over. "It's like this — you see — I've been involved with a play which features First Lady Edith Wilson. I have her antique dollhouse and now it's at my home." I collected my thoughts. "You see — I've received threats, been harassed and had all sorts of things happen by someone who seems to think that I'm either smarter than they think I am or dumber." I noticed that he looked ready to salivate, so I said, "Are you following? Are you getting this all down?"

"Yes, ma'am." He gulped, and his fingers shook when he wrote.

I continued, "Supposedly they want something that they think I have, and I haven't any idea why or for sure what it is. I believe it's some papers which the First Lady wrote and came from her hidden diary. Supposedly I have them. Don't know."

"Finished?"

"For the time being." I ran my fingers through my hair, and asked, "So now what?"

"I'll take pictures, and then remove it for evidence."

"That's it? You'll take pictures and save it for evidence?" I wanted to strangle him. I started making fists inside of my pockets when Aaron arrived. He must've read the look of murder on my face, because he jumped from his car as fast as lightning and was by my side. "I'm glad you're here."

"Now what?" He took a good long look at the paper. "Called the detectives?"

"Yep. No reply."

"Hmm," Aaron rubbed his whiskers. "I say it should be removed and placed in a plastic bag." He turned to the officer. "Got one?" He smiled. "I'm also a policeman."

"Right." Within a few minutes, the officer had safely removed the item, placed it in the evidence bag, and left.

"Now what?" I asked, hands on hips.

"I'll have a smoke," Max said.

"Yeah, then we'll try and decide what to do next." I opened the back door and went inside, leaving the two behind.

No sooner had I made my sweep of the showroom when my store phone rang. I answered only to have Detective Erlandsen on the other end.

"Tell me about the paper," he said.

"You have the report," I replied, with a slight edge to my voice. "Something's happening around here and I'm getting mighty tired of it! You guys aren't doing anything to remedy the situation, either!"

"The print guy is on it. We've got all sorts of stuff but no actual crime to give us anything to investigate."

"No crime? So the break-ins don't count or this paper? What about the postcard? The e-mails?" I saw red when I glanced to the back as the door opened and closed. "How about Nancy's death?"

"We don't have anything tying them together, that's the problem. No connection." I heard frustration in his voice as he continued, "We're going to have a patrol car drive by the neighborhood more frequent.

We'll also have a plainclothes officer in the audience tonight. It's your last performance, isn't it?"

"Yes, thank heavens." I frowned. "I sure hope nothing happens."

"We'll be in touch."

We disconnected, and I glared at the phone before cradling it. "The man drives me nuts." I crossed my arms and stared into space. After a few minutes, I strolled to the workroom where Max busied himself clearing off the counters.

"Honey, it'll work out," Aaron said. He pulled her into his arms and kissed her. "I'm so sorry that we haven't found the killer, but it'll happen soon."

"I hope so," I said. "I wish it was a week from now. Promise me that if I'm ever offered another part in a play that'll I'll turn it down."

"That's up to you, isn't it?" He grinned. "I'm not the boss."

"Ahh, yes you are over this one! Don't let me. No more acting. Got it?"

"Yep."

Max left to run errands, and Aaron went back to work. Jane called to say that she couldn't make it in because of a sick baby. Actually, I didn't mind. For a Saturday in July, it seemed odd to have few customers, but that suited me okay. I took the time to run through my lines for the last time, and shuffle inventory around. I made sure that a few extra boxes for the most sold houses were ready upon sale.

I hadn't wanted to be the first to arrive for the evening's performance, but I felt like I needed to do something, so I arrived early. It actually was kind of creepy to be there an hour before anyone. I was surprised that Linda wasn't present. Since I was alone, I took the time to once again go up to the tech area. The lighting board had so many levers and switches, that I wondered how on earth they managed, but figured it was preprogrammed. I read through the written notes, and didn't see anything untoward. I continued riffling through items until coming across a few scripts from other productions. After tossing them aside, I went back toward the main offices.

I hadn't heard voices before, but I thoughts I did so now. I tip-toed toward them and noticed Linda and Joan discussing something over behind the stage. I chose to keep quiet with hopes of hearing the discussion so I stopped behind a slat.

"She doesn't know anything," Joan said. "I'm positive."

"Let's keep it that way," Linda said.

My eyes opened wider, and I didn't move. My heart beat loud, and I worried that it would jump out of my throat. *Are they talking about me?*

"Let's keep it between us."

"Should we invite her out tonight? You know, a cast party?"

I accidentally backed into a garbage can and it scraped the floor.

"What was that?"

I inched backward, staying out of sight and headed for the dressing room, and was stepping from my capris as the door opened.

"You're here early," Joan stated. Her face looked pale as her eyes darted around the room. "Did you just get here?"

"Yes," I replied innocently. "Why?"

Shaking her head, she walked back out of the doorway. I fell into the nearest chair and stared into the mirror. My pink cheeks could be blamed on the makeup, but my heart still pumped hard. After a few minutes, I finished dressing and was mid-way through makeup applications when she reappeared.

"I'm ready for tonight's performance to be done. I can't wait to dismantle the set, strike it." Joan started changing clothes. "That's what it's called, set strike. You staying?"

"You betcha." I finished with the rest of costuming, and headed out to the stage area, stopping when I spotted Linda. "I'm going to my place, so don't worry about me."

"Gotcha."

As I stood peeking out into the crowd, I searched for the undercover policeman. I wasn't sure, of course, but thought he sat in the middle row and on the end. When Detective Erlandsen mentioned the undercover policeman, I thought Aaron may be the assigned person, but now I saw that he wasn't. I removed my phone to make sure that it was off, but first checked messages. Grandma sent one, telling me to break a leg. I'd be deliriously happy if I never hear that phrase again. Maggie sent a similar one, only she said to eat cyber cheesecake and drink cyber champagne from her. I wrote back, '*thanks*'.

I slipped the phone into my pocket and glanced around. Dan wasn't where he should be, but it was still early. I didn't expect Joan, either. My thoughts went to the previous conversation. I wondered who, "she" was? I was all but certain that I was the person in question. So far, no one had mentioned a cast party to me. I sure wasn't in the mood for one. I wanted to get as far away as possible from these people and just as fast.

Linda walked across the stage, stopping dead center, and stared at the set. I watched as her eyes shifted from one item to the next, presumably to make sure that everything was in its correct place.

The pre-set opening background music began along with the change in lighting. I peeked out, and noticed that a woman sat with the man I thought of as the policeman. Strike him from my list. I searched again, but didn't see anyone who fit the predisposed image of one. I didn't see anyone known to me in the audience. I took the rest of the time mentally running lines. Soon the stage lights and music diminished and I readied myself for the final performance.

The evening happened without a hitch, thankfully, and after curtain call, we rushed to change our clothes. Following the performance, the cast and crew stayed to strike the set. It took at least two or three hours for dismantling and replacing of furniture and other lighter weight props to be returned to their correct units.

Afterwards, I declined an invitation from the stage crew to stop by Pracna on Main for a beverage with the excuse of being overly tired and worn down. I couldn't stop yawning as I drove home.

On the short drive home, I realized that I was starved and decided to purchase a hamburger and fries from the nearest drive-through so that I wouldn't have to cook. After letting myself inside the kitchen, I ate what was left of my food in the living room.

I went to the bedroom, and before stepping into the shower, I realized the towels were still down in the dryer. As I started for the basement steps, I thought I heard a crash, but attributed it to outside cars driving past. A chill swept through me, but I shagged it off. At the top of the stairs, I listened for sounds for a few minutes. When I didn't hear anything else, I switched the light on and climbed down the basement stairs. A dim light shone from the storage room, and I wondered if Aaron hadn't forgot to shut it off when he carried the antique dollhouse down. As I neared the room, the light disappeared.

I silently inched ahead and heard footsteps coming from behind. The only source of light was shut out. My legs felt like heavy bricks. I couldn't move. My phone was still in my pocket, and I wondered if I could contact Aaron without this person knowing. Since the brightness of it would show my position, I left it there, and touched certain points on the phone.

"Give me the phone."

I gasped. "No!" A sharp knife point poked my back, and I hollered, "Ouch!" The tip hurt, and the force pushed me forward.

"Where is the diary?"

"Don't know." *How is the passcode so easily broken?* I wished for some kind of an inspiration to get me out of here, but nothing came. "First Ladies keep journals, not diaries. You should know that."

"Listen, missy," she growled, "it's mine. Hand it over."

"I don't have it." I slipped and fell right into the dollhouse. The crash sent a roar to the heavens, as the walls broke into splinters. "Ouch! Now it's in ruins." I pulled myself up as my eyes slowly adjusted to the darkness.

"Hand it over."

"I don't have anything," I said. "Joan? What are you doing here?" Then it started making sense. Ann Michel. "You're the playwright, aren't you?"

"Yes, and a Suffragette descendant."

"You said it was your husband."

"I did, didn't I?" Joan cocked her head. "I lied."

"You murdered Nancy and Russ and tried to poison me?" I said. "This is what it's been all about, isn't it? Revenge?"

"My family was never the same, thanks to Edith Wilson and the President." She grabbed my hair. "Where is it? Where are the sheets?" She grabbed my arm, and I bit her wrist.

"Ouch!" She grabbed me by the collar. "You'll pay for that."

"Ever hear of the First Lady desk? Maybe it's hidden in it? You know?"

"Never heard of it."

"It's a secret."

"You're wasting my time." She began dragging me from the area. The basket of towels sat on top of the dryer, and I stretched to reach it as she tried to slit my upper arm with a held knife. At the same time, I yanked her hair with my other fist, and kneed her gut, which sent the knife flying. I grabbed the full laundry detergent bottle and struck her alongside of the head, knocking her hard. She banged her head on the dryer before falling to the floor and tipping an old water bottle onto the smashed dollhouse.

I knew there was a roll of packing tape nearby and quickly located it. In a matter of a few minutes, I had it wrapped around her arms and connected with the washing machine sewer pipe.

By the time I'd slipped out my phone to call Aaron, the basement light was flipped back on and he and two other policemen were running down the stairs.

"Liv!"

"Aaron!" I rushed into his arms. "It's her—Joan or Ann Michel. She was doing this all along."

"I'm glad you're okay. The detectives are coming, also."

"How did you know?"

"The phone. I caught some of it."

Chapter Twenty-Eight

Once Ann, alias Joan, was taken into custody and I'd given my statement, I was left with my grandparents. They insisted that I spend the night with them. My fingers itched to get down to my basement and take apart the dollhouse remnants. After Grandpa brought me home the following afternoon, with the reassurance that I'd phone if something new developed, I went straight to the basement.

Aaron followed me down the stairs, and we stood with hands on our hips and stared at the mess in front of us.

"You don't actually think there's something worthwhile inside of this trashed thing, do you?" Aaron picked up the splinters of a bookcase.

"Look at the chinaware. All wrecked and broken into a zillion tiny pieces." I reached down and lifted the house. "I'm tipping it over."

"Let's pick out the pieces and place in a separate box first."

"Good idea." I went for one, and soon Aaron tipped it on its side, and all the broken pieces slid out. I removed the rest. "Ready?" We both held it from either side. "On your mark..."

"One..two..three..."

We tilted it upside down, and a false bottom board fell out, revealing sheets of paper which sailed across the floor.

"Oh, my God." I bent over to retrieve them. The non-waterproof ink stained the paper and all that I read was the date: November 15, 1917. The rest was dissolved by water.

"This date. Right here," I said, my hands trembled, "with her signature, confirms that she knew what happened that night."

"The Night of Terror."

"Her thoughts are lost to history." I studied the other sheets, but could only make out a bit of writing at the top of another. "This one reads, 'Fourteen Points.'"

"Let me see." Aaron studied it. "This must be from the president. He didn't have his stroke until after the Fourteen Points were written." He shook his head and said, "Now what?"

"We turn it over, but to whom?"

"We'll contact the Presidential Library and Museum."

"Then, we'll deliver it all in person."

"Sounds good." I thought for a moment, and said,

The End

WORD to DEATH

A White House Dollhouse Mystery
By Barbara Schlichting

I expected Blanche at any moment, the Mary Lincoln impersonator from the Mary Todd Lincoln House in Lexington, Kentucky. Blanche needed a place to dress for the afternoon engagement at Inga's Antique Store, located at the end of the same block as my own shop. I own the White House Dollhouse Store in downtown Minneapolis, so it seemed fitting that she should dress here. Blanche's grand entrance for the tea party and diary reading would delight the audience.

Putting on my own period dress had taken all morning. The crinoline and hoop made me almost nuts from all the pulling, straightening, and latching. Fortunately, Inga had loaned me a shoe hook, which worked nicely.

The skirt swept across the floor as I walked around the showroom, circling my dollhouses carefully. "I'm busy this afternoon ladies, but Grandma will tend to things," I told the miniature dolls. Dolley Madison was my favorite, not only because of being distantly related, but because she had so much personality and character. Glancing at the nearest modern-day White House, I commanded, "Laura, stand straighter." I picked up First Lady Laura and set her closer to President Bush. "Much better." The overhead doorbell rang, and a short woman the size of Mary Lincoln walked in toting a very large hatbox.

"Hi! You must be Blanche. I'm Liv, and let me help you. I'll get Max to carry in your remaining boxes."

"Thank you," Blanche said. She glanced around the store. "What lovely miniature period White House dollhouses. I love them. You must show them to me before I leave tonight."

I thought her southern accent charming. "Thanks! I'd be glad to show you around after the shindig is over. I have Tad's play uniform and other Lincoln memorabilia left for unpacking later to share." I took the box out of her hands. "Follow me into the back room. That's where you'll dress."

"Max," I said, "how about running out and carrying in the other large box with her dress? She's right out front." I set the hatbox down on the counter. It was large enough to mail a large nest of baby chicks or a potted plant.

"Sure," Max said. "I think you should really park out back. It will be easier for you to return your costume to the car later."

"You're right," Blanche said. She handed him the keys then placed her briefcase and purse on the counter.

"It's a little dusty in here but not bad. Max carves the doll heads at those benches and lives upstairs. At the moment, he's carving Eleanor Roosevelt's head. He and Grandma will mind the store while we're at Inga's shop."

"You look magnificent, by the way," Blanche said.

"Thanks. I'm looking forward to the afternoon." I made a slight curtsey.

It wasn't long before Max had the remaining boxes stacked on the counter.

"I'm going upstairs but won't be gone long," Max said. He handed Blanche the car keys.

"Changing room?"

"Oh, right. Across, in here." I pointed to the restroom. "It's small, that's why you'll have to dress in this room. The back door is locked. You can leave your things here during the engagement. I'll be in the showroom if you need anything."

"Okay. I'll get started."

This short moment left me time to leave a note for Grandma.

    A.   Dust if time.

    B.   First Lady Wilson should be visible and out of the bedroom.

    C.   First Lady Nixon needs a hair tune-up.

    D.   Do you have time to:

        A – Y or N?

        B – Y or N?

        C – Y or N?

I busied myself after that by reading through my latest emails until I heard Blanche call my name. I went to see how she was doing.

"Please help me hook the hoop before I break something!"

"Sure." I helped her adjust and latch things up. "Almost ready for the shoes." Together, we pulled the dress down over her shoulders and fanned it out over the hoop. "You're even wearing pantaloons! I'm impressed."

"This Victorian style dress is horrible."

"True. Thank heavens it's outdated."

"Anyway," Blanche said, "we can talk while I'll fix my hair."

I followed her across the hallway and stood outside of the bathroom as she swirled her hair into a bun.

"Ever heard of the Lost Speech?" Blanche asked. I shook my head and she explained. "The Lost Speech of Abraham Lincoln has never been found. I received an email from a close historian friend who believes it's still within reach, like it's ripe for discovery." She pushed in a hairpin. "There's also a newly found letter of Mary Lincoln's at the Presidential Library. They, of course, notified The Mary Todd Lincoln House. I'm going online to search for the speech once I return home."

"I've never heard of the Lost Speech." I cocked my head.

The letter piqued my interest also.

"I should show you the puzzle from her published diary. Mary Todd Lincoln's diary, that is. I brought a stack of copies and left them for sale at Inga's. The puzzle is made of letters arranged within circles. Most unusual."

"Do you have a picture of the puzzle?"

"Yes. I'm excited to show someone." Blanche opened her laptop and brought up an image. Rings of letters circled smaller rings, and in turn were circled by rings yet larger.

"Wow," I said. "This picture looks like the puzzles that Luke has at his coffee house, Brew Café, two doors down."

"Goodness. I should like to see them."

"I'm not sure if they're a perfect match, but close," I said. A thought came suddenly to me. "Wow, that speech would be worth a fortune, wouldn't it?"

"It certainly would be. People might even kill for it."

I shook my head. "I have to admit that I've never heard of it, and I have a doctorate in American History."

"What was your specialty?"

"The first ladies."

"Then your store certainly makes sense. I'm going over to that café now, and then head to Inga's. It's the only available spare time before my flight leaves, unless there's a few minutes after the tea."

"Sure, go right ahead. Don't forget to turn sideways as you enter and be ready for a few gawkers!"

"I'll tell them I'm Mary Lincoln's ghost!"

"Grandma should be walking in any minute. I'll meet you at Inga's."

The front bell rang.

"She's here. See you in a bit."

If anyone saw us embrace, they would've thought it hilarious. Two women wearing hoops! We must've looked like two question marks embracing with our butts sticking out.

I went out to the showroom. "Hi, Grandma," I said, bending over to give her a peck on the cheek and raising my hoops again. "Thanks. I left you a note of things to do." I grabbed a heavy shawl to wrap over my shoulders. "Max should be down shortly. He's right upstairs if you need anything."

"Don't worry. I know how to stay busy. Have fun," Grandma said. "It's getting slippery, so Grandpa may pick me up early."

"That's fine." I adored my grandparents, who raised me from the age of eleven when my parents were killed in a car accident. Last year, Grandpa walked me down the aisle when I married Aaron. Since then, Aaron and I moved to another location which was closer to my business. I could walk to it, weather permitting.

The weather was terribly cold, and I had to steady myself on the icy sidewalk to Inga's.

As I walked, men stepped sideways to allow more room to pass and nodded. Women smiled. One woman stopped me, and said I reminded her of Charlotte Bronte.

The warmth inside Inga's store greeted me as I entered.

Because of the hoop and crinoline, it was difficult to squeeze myself behind the counter. Holly, Inga's young employee, also wore a period dress, though my fingers itched to yank out her nose and hoop earrings. Meanwhile, Inga greeted her guests–mostly local historians and Civil War buffs. She had prepared a stylish offering of tea and scones as part of the festivities for the afternoon. I stood next to the counter where stacked copies of Mary Lincoln's diary were displayed and picked one up to ensure I got a copy before they were all purchased. I paid Holly, slid the receipt inside, and tucked it under the counter to take home later.

Inga swept up just then.

"You look great in that dress, Inga. You're the spitting image of Mrs. Lincoln." I looked around. "Where's Luke? I don't see him."

"He had to return to his café for a minute, but an employee is still here. She's that young Asian woman over there, helping to serve the refreshments. He said she's his cousin from Cambodia. Luke and his wife certainly seem to have a lot of cousins.

Someone waved to her from across the room. Inga waved back, and then confided in me. "It's a great crowd, but they're keeping me busy." A door slammed somewhere. "Oh, that's the back door." She looked around the corner. "Yes, Luke's back."

Mrs. Olson interrupted our privacy in her usual style. "Goodness, Inga, you look just like our famous

First Lady." She picked up the china plate and silvered fork. "Is it true she was very short?"

"Only five feet, two inches tall," Inga agreed. She began pouring tea for guests. "Go ahead and mingle, Liv."

I began the process of turning around, not an easy thing to do when wearing a hoop.

"No, wait," said Inga. "Where is Blanche?" She glanced at the nearest clock. "She should have been here by now."

"That's true." I backed out from behind the counter to join the guests. "I'll text Max and Grandma. They might know." Within a few seconds Grandma's reply came:

Don't know. She never returned for her hat. Grandpa circled the block and came back for me. I have to leave. He's having a terrible time driving. Talk later.

That made sense. She had her laptop and probably didn't want the bother of holding onto the hat in the wind. Still, she should've been here. Perplexed, I went to the window to look outside, but few people were stirring in such awful weather.

"I wonder where she's at?" Holly said. She'd joined me.

"Do you think something happened?" I asked her.

"I hope not. The weather's awful out there."

I walked over to Inga and whispered, "Grandma doesn't know where she is."

Inga looked at me and then turned away to finish pouring tea for a woman, then she beckoned me toward a quieter area.

"Something isn't right," Inga said. "I can feel it in my bones." Inga is one of Grandma's oldest friends, at least sixty years of friendship. I suspect she still regards me as a child to be commanded. "Go investigate."

"Plan to."

It was well after the event's starting time of two o'clock by the time I was finished dressing for going outside. I opened the door and the frigid air took my breath away. A crowd of people was gathered at the end of the block, which was odd, considering the bitter cold.

My full skirts swayed backwards against the powerful north wind. Sirens blared from a distance, becoming louder, propelling me to hurry. I slipped, barely catching myself. My hoops worked to my advantage and I easily pushed through the crowd. As soon as I saw the heavy, full skirt billowing from the wind, I knew who it was.

"Blanche!" I shouted, kneeling down. "Oh dear God! Did someone call an ambulance?" It seemed as if her neck was at an odd angle. I took off my mittens and took her hands in mine to warm them. "Blanche? Speak to me."

The crowd jostled me and made it hard to take care of her, plus my attire was in the way. Soon two police officers stood over me.

"Liv?"

"Aaron?" My husband, a police officer, was first on the scene. "Thank God, you're here."

"Let us take over. Go to the store and stay." Aaron held out his hand and helped me to stand. "Don't worry. An ambulance will soon be here."

"Okay." I nodded, turned, and fled to my store.

I quickly punched in the security code and entered. I made a beeline to the back room where I fumbled with the ties and tangled strings of my dress until at last I stepped out of it. I was thankful I hadn't tied anything into double knots. Though in a hurry, I took time to hang the dress properly. The dress had belonged to Mary Lincoln. I had purchased it recently when an assortment of her dresses were sold on an online auction. She wore it after she had served as First Lady, so the value was much lower than I'd expected. It seemed we were similar in height but not girth. She had to have weighed much more than me — otherwise I would never have been able to get into it.

I glanced down the street when dressed. People were coming and going. Holly walked past, and so did Luke. The sirens blared louder. Police car lights flashed along the blocked street, and rings of spectators huddled together to stare down the street.

Two detectives headed my way and I waited for them to enter.

"Liv Reynolds, Aaron's wife," I said.

"Detective Mergens. Remember me from the other case?" He showed his badge.

"Yes, of course. And Detective Erlandsen." "What can you tell me?"

"Her name is Blanche. She's a Mary Lincoln impersonator. Is she going to be all right?" I glanced toward the back room. "Come with me. Some of her stuff is in the back room."

They followed me to the room.

"What happened?" I asked. *Was it possible she might have a broken neck, since the angle of her head seemed odd? Something didn't seem right about the scene.* "She's a representative from the Mary Todd Lincoln House in Lexington, Kentucky. They could tell you more." Tears filled my eyes.

"Are you saying she's from out of state?"

"She was invited to an event here, to read from Mary Lincoln's diary at Inga's down the street..." I trailed off for a moment. "She's dead, isn't she?"

He continued to ignore my questions. "Inga from the antique store?"

"What? Oh, yes." I wiped my eyes. "Sure, that Inga. She gave a tea and had invited Blanche."

"Anything else?"

"Take a look. Her hat is still here. This is where she dressed. That's her purse, but she had her laptop with her."

"We'll have to look into that," Erlandsen said and made a note.

"Hate to bother you, but," Mergens said, "can we use your store for a base for a while?"

"Sure."

"We'll probably need to warm up. Got coffee?"

"Okay, I'll put on a pot."

"Leave everything of hers as it is while we're gone," Mergens said.

The two detectives left.

Naturally, curiosity got the best of me. I felt drawn to Blanche's hatbox. It was made of heavy cardboard that was gray with age. Peering closer, I noted that dirty smudges abounded, but were smoothed over. Inside the first box, I found jagged handwriting, reminiscent of an elderly person's script. The written name was Mrs. Tindall. The smeared ink was right beside a miniature drawing of a staircase, yet another thing to pique my interest. I grabbed for a blank sheet of paper from the printer on the counter and quickly made a sketch before replacing the lid. I slid the sheet inside of my cash drawer just as the police entered.

The name of Mrs. Tindall was familiar, but I couldn't place it. I pondered the question of who she was as the coffee brewed.

Disclaimer

As far as I know, there's no diary or journal hidden away by either the First Lady or President. My only intention was to make the public aware, and most especially young women, of what these brave and courageous women had to do to force the voting rights in this country for women.

We still haven't passed the Equal Rights Amendment.

Everything has been made up except for the information about the Suffragists. It's all a work of fiction.

9 780999 563090